UNWANTED

AGENDA

Book Three of
The Unwanted Series

Also by Sandra Denbo and Tamarine Vilar:

In *The Unwanted Series*:

Unwanted Discovery – Book One
Unwanted House Guest – Book Two
Unwanted Agenda – Book Three

UNWANTED

AGENDA

Book Three of
The Unwanted Series

by

Sandra Denbo

& Tamarine Vilar

Book Lamp and Chair, LLC
Portland, Oregon

Scan this QR code
to learn more about
this series or visit our website at:
www.theunwantedseries.net

ISBN- 978-0-9967895-0-9

Published in 2015 by Book Lamp and Chair LLC
Printed in the U.S.A.

Acknowledgements

Personal thanks to Emery Denbo who inspired the subplot and provided many suggestions and much encouragement.

Chapter 1

Outside the steamy windows, rivulets of rain shivered from the gusts of howling December wind. It was well after breakfast time, but the cozy diner was still busy. The aroma of bacon, hot maple syrup, and fresh coffee filled the air. Just outside of Portland, Oregon, this was Sharon Cooper's favorite place to meet, and it was convenient for the whole family.

Although she was nearing fifty, Sharon looked much younger. Those genes came from her mother, Alice, who died last year. Thankfully, that was the only trait she got from her — in character, there was no resemblance. Sharon's kind, hazel eyes and proper sense of right and wrong came from her father. Although he had died almost twenty years ago, she still treasured his life lessons. She always looked for the good in people and situations. Most of all, she cherished her family — her devoted husband, Jack, her son, Mark, who was away at college, and daughter, Callie, who was two years younger than Mark.

Yet here in front of her were family members she was just getting to know. Sharon unconsciously twisted her strawberry-blonde hair as her mind wandered back to just over a year ago, when she first met these women sitting with her in the big corner booth. After living most of her life as an only child, she was still in a bit of shock at how much her life had changed since she found out about her father's previous life and that she had three half-sisters. Stranger still, she was surprised at herself that she had started to like the idea of getting to know them.

Arlene Rand was the oldest, sitting across from her along the left side of the table with her back to the wall. Arlene had recently started to get her hair done regularly with highlights, which was a definite improvement over the mousy brown her hair had been when they first met. If she wore makeup, she would definitely look better, almost pretty — if it weren't for the constant sneer on her thin lips. Her blue eyes seemed devoid of emotion except for disdain. That and her bifocals gave her the look of the proverbial spinster librarian. Arlene had already let Sharon know that as far as she was concerned, Sharon was the outsider. Sharon hoped that as time passed, Arlene would eventually accept her — or at least tolerate her.

Bonnie Parker was the middle sister and sat to Arlene's left. Sitting between her taller sisters, Bonnie's petite frame made her look even shorter, as if she were a child between them. Unlike Arlene, Bonnie was always cheerful and upbeat. Sharon watched as Bonnie pulled out her compact. When Sharon had first seen it, she had thought that Bonnie must've bought it at some high-fashion boutique. The crystals, beads, and stones were arranged in a delicate paisley pattern. She smiled as she recalled Bonnie telling her that she had created the design. It was then that Sharon realized that, aside from Bonnie's somewhat clueless demeanor, she had an extraordinarily creative imagination. Sharon watched as Bonnie opened the compact to primp her short, wavy, dark brown hair. Sharon always enjoyed being around Bonnie — she made her laugh, even if it was sometimes unintentionally.

Visibly annoyed by Bonnie's jingling charm bracelet, Arlene sighed loudly and gave her younger sister a contemptuous look. Sharon groaned inside, thinking that Arlene would probably never appreciate Bonnie's abilities, and she twisted her hair again.

She turned to look at Charlotte Knapp, who sat to her right at the end of the table. Although Charlotte was the youngest, she was the tallest of the three. She had slouched down, with her long, blonde hair draped on either side of her face. Charlotte looked at her hands folded in her lap. She glanced up occasionally with those long-lashed, blue eyes. Even though Sharon and Charlotte were the same age, Sharon thought that if she wore makeup and dressed a little more carefully, she could pass for a model. Still slouching, Charlotte shifted her weight and crossed her long, slim legs. Sharon wished Charlotte had a little more self-confidence. Sharon looked at her watch and leaned forward anxiously. "Nobody spilled the beans, right?"

Arlene raised one eyebrow above her bifocals. "You worry too much. She thinks this meeting is about Callie's wedding plans. Remember? It was your idea."

Since Sharon's back was to the lobby, she realized that Karen Frainey had arrived only when Bonnie waved to her mother. Karen was tall, gentle, and beautiful with or without makeup. Charlotte looked the most like her. Unlike Charlotte, Karen carried herself with confidence. Her hair was pulled back in a soft bun except for short curls that framed her face. The relentless gray had been winning the battle over the once-blonde mane she had so proudly displayed in her younger days. Just last year, she had given up the battle and stopped dyeing her hair — much to the objections of her daughters. She told them she didn't want to bother with the effort and expense anymore.

Karen closed her umbrella and shook off most of the raindrops. When she saw her girls and Sharon, she smiled, crinkling the corners of her bright, green eyes. She sat down at the left end of the booth and glanced at the coffee awaiting her at her spot. "Sorry I'm late. I got a phone call just as I was leaving the house. Thanks for ordering coffee for me." Looking at Sharon, she smiled politely. "I'm so glad Callie's going to marry Roy. He's such a nice boy."

"So am I," Sharon said. She smiled and looked at everyone else around the table.

Bonnie bounced in her seat, her green eyes wide with anticipation. "I can't stand it anymore; we lied to you. We all wanted to be together when we told you."

Arlene rolled her eyes. "You just can't keep a secret, can you?"

Bonnie tilted her head. "What?! We're all here now. Why not tell her?"

"Tell me what?" Karen squinted at her. "What are you all up to?"

Bonnie giggled. "We have something for you."

Sharon leaned forward with a twinkle in her eyes. "Remember how it took so long to inventory Alice's — well actually, Dad's — estate?"

Karen nodded.

"Well, as soon as it was settled and we all got our shares, we started talking."

"Yeah, and we all agreed," Bonnie jumped in. "We each want to give you a fifth of what we inherited. That way we'll each have four-fifths." She leaned over and whispered to Arlene, "Four-fifths is right, isn't it?"

Arlene slowly turned to look at Bonnie. "Oh, Honey, you're so lucky you're pretty."

Proud of herself, Bonnie smiled as she straightened up. "Thanks!"

Ignoring that, Karen looked around at the girls with shock. "Oh, girls, you don't have to do that."

Charlotte blushed. "We know that. We want to." She leaned forward and begged, "Please Mom? We really want to."

Bonnie giggled. "And that's what makes it so fun."

"I can't believe this. And you, Sharon — you hardly know me." Karen's voice was soft and low.

Sharon became aware that Arlene was staring at her ambiguously. Uncomfortable, she looked away and shrugged. "We all agreed it was the right thing to do."

"So the wedding was never going to be the topic?"

"Well, I do have a couple things I wanted to discuss, but, no, it wasn't why we got you here."

"I never would've guessed." As Karen removed her coat, the rest of the women reached into their pockets and purses and pulled out envelopes, each containing a check. "I feel guilty taking this from all of you. Shouldn't you be taking care of your families?"

Bonnie looked puzzled. "Mom, I think that's what we're doing. Aren't we?"

"You know what I mean. Your kids."

"They're fine. Don't you worry about it."

"But, Charlotte, your boys are still in school. And I know for a fact how expensive college is."

Charlotte smiled shyly. "We have enough left over and then some. Go ahead, look."

When Karen opened the first envelope, she gasped. "Oh! You can't be serious! You each got five times this?"

Sharon smiled. "Well, you saw The Mansion. Alice had a lot of antiques, fine art, and collectibles. And then The Mansion sold for almost two million."

Bonnie giggled. "You wouldn't believe the dance John and I did when we got the check. His special-order Corvette Stingray is being shipped in next week." Then she rolled her eyes and sighed. "You know what he said? He said that even with giving you a fifth, we'll still have too much for me to spend it all on clothes. Can you imagine?"

Charlotte grinned.

Karen wiped a tear. "I'm astonished. To say thank you isn't nearly enough. What can I do to repay you?"

"Oh, good grief, Mom. We don't expect anything in return. It's a gift. That's the point — you aren't obligated. Okay?" Arlene said.

Karen's lip quivered and she looked at each one. "Thank you. All of you," she whispered.

Arlene took a sip of her coffee. "So, Sharon, didn't you just say you wanted to talk about the wedding after all?"

"Oh, yes. Callie wanted to know if any of you would like to be involved in the wedding planning."

Karen took her hand. "I'd be delighted to. Just tell me what you'd like me to do."

"Thanks, Karen. I'll ask Callie what she'd like. Since she hasn't decided on anything yet, it's pretty wide open." Sharon saw Charlotte shrink back and bite her lip, so she asked her, "Charlotte, what do you think?"

"Well, I've never had a wedding. I eloped the first time, and then with Hal, we went to the Justice of the Peace to get married. I wouldn't know how to plan a wedding." She paused for a moment. "Well, Arlene and Bonnie had big weddings, of course — but I really didn't do any of the planning. I was just a teen-ager."

Arlene scowled at Charlotte. "Why'd you marry Kurt anyway? You knew we didn't approve of that jerk. You couldn't even sneeze without his permission. And heaven forbid you have an opinion. Did he pick out your clothes for you, too?" She huffed. "I'm so glad Josh ran away so you could get out of there."

Charlotte blanched and fingered her locket.

Karen frowned at Arlene. "Don't talk to your sister like that. Yes, she made a mistake, but it's in the past now. It doesn't do any good to make her feel worse about it."

Feeling bad for Charlotte, Sharon leaned over to her. "Charlotte, I have a confession. Callie said I was supposed to do anything to get your help — even if it meant bribing you."

With her head down, Charlotte glanced at her sisters and her mother, and then she fidgeted. "I guess. But I don't know how much help I could be."

Bonnie leaned forward. "I'd love to help pick out the dresses! Callie's so lucky — she won't need a booster like I did."

"A booster?" Sharon squinted at her.

"Yeah, you know, one of those things that sucks in your waist and makes you look skinnier and pops your boobs up to your chin?"

Arlene rubbed her temples. "Bonnie, that's a bustier."

"Yeah, that!"

Sharon giggled. "I think she'd like that, Bonnie, I'll have her call you."

"One of my co-workers makes cakes as a hobby. Well, she's actually trying to get a business started. She even has a portfolio. I can give you her number," Arlene said.

"That would be great."

They talked for another half an hour about the wedding plans and how they might spend their inheritance money. Then they made arrangements for another meeting. They headed for the door and paused in the entryway to put on their coats.

Without looking at Sharon, Arlene said, "I'll get that phone number, you know, for the cake."

"Thanks." Sharon turned to Charlotte. "I'll have Callie give you a call, too."

Charlotte nodded.

"Sharon, what are you doing on Sunday?" Karen asked.

"Well, I help Jack get snacks ready for the game on TV, but then I usually read a book or go shopping."

"Oh, good! It isn't just me and the girls. What do you say we arrange for the men to gather at one of our homes, and we can meet at another for cheese and wine? How big is your TV? They'll want the one with the biggest screen."

Bonnie raised her hand. "John just bought one that takes up, like, the whole wall in the living room. It's totally ridiculous. I had to move all the pictures and stuff to make room for it. I feel like I live in a theater now."

"Do you think he'd mind having all the guys over for the game every week?"

"As long as he doesn't have to get up to get his beer. Which isn't a problem now since he put a mini-fridge next to the couch."

Arlene frowned. "I don't know why you put up with that. A fridge in the living room? Now that's downright lazy — and tacky."

Bonnie shrugged and then smiled. "It's okay. He's happy, and I don't have to go fetch for him."

Arlene frowned and shook her head. "He's got you wrapped around his little finger."

Bonnie's eyebrows knitted for a moment. "I don't think that's possible," she said slowly.

Arlene rolled her eyes.

"I'm sure the guys would love it. We'll just make sure they have their snacks before we take off for girl time." Karen said.

Sharon grinned. "I'd love to have all of you over to my house. I can put together a cheese plate as long as you each bring a bottle of wine."

"That sounds perfect. With the giant TV, I don't think they'll miss us. Let's all leave for your place right after the men leave for Bonnie's."

"Okay. It's a date."

The rain had turned to a downpour, so Charlotte, Bonnie, and Karen ran to their cars.

Sharon walked up behind Arlene as she buttoned up her coat to leave. "Arlene, could we talk for a moment?"

Arlene sighed and her shoulders slumped. "I suppose." She turned around. "What do you want?"

"I wanted to thank you for coming."

"Well, I'd do anything for Mom." As Arlene stared at her, she seemed a little less tense. "By the way, that was big of you, sharing your part of the inheritance with our mom. You didn't have to do it, you know. So thank you. She really needed it."

"Well, after everything that happened, I just felt it was the right thing to do." Then Sharon frowned. "That stuff you said about Charlotte and her ex — just how bad was it back then?"

"Well, if you have to know, she was damaged — still is. Kurt was a real control freak. He didn't beat her, but he might as well have. We were all glad to see her get away from him."

"How'd she manage that?"

"Well you know she had the two boys with him. Josh, being the oldest, was a pretty headstrong kid. But it turned out to be a good thing. When he was nine, he assumed he was the reason Kurt was mean, and he ran away. He did it to save his mom — he thought that if he wasn't there, then Kurt would be nice to her and Cal.

"Well, when that happened, the police and Child Protective Services got involved. Then the boys started to tell everything that Kurt did to them, but mostly Josh. The authorities said that she had to leave Kurt or she'd lose the boys. The only way he could see the boys was under supervision, but he never even did that. It just proved what kind of jerk he was!" Arlene clenched her jaw, shook her head, and took a deep breath. "I don't think she would've had the courage to leave him on her own." She paused and shook her head even more quickly. "No — I *know* she never would have."

"Oh, I'm so sorry."

"You couldn't have known. But I suspect that a lot more went on in that trailer than we know, and we may never find out. The records are sealed, Josh and Charlotte won't talk about it, and Cal doesn't seem to remember much. No one else knows how bad it really was. But I know it must have been awful because Josh gets really angry if the subject comes up. And Charlotte, she can get an anxiety attack. Mom can't handle it, so she pretty much forbade us to talk about it.

"Mom and Dad paid for the divorce, but it was long and ugly. Kurt didn't want to admit that anyone would dare leave him so he fought tooth and nail for the boys. *He* didn't want them — he just didn't want *Charlotte* to have them. But Mom and Dad had a good lawyer, and we won. Charlotte was able to get therapy for the boys because the State paid for it, but she didn't have insurance, so she never got any help. She felt bad because Mom and Dad spent so much on the divorce — she refused to impose on them to pay any more for her to get counseling. We were all relieved when she married Hal. I'm really glad I introduced them."

"You did? How'd you know him?"

"About four years ago, Mel's contracting business picked up, so he hired Hal to do the books and the taxes. I'd been doing the books up until then, but it just got to be too much with me working full time. When I found out he was single, I took a chance and invited Charlotte over when he was going to be there. One thing led to another, and they made a connection. They've been married for almost two years now. He's really good to her and the boys." Arlene's face softened. "Like a knight in shining armor rescuing the damsel in distress. He really loves and encourages her, but she still doesn't have any self-confidence."

"I'm glad for her. The only thing I knew about Kurt was the hint I got when I first met all of you, and Karen said everyone was glad Kurt was out of the picture. I was curious, but I didn't ask since I didn't know you then."

"It's okay. But just keep it in mind that she's our little sister and we protect her."

Sharon nodded.

"Well, I guess you're our little sister, too."

Sharon sensed a trace of animosity.

"But you're pretty stable, and you don't seem to need protection. That and your perfect husband would kill anyone who tried to hurt you." She turned to leave.

As Sharon buttoned her coat, she thought, *What's eating her?* But then she decided to stay positive and give her the benefit of the doubt. *Maybe I'm just imagining things.*

Arlene looked back at Sharon. "I guess we'll see you on Sunday."

"I look forward to it."

She saw Arlene rolling her eyes as she turned away to leave.

By evening, the rain had stopped, and the temperature had dropped to near freezing. The oven in Bonnie's kitchen had warmed the house and filled the air with the aroma of herb-roasted chicken and scalloped potatoes.

She hummed happily as she set the table for dinner. When she heard the door to John's car close, she grinned and walked over to the front door. She pulled aside the curtain to see when he'd get to the porch and opened the door for him. She looked up at him and smiled.

"Hi, Bonnie." Although John was less than average height, he still had six inches on her. His styled, black hair created a stark contrast to his pale complexion. That and his slight frame almost made him appear sickly. He started to unbutton his overcoat with his manicured fingers.

"Oh, John, that big TV of yours is going to come in real handy," she announced as she closed the front door.

He turned around from hanging up his overcoat in the hall closet. His hazel eyes narrowed to slits, almost closing them. "Huh? What're you talking about?"

"We girls decided that it will be just perfect for all you guys to watch the big game here every Sunday. And all us girls are going to go to Sharon's house while you're all here. That way we won't get in your way. But don't worry, we'll all make snacks for you, so you won't go hungry." She smiled proudly. "Pretty smart, huh?"

"I don't suppose you thought about asking me first?" He took off his suit jacket and silk tie.

"Well, that huge TV just begs for an audience. You'll have fun."

He sighed. "Okay. Whatever."

"Good, it's all settled then," she said, satisfied with herself. "Oh, dinner's ready."

He followed her into the dining room and sat down as she placed the food on the table.

"Mom was so surprised today. You would've been so proud of me. I didn't tell her until we were all there at the diner."

"Will wonders never cease?" he mumbled.

"Oh, and I'm going to help Callie pick out her wedding dress."

He paused and raised his eyebrows. "Well, that's no surprise. You and shopping go a long way back." Then he frowned. "Just don't you go buying any more stuff for yourself."

"Well, I'm going to have to get a bridesmaid's dress." Then she paused. "Maybe — she hasn't asked me yet." She frowned and stopped to think. "Maybe she'll ask her friends."

"I'd say that's probably a safe bet."

"They haven't picked a date yet, so it'll be a while anyway." After a brief silence, she smiled. "How was it at work?"

"Nothing new. We still have trouble getting applicants to qualify for home loans."

She looked up. "Well, you're the manager. Just lower the rates. Then they could afford to buy a house."

"Bonnie, the recession has reduced people's income and assets. That's why they can't qualify."

"Exactly. If the rates were less, then they could afford it." She smiled proudly as she tilted her head.

He stared at her blankly as she started chattering about the rest of her day. Each time she giggled, his attention faded a little more. The longer he brooded, the more he tuned her out. During a lull in her monologue, he picked up his plate and plopped down in the living room. He reached over, pulled a beer out of the mini fridge, turned on the TV, and cranked up the volume.

Bonnie, oblivious, hummed happily as she cleared the table and washed the dishes.

Chapter 2

The morning air was cold, so Charlotte quickly shut the door when Callie came in. Callie's long, red hair curled out from her knit cap and draped over her ski jacket. Her hands and fair cheeks were red from the cold. When she took off her jacket, the curve of her hips was emphasized by her black jeans being tucked into knee-high boots. Anticipation seemed to electrify the sparkle in her green eyes as she took off her knit cap.

"Callie, I don't know what I can do to help you plan your wedding. I literally have no ideas." Charlotte nervously fingered the locket that hung in front of her turtleneck sweater.

"That's okay, Aunt Charlotte. I've never had a wedding either, so I brought some magazines for ideas."

Charlotte closed her eyes and groaned. "Oh, goodness, please don't do that anymore."

Callie's eyes widened with concern. "Do what anymore?"

"Don't call me 'Aunt' anymore, it's too weird. Just Charlotte is fine."

Callie let out a sigh of relief. "Oh, okay. It felt kind of funny calling you that anyway."

Charlotte smiled shyly. "You really think I can help you with this?"

"We can figure it out together." Callie grinned.

"Okay. Well, let's spread out those magazines on the coffee table, and I'll get some scissors and a binder. Would you like some coffee while we look?"

"Sure, with cream and sugar, please."

As Charlotte poured the coffee, Callie put everything on the coffee table. "Charlotte? Is this your purse?"

She peeked around the corner. "Oh, yeah. I love it."

"Where'd you get it? It's so cute."

"Bonnie made it. She has a real knack for that kind of thing."

"Wow, that's amazing! Do you think she'd make one for me?"

"Sure. She'll be flattered."

"I've got to talk to her. Oh! I should ask her to make a bridal purse, too!"

"That's a really good idea." Charlotte brought in the coffee and sat next to Callie. The couch faced a large picture window with lace curtains. The morning sun shone directly onto the magazines in front of them. They each picked up a magazine to leaf through, and Callie took a hair tie off her wrist to pull her hair back into a ponytail. They discussed each idea before approving and cutting it out to put in the binder.

"Oh, Charlotte, look at these flowers. I've always loved lilies, and the baby's breath is arranged so beautifully. I'm cutting this out for sure."

"And the color of those lilies would look so good with your hair. Oh, look at this. There are places that you can rent for the whole thing: the ceremony and the reception. Bringing these magazines was a great idea." She glanced up toward the window. "I never would've …." She gasped. Her eyes were wide as she craned her neck to see more clearly.

"Charlotte, what's wrong?"

Still looking, she sat up straight, "I thought I saw someone I used to know," she mumbled. "But it couldn't be." She stood up to see better. "Could it?" She slipped her locket inside her turtleneck sweater. "I'll make some coffee," she blurted out as she hurried into the kitchen.

Callie looked at her full coffee mug as she mouthed, *Make some coffee?* Then she stood up to look outside. A dark green GMC pickup with oxidized paint was parked at the curb. The large camper on the back reminded her of a hunter. Then she saw a man emerge from the other side of the truck. "Charlotte, someone's coming up the walkway." She looked toward the kitchen and saw her leaning on the counter with both hands. Her head hung down with her hair draped over her hands. She jumped when Callie came in and put her hand on Charlotte's shoulder.

"Whoa! What's wrong?!"

Charlotte's wide eyes shot towards Callie. "Hide the scissors!"

"O-o-kay. Do you want me to get the door?"

There was a knock and Charlotte's body tensed.

The doorbell rang.

Charlotte's eyes darted around. "No. Yes. He won't go away if you don't."

"You stay here." Callie put the scissors into a drawer of the secretary desk before answering the door. When she opened it, she made sure to memorize his description. He had a clear olive complexion and hooded, dark brown eyes. He was running a small black comb through his greased, collar-length, black hair. Then he slid it into the back pocket of his faded-blue jeans. His bulky flight jacket was tight at the waist, making his shoulders look extra broad for his six-foot frame. His black cowboy boots were slightly worn, but they looked like they had a spit shine. She thought the sideburns were a bit much, but it added to the whole young Elvis image. "Hello, can I help you?"

"Is Charlotte here?" Steam blew out of his mouth as he spoke.

"What do you want?" She tightened her jaw when she saw his eyes check out her hourglass figure.

"I need to talk to her." He smiled, bringing on two deep dimples.

"Obviously. Can I tell her who's asking?"

"Just tell Chickie-baby that I need to talk to her."

Callie turned around and called out. "Uh, Chickie-baby? Someone's here asking for you."

Silence.

"Just a minute, I'll be right back." She pushed the door so that it was almost closed. Then she hurried into the kitchen. Charlotte was standing now, with her back against the wall. She trembled as she held her face in her hands.

"Charlotte, what's wrong?!" she whispered.

"I can't do this."

"Do what?"

Charlotte put her hands down and pressed her head back against the wall. She whispered, "That's Kurt." She squeezed her eyes shut again as she grimaced.

No way. "I'm going to send him away," she whispered back.

Charlotte crossed her arms, gripping herself tightly. She shook her head quickly. "It won't do any good," she whispered. "He won't take no for an answer."

"He will this time!" Callie boldly marched back to the front door. "I'm sorry. You can't see her right now."

Although he smiled, Callie saw a flash of disdain in his narrowed eyes. "Okay. I'll just come back later. Thank you." He saluted.

Callie locked the door and watched him through the blinds until he drove away. She went back into the kitchen. "He's gone."

"He only wants you to think so." Charlotte stared at her and her voice seemed dead.

Callie put her arm around Charlotte's waist. "Come on. I'll help you to a chair in the living room."

When they got to the living room, Charlotte pulled away from her and went to the front window to look up and down the street. Only then did she sit down. She looked up with urgency in her eyes and begged, "You can't tell anyone about this."

Callie frowned as she sat down next to her. "Why not?"

"You just can't." She leaned towards Callie, pointing her finger. "Promise me you won't say anything! To anyone!"

"I can't. I know too much about him for that."

Charlotte froze for a moment, and then she shut her eyes. "Okay, how many people know?"

"My mom said that Arlene told her. And we talked about it at dinner last night. Why?"

Charlotte seemed to wilt as she muttered to herself incoherently.

"Charlotte, what's going on?"

Her eyes darted quickly from the window to Callie and back to the window again. "Nothing! Nothing at all!"

"Okay, Charlotte, I know better than that. You're acting just like my friend Ally. It turned out that her uncle was a real creep. I made her tell me, and he went to jail. I can't stand to see anyone suffer like that. I know there's a story here. If you won't tell me, then you have to tell somebody."

Charlotte's eyes got wide, and she shook her head. "No! No, I can't!"

"What about your family?"

"Not Mom. She couldn't handle it. She almost lost it about what little she found out. Not her."

"I can ask my Mom. She's really good with people. She'll understand, and she's so easy to talk to."

Charlotte's lip quivered. "I don't think I can talk about it. To anyone." She leaned forward and sobbed into her hands.

Callie slipped into the kitchen to call her mom.

Ten minutes later, Charlotte was on the couch, hugging a pillow and biting her nails. She didn't hear Sharon quietly slip in the back door.

"She was terrified," Callie whispered.

Sharon whispered back, "Like I told you, Arlene said they don't know what really happened with him. No one will talk." She paused, twisting her hair, "If there was a restraining order, it would have expired a long time ago. And he hasn't done anything — that we know of. I'm pretty sure we can't call the police."

"But what can we do to help her?"

"I don't know. Did he say what he wanted?"

"No, but he said he'd come back. I didn't tell her that."

Sharon frowned. "Oh, great." Then she put her hand on her daughter's shoulder reassuringly. "But it was good you didn't tell her."

"Why don't we ask the guys to check up on him? Maybe they can find out what he wants. You know, unofficially."

"Good idea. But we won't tell Charlotte yet."

The front door burst open, and Charlotte gasped as she recoiled.

"Hi, Mom. Is lunch ready?"

"Oh, Cal. I'm sorry, I got distracted. I'll make it now." Charlotte got up and went into the kitchen.

Cal was slim and almost as tall as Sharon. All it took was a glance at his mother's nails to know that something big was bothering her. His dark eyes watched her suspiciously as he took off his coat. When he removed the knit cap, it electrified his dark-brown hair. His nose, cheeks, and hands were red from the cold.

Sharon held out her hand. "Hi, Cal. It's good to see you again. Do you remember me?"

"Sure, I remember. The picnic. Sharon, right?"

Sharon smiled. "Yep. You've grown since we saw you last time. You're practically as tall as I am."

Cal smiled. "Yeah. Mom says she can't keep clothes on me."

"Well, that happens with growing young men."

He turned redder as he grinned.

Sharon smiled again and turned to help Callie and Charlotte make lunch.

Cal grabbed his mom's hand to look at her nails. "Mom, what's wrong? You've been biting your nails again."

She took a quick breath as she looked at her nails. "Oh. Uh, nothing. You'd better go wash your hands."

He frowned. "Yeah." He backed out of the kitchen so he could watch her as he headed toward the bathroom.

When Charlotte heard the bathroom door close, she put her finger up to her lips. "Don't tell him!" she whispered loudly.

Sharon put her hand on Charlotte's shoulder. "Don't worry, I won't."

When Charlotte saw Cal return, she put on a brave face. "Cal, isn't this nice, having company for lunch?"

"Sure, Mom."

They sat down and had a quiet lunch. Cal watched his mother out of the corner of his eye.

Eventually, she smiled and assured him. "You don't have to help with the dishes. Sharon and Callie will help."

He reluctantly left to go back to his friend's house.

When the front door closed, Charlotte hung her head like a beaten puppy. "He knows something's up. He's going to tell Hal and Josh. What am I going to say?"

Sharon put her hand on Charlotte's shoulder. "What's wrong with the truth? They're your family — they'll support you. And you're going to need that."

"But I don't want to worry them."

"You know you can't handle this alone. They'll be there for you. They love you. You have to do this together."

She stared at her for a moment, tears welling up. "I wish you'd been around a long time ago."

"I'm here now."

"Are you sure you can't talk to someone?" Callie asked.

16

Charlotte pinched her eyes shut and a tear leaked out. "Not really. I can't tell Hal. He'd want to kill him, and Kurt is …. Well, Hal would be the one to get hurt … or killed. Mom can't handle it, and I'd wind up having to be the strong one and reassure her. Arlene always gets angry and tells me how to handle it, but I can't do things her way. She just makes me more anxious. And Bonnie — well, she just doesn't get it."

Sharon held her and Charlotte hugged back. "Thank you. Thank you."

"Just remember. If you want to talk, I'm here to listen."

"I wish I'd known you all along."

"Me, too." Sharon gave Callie one of her signals, and Callie winked back.

"Oh, Mom, I just remembered. I have to go to the mall and critique a photography exhibit for a homework assignment. They close in an hour, so I have to go now or I'll miss it."

"That's okay, Callie. You go."

After Callie left, Sharon comforted Charlotte as best as she could, and Charlotte allowed herself to sob on Sharon's shoulder for a while.

Several minutes of gasping passed before she could catch her breath. "Will you stay until the boys get home?" Charlotte eventually asked.

"Of course I will. Are you going to be okay?"

Charlotte nodded.

Cal walked in the door just after five. "Mom?"

"I'm in the kitchen."

After giving his mom a hug, he picked up her hands and pointed out her chewed nails. "What started this?"

She put on a weak smile. "Nothing important. Dinner should be ready soon, okay?"

"What happened to your locket?"

"Oh. Uh, it must've slipped under my sweater." She pulled it out.

He cocked an eyebrow and watched her carefully. Biting her nails *always* meant something was serious. Even after he turned to go toward his room, he watched her over his shoulder until he rounded the corner.

"Are you sure you're going to be okay?" Sharon asked.

"Yeah. Thanks for staying. I really appreciate you being here. Please thank Callie for handling him. I don't know what I would've done if she wasn't here." Her eyebrows pinched together. "I know he'll be back." Charlotte took a deep, shaky breath. "What am I going to do?"

"I wasn't going to say anything, but my uncle is a private investigator. I can ask him to watch the place. That way if there's an emergency, he'd be here."

"Oh, I couldn't ask you to do that."

"You don't have to ask. I'm just going to do it."

"Do you really think he would? We can afford to pay him now."

"Pshh. He's mostly retired now, and he doesn't need the money. He'd be glad to do it for family. And there's Roy, too. He's a cop, so he can get information that we can't."

Charlotte gave her a bear hug. She pinched her eyes closed. "Oh! Oh, thank you! You don't know what it means to know there's someone here for me."

Sharon held her tight. "I'm glad to do it. I'm here for you from now on. We're sisters, right? If you ever want to talk, I'm just a phone call away. Any time, day or night."

Charlotte nodded enthusiastically.

Chapter 3

Rudy Burke held the front door open for his wife, Georgia. When he closed it, he caught the aroma of chicken and dumplings and fresh baked bread. He inhaled deeply and let it out with a long, "Ahh." Then he called out, "We're here." He brushed the raindrops from his black hair. He had tried dyeing his hair last year when they got married, but he decided it was too much work and let it grow out again. Although his graying temples made him look like a distinguished gentleman, he could give the most menacing of looks with his dark eyes. Of course, he'd never give Georgia one of those looks, but it worked to his advantage when working as a private investigator. He hung his coat on the coat rack in the corner. Even while wearing a bulky sweater, it was obvious he was fit — especially for a man in his sixties.

Georgia put the foil-topped baking pan down on the table by the door so she could take off her coat and scarf. Her auburn hair was cut to shoulder length, making an attractive frame for her happy, blue eyes. She was of average height and build, but nice for a woman in her sixties. The red sweater and black slacks almost disguised some of the curves of her European figure.

Rudy saw her unbuttoning her coat. "Oh, here, let me help you." He helped her take off her coat and hung it up.

"Thanks, Honey Bear," she whispered. She turned around and picked up the pan to bring it into the kitchen.

His eyes twinkled, and he gave her a pat on the rear as she started to walk away. When she looked over her shoulder to wink at him, her hair swung around, and she blew him a kiss.

Sitting on the couch, Jack Cooper smiled at the scene, making laugh lines appear around his blue eyes. He was a little taller than Sharon and wiry. Being a maintenance mechanic meant that he had to climb over, under, and around a lot of equipment at work. But it was his kind face, tender voice, and sensitivity that attracted Sharon when they met. He resembled the comedian, Jeff Foxworthy — right down to the mustache. Jack's hair was the big difference, though. He always had his sandy-colored hair cropped short so he could control its unruliness. He got up and shook Rudy's hand, and they sat down to talk. "Welcome back, Uncle Rudy. How was the trip? You guys were gone for over a month."

Rudy leaned back to get comfortable. "Most of it was good — and don't ever call me 'Uncle' again."

Jack chuckled before asking, "What did you mean that most of it was good?"

"The not-so-good was Easter Island. The stone monuments were interesting, but that was about it. There wasn't much else to see or do. But I really enjoyed going to Machu Picchu. You wouldn't believe how amazing their civilization was. The hard part was just getting there. We had to climb the trails — *lots* of steep trails, mind you — just to get to it. It's pretty high up there, but it was worth it. You and Sharon should go sometime."

"We've been talking about taking a second honeymoon. That's a good suggestion. We'll have to talk about it." He nodded. "I'd say going out of town was good for you. You look relaxed."

"Actually, I'm kind of glad to get back to the grind."

"Already? What's so pressing?" Jack slapped his forehead. "Oh, yeah. Kurt, right? That's all Sharon talks about nowadays."

Rudy nodded. "When I retired, I really was kind of relieved to quit. But when Sharon called me about that scumbag, it stirred up the need to fix things. And this situation sure needs fixing. I've got a gut feeling that there's a lot more under the surface. There usually is with snakes like him. The only thing that gets in the way is that I just don't have the gumption to be away like I used to. Georgia's company is a lot more appealing than sitting alone in a car on surveillance all night."

Jack shook his head, grinning. "I remember that feeling. When Sharon and I were first married, the only thing I could think of was getting home when my shift was over. So it's the same even at your age, huh?"

"Hey! I'm not that old." He leaned in to whisper. "And don't you let Georgia hear you say anything about us being old."

Jack laughed.

After Georgia set the pan on the counter, Sharon gave her a hug. "You don't have to bring a dessert every time."

"That would be like asking the tide not to come in. You know I enjoy it, and I know Jack does."

"Yeah, he does love your baking."

"And don't sell yourself short; you're a good cook, too."

"Thanks." Sharon grinned as she lifted the foil and sniffed. "Mmm." Then she turned to Georgia. "You always make such great desserts. How'd you learn?"

"Well, Mom started teaching me when I was about six. She worked as a cook and housekeeper, so she gave me a lot of tips. But Alice wasn't interested; she thought cooking would make her look like a servant." Staring into space, she paused for a moment. Then she put on a smile and continued. "At first, Mom helped me do the measuring, and it just grew from there. We were pretty poor, so we'd walk around the neighborhood and ask people if we could pick the fruit that fell from their trees. My first desserts were pies and such. And she always took us with her to the fields where she picked every summer. We picked everything, fruit, vegetables, nuts. Alice hated that. But Mom always made sure we went back to school in the fall, even when she was still going to the fields." Georgia cupped her hand to her mouth and grinned. "Don't tell anyone, but we always snuck some of the produce to take home."

Sharon laughed. "I'll bet your dad liked your cooking."

"He'd already died by then," she said quietly.

Sharon turned red. "Oh, I'm sorry. I didn't mean to bring up bad memories." She put her hand on Georgia's shoulder. "Is it too painful to ask what happened?"

"No, it's okay. He had two jobs — Mom said he worked himself to death. I was only four when he had the heart attack."

Sharon gave her a hug. "I'm so sorry."

"I have one good memory that I treasure. Even though he was gone most of the time, I remember how he would tuck us in at night. Mom said that he stopped at home between jobs just to make sure of it." She became lost in her thoughts, smiling briefly, but then she frowned. "But I can't remember what he looked like anymore."

"You don't have any pictures of him?"

Georgia slowly shook her head.

"Aw, I'm sorry." Sharon took a deep breath, trying to look cheerful. "Callie and Roy should be here in a few minutes." Then she turned around to check the time left on the dumplings.

Georgia started chopping vegetables for the salad. "Have the lovebirds set a date yet?"

"Not yet. Charlotte was going to help her with some ideas on the theme and decorations, but that came to a screeching halt."

"Isn't that when Kurt showed up?"

"Yeah. And then Charlotte called me last night to tell me he showed up again. He scared the wits out of her. It's a good thing Hal was there, or she would've freaked out."

"Kurt's the one that was so abusive, right?"

"Mm-hm."

Georgia fumed for a moment. "If we were in the vigilante days, he'd have been buried long ago!"

Sharon raised an eyebrow and turned around to look at her.

Still agitated, Georgia inhaled slowly. "Why is he back after all these years?"

"I don't know! It sounds weird, doesn't it? He's been absent for over six years, and now all of a sudden he shows up? Charlotte's really apprehensive, and I don't blame her."

Georgia cocked an eyebrow. "I'll bet he's got an agenda."

"Charlotte said the only thing he asked about was to see the boys again. Has Rudy found out anything on him yet?"

"I don't know. He doesn't talk to me about work. You'll have to ask him at dinner."

When Callie and Roy arrived, Jack got up, greeted them, and gave Callie a bear hug. "How's my favorite daughter?"

She giggled as she him hugged back. "That's pretty easy for you to say since I'm your *only* daughter!" Then she saw Rudy on the couch and waved. "Hi, Rudy."

He waved back.

"Hi, Rudy," Roy said as he helped Callie with her coat before he took off his own and hung them up. His red ears and nose clashed with his V-neck maroon sweater. At six feet tall, he was taller than everyone here, yet he never flaunted the fact. His humility was one of the reasons Callie said yes when he proposed. Besides, with him recently graduating to become the youngest detective on the force, Callie felt safe with him. When he turned around, he rubbed his hands together. "I think it might freeze tonight. Would you like me to build a fire?" His green eyes lit up with anticipation.

Jack waved him to the fireplace. "Thanks, Roy. That'd be nice." Then he called out, "Callie and Roy are here."

"Good. It should be another two or three minutes," Sharon said loudly from the kitchen.

As Roy picked out several pieces of wood to arrange them in the fireplace, Callie watched him from behind and gazed at his toned physique. When he squatted down like that, his jeans hugged him in all the right places. She smiled.

Jack saw her watching Roy and walked over to whisper in her ear. She blushed and hurried to the kitchen. Jack chuckled as he returned to the couch.

"What was that all about?" Rudy whispered.

"I just told her to save it for the honeymoon," Jack whispered back.

Rudy laughed out loud.

Roy looked up. "What's so funny?"

Jack grinned. "I'll tell you after the wedding."

Roy sat back on his haunches and scratched at his dark brown hair. "Huh?" He shrugged his shoulders and went back to lighting the fire.

When everyone sat down at the table, Callie said, "Oh, Mom, you were right. Having Roy pick me up after he gets off work was a great idea. Thanks for the suggestion." She passed the bread.

"I'm glad it worked out so well."

Looking serious, Callie turned to Rudy. "Did you find out anything about Charlotte's ex? I've been worried about her."

Rudy's demeanor instantly changed from charming to intimidating, as he always did when discussing business. This image always gave the impression that no one would dare to mess with him. "Well, after he showed up at Charlotte's last night, I followed him. He's living with a young woman at a trailer park. I don't know what she sees in him. I only got a glimpse of her, but she looks like she's not even in her twenties yet. I'll try to find out what he's been doing since Charlotte divorced him."

Georgia shook her finger at Rudy. "Whatever you find out, you make sure he gets what he deserves!"

"You know I always try to make things right. Don't worry. I'll take care of it."

"You'd better! From what Sharon told me, he doesn't deserve any mercy."

"I just need to find out what's happened since they split."

"Good." She smiled at him. "I trust you." She gave him a peck on the cheek.

Roy smiled ambiguously. "You're a pretty tough cookie, you know."

Georgia played with the food on her plate, showing no emotion. "You have no idea."

Roy raised his eyebrow for a moment, then turned to Rudy. "What's the plan? What'll we do first?" Then he turned red. "Uh, I mean, what're you gonna look for?"

Rudy folded his arms, leaned back, and raised an eyebrow. "You want a piece of the action, huh? I'd be okay with showing you the ropes on this one."

Roy smiled sheepishly. "Yeah, I want to help. What can I do?"

"Why don't you come over tomorrow, and we can go over the game plan?"

"How early can I get there?"

Rudy chuckled as he looked at Georgia. "When do you think we'll be decent?"

Georgia gave him a playful shove on the shoulder. "Oh, you little devil."

Roy blushed. "I'm sorry. I don't want to intrude."

Georgia turned to Roy. "It's okay, just not too early. As long as you're not there before the sun comes up, you'll be fine."

Sharon chuckled. "Not to change the subject, but I want to make sure we're all still on for Sunday."

Jack grinned. "Oh, yeah! I'm really looking forward to that. Roy, are you and Callie going to join us?"

"As appealing as it sounds, Callie and I already made plans. We're going roller skating at Oaks Park," Roy said.

"Well, I guess that beats out the game. Are you going to be busy every Sunday?"

Callie snuck a quick glance at Roy as he blushed. "Well — you know how it is, Dad."

"Yeah, we understand. Young love and all that. Your mother and I were young once, too, you know," Jack reassured them.

Roy let out a sigh of relief. "Thanks. Anyway, after that, we planned to take a stroll on the Esplanade."

Jack leaned his elbows on the table and pointed at him. "Remember, just 'cause you're a cop doesn't mean I'll let you off the hook if anything happens to Callie."

Callie looked at Roy. "You know he's teasing you. He wouldn't do that if he didn't like you."

"Teasing? Heck, I'm serious. I'll hunt you down if you hurt my baby."

Roy leaned back with a twinkle in his eye and folded his arms. "This is your way of saying you like me?"

Jack tried to look stern. "Hey, those were Callie's words." He buttered a slice of bread and then grinned. "Yeah, you meet our approval." He gave Roy a thumbs-up as he nodded.

Sharon looked at Georgia. "Will you be here on Sunday?"

The corners of Georgia's eyes crinkled as she smiled. "Oh, no. Rudy and I will be just fine." Then she looked at Rudy. "Unless you changed your mind?"

"Nah, I've never been into sports." Then he did a double-take, "Does that mean you want to go?"

"Not if you have a reason to stay home."

"Maybe we should discuss this in private."

Georgia giggled. "I guess that means we're not going." She cleared her throat. "I think I'll go serve up the apple cobbler."

Roy leaned over to Rudy. "I hope Callie and I will still be that disgustingly gushy when we get that old." He turned red. "Sorry. No offense," he quickly added.

Rudy chuckled. "No offense taken, but don't let Georgia hear you talk about how old we are," he whispered.

"Well, they're still newlyweds, so they don't count. Do they?" Callie piped up.

Roy grinned as he stared at Jack and Sharon. "Ah, that's right. The old fogeys in love are you two."

Jack shook his head. "Since you're putting the digs on us, does that mean you approve of us?"

Roy shrugged. "Maybe." He unsuccessfully tried to look noncommittal.

"You learn pretty quick."

Chapter 4

Rudy pulled into the driveway and gave Georgia a kiss before she got out. "I've got some business to take care of. I should be home in about an hour and a half." He waited until she locked the front door behind her. He drove off with a frown. *I should've done this before we left on that trip. Risky leaving it like that. I really should retire; I'm starting to slip up.*

He turned onto the tree-lined street in the Alameda district. When Rudy saw the SUV parked in Pierre's driveway, the hairs on the back of his neck stood up. *Is that the same one?* He passed the one-story house and parked around the corner. He turned off the ignition, grabbed his phone, and opened an app. He put the ear buds in, turned up the volume, and set his phone to record. He listened as he put on a pair of black latex gloves.

"I'm telling you, man, they were real."

"You always think they're real," said a deep voice.

"Yeah, but these were."

"You know, we all like hearing about everyone's strip club experiences, but we need to keep focused on task, and right now no one's looking for it."

"Okay, okay. You got any idea where he'd put it?"

"I don't know. He's pretty clever. Could be anywhere. We don't even know *if* he made a copy."

"He may be clever in business, but when I tried to train him on how to use the computer, it was like trying to teach a donkey to do a crossword. I'm pretty sure he had no idea how to make a copy."

"We just hafta make sure."

"This is a waste of time," a third voice chimed in.

"Look!" shouted the deep voice. "When Frankie says 'Jump,' you jump. You don't even take the time to ask how high. Go check the master bedroom. Fingers, you check the other bedroom. I'm goin' to the kitchen."

Rudy put the phone in his pocket, got out of the car, and quietly closed the door. He only heard random shuffling sounds, footsteps, and what sounded like drawers being pulled open. He hurried through the neighbor's back yard and climbed over the fence, making sure to use shrubs and trees to cover his approach. Since he'd been inside only once last year, he had to think hard to remember the floor plan. He was pretty sure he was nearing the second bedroom window. Since it was dark, he knew that he wouldn't be seen looking in. He saw a tall, lean man checking the bureau drawers. He had a long, hooked nose that almost touched his upper lip. His black hair covered his ears and turned up slightly just below his collar. He had a tattoo on his left hand.

Rudy gasped. *That's it! That's the same tattoo!* He was thankful that he couldn't be heard by the men inside. He continued memorizing the thin man's features.

He had narrow shoulders, a short torso, and very long legs, almost abnormally long, making Rudy think of a clown on stilts. He looked like he'd been put together from two different people. Even with the loose sweatshirt, he still looked too thin. The baggy black pants flowed like a skirt as he moved around.

"Brick, Fingers, I think I found it," called the deep voice from another room.

When the man grabbed a laptop case and ran out of the room, Rudy hurried over to the kitchen window. He looked in through a bush and let out a silent whistle when he saw the muscular man with a blonde ponytail digging through a drawer. *I thought I recognized that voice.*

More steps. A short, thick man with red hair and mustache entered the kitchen just before the thin man came in carrying the laptop. The man with red hair had a short neck and tiny ears, which created the illusion of an oversized head. His hair was shaved on the sides but flat on top, as if someone had cut his hair with a chainsaw. His short arms and pecs bulged unnaturally under his brown T-shirt. The sleeves were rolled up as if to emphasize the muscles, and it appeared that a pack of cigarettes was rolled up in the left sleeve.

"Here, Fingers. Check it out. We can't go back sayin' we got it and it winds up bein' somethin' else." The man with the deep voice turned to hand something to the thin man. The man with the deep voice had the blonde hair pulled back into a ponytail. He had broad shoulders under a denim jacket and tight-fitting blue jeans. Below his arm, Rudy noticed a bulge under the jacket and assumed it was a gun. When Rudy turned to Fingers, recognition gripped him. He was certain it was the same man from the bus; no one else had such pale blue eyes. They were almost unnatural in lack of color, as if his life had been drained out of him.

Rudy realized "it" was a flash drive when Fingers plugged one into the laptop.

A couple minutes later, Fingers stood up straight. "These are the training files I gave 'im. We gotta keep lookin', Shiv."

His name is Shiv, eh. Gotta be a nickname.

Shiv sifted through the contents of the drawer carefully and went on to the next drawer. "Well, don't just stand there; keep lookin'. We can't be here all night."

I'd better wait and see if they find a copy.

"How come the cops didn't swarm all over this place?" Brick asked.

"'Cause the cops don't know Pierre was ever here."

"How come?"

"You sure got a lot to learn. Frankie never lets anyone have a house in his own name. The title belongs to a company with layered ownership. That way nobody finds out anything. Besides, when he checked in with his parole officer, he told him he was registered at a fleabag motel."

"Oh."

"When are you gonna get one of these?" He turned around and pointed to the tattoo on the back of his hand. "I thought you'd be jumpin' at the chance to get branded. You earned it."

Brick winced. "I just wonder if it's a good idea to flash it around. I mean —"

Shiv crossed his arms. "Are you questioning how we operate?" he growled.

"No, never! I just — I just don't think it's a good idea."

"Are *you* gonna tell that to Frankie?"

He shook his head quickly. "No! No."

"Besides, there's no one outside the family that knows what it means."

His face fell. "I'll go tomorrow."

"I'll call Freddy tonight and set up your appointment."

Rudy flinched. *Freddy knows a lot more than he's letting on. They've gotta have him on the hook somehow. I think I'll call on him.*

Fingers shook his head. "I can't believe we have to do this. We should've made him tell us *before* Brick smoked 'im."

"Look, he was stealing from Frankie. Do you really think he'd tell us anything?"

Rudy cringed, knowing he was responsible for Pierre's death.

"Besides, he was hiding from us up till the time the cops grabbed him."

Fingers sneered. "I only wish he was still alive so I could kill him myself."

"Yeah, I told Frankie not to trust him."

Finally, after two hours, Shiv laughed with his deep voice. "Well it looks like he didn't make one."

"Yeah. I don't think he even knew it was possible," Fingers sniffed.

"It's a good thing Todd made sure the cops couldn't read the one they found on 'im. I just wish he had a way to get rid of Bart's files."

Brick frowned. "What? Why can't he do what he did on Pierre's flash drive?"

"'Cause the files were on Bart's computer, not on a flash drive. Todd already let us know there's another cop assigned to work on it with him, so they have to work as a team. He can't do anything to those files."

"Yeah. Frankie's not sure how we're gonna get around that. At least Bart's information was only on *his* business. Pierre's files had everything. That's why we're here, to make sure nobody can get it."

"I'll have to ask Frankie to give Todd a bonus for what he did."

Brick sneered. "He doesn't deserve a bonus. He never warned us about Big Bart's takedown. And the captain — he didn't either. What's the point in buying those guys if they can't deliver?"

Shiv shook his head. "I know you're still green, but you gotta pay more attention. The captain was out of town on his vacation. And the cop in charge of the operation kept Todd in the dark. Besides, Bart's operation wasn't as profitable as it used to be. He's no big loss."

"What's in the works to launder the dough now?" Brick asked wide-eyed.

Shiv glared at him through slitted eyes. "If Frankie wanted you to know, he'd tell you."

Brick cringed. "Okay, I get it."

Fingers scratched his head. "Are you sayin' Bart was a liability?"

Shiv stared at them for a moment. "This doesn't go beyond these walls — right?"

Brick and Fingers nodded.

"After Bart was arrested, he tried to rat us out to make a deal. He just talked to the wrong cop, and it got back to Frankie. He was more than a liability; so yeah, he had to go."

"So the riot was staged — to get rid of him?"

"Yup."

"Why'd his crew have to go too?" Brick shook his head. "I lost a good friend in that riot."

"They were loyal to Bart, not to Frankie. 'Nough said?"

Brick nodded reluctantly.

"Besides them getting Bart's files, there was a big downside. When the cops searched the pawn shop, they found the connecting door to the machine shop."

Brick looked up quickly. "How are we gonna clean weapons now?"

Shiv glared at Brick. "Ask Frankie," he said in a firm, threatening tone.

Brick stepped back and shook his head.

Fingers zipped his laptop into its case. "Too bad how it went down. Maybe Frankie should put more of our moles to work."

"I think he's already planning it."

Rudy shook his head as the men left. *More moles? I hope all those names are in the flash drive. But Todd? I wouldn't have believed it. I've known him ever since he started at the precinct. And I thought he was okay. I guess you just never know.* His heart sank as he tried to remember all the information he'd asked Todd to look up in the past, and he groaned. *Roy asked about that license plate. He might be in danger. I'll have to warn him.*

He waited for a while before he jimmied the back door to retrieve the bugs he planted last year. *Whew, that was a close call. I'm glad they didn't find these things.* He had just removed the first one when he stopped. *Wait a minute!* He smiled and reinstalled it. *There. Let's see what you've got to say now.* He made sure everything was as he found it, locked the door, and left. When he got to his car, he made a note to check out the layers of ownership on this house.

He drove to the tattoo parlor, walked in, and waved at Freddy. "Hey."

Freddy's shirt was sleeveless. The sleeves had been torn off to advertise the tattoos from shoulder to wrist on his arms. Multiple studs punctuated various places on his face and body. Today, his spiked hair was blue. A chain hung from his belt to his right ear and his blue jeans were cut in so many places that there were more holes than fabric. "What can I do for you, Rudy?"

Rudy eyed him. "New tattoo?" He pointed to the skull and crossbones on Freddy's neck.

"Yup. Gotta advertise."

Rudy shook his head. "You're just never gonna quit adding to them, are you?"

"What can I say? I like ink."

"Speaking of art, remember when I was in here last year?"

"Yeah."

"I just thought I'd run this by you again, you know, that design that I showed you." He pulled up the picture on his phone and showed it to him.

Freddy looked at it and shook his head. "Nope, still don't recognize it."

Rudy stared at him for several seconds.

"What?!" He stepped back, his breathing shallow.

Rudy leaned over the counter so that his face was just a few inches from Freddy's. He saw his forehead start to shine from perspiration. "We need to meet on neutral ground." He inched closer. "Murphy's, two o'clock."

Freddy swallowed hard.

"Well?"

He took a deep breath. "Okay. But make it two-thirty. I have to make it look natural. I close at two and I don't want to rush over there." He pressed his lips together. "Now get outta here before someone sees you."

Rudy nodded and left.

Rudy sat in the far corner booth, where he could see the front door and everyone in the place. A flickering, pool table light hung over the pool table where a couple was playing 9-ball. The man had a long beard, and his open flannel shirt emphasized the dirty T-shirt that almost covered his gut. He was flirting with the plump woman who cooed over his minimal playing ability. She wore a tight mini-skirt that hugged every bulge. When it was her turn, she stood in front of him and bent over to shoot with an unnatural sway to her backside. Rudy shuddered and turned away to look at the three men sitting at the bar. One was absorbed in playing video poker. The other two were nearing their limit. The old man with obviously dyed black hair was unaware that he was failing at his attempt to flirt with the bartender. He didn't seem to realize his words were running together. The bulky man at the end of the bar rested his chin on his hand with his elbow on the bar. He looked like he could fall over at the slightest nudge.

Freddy didn't arrive until almost three. He ordered a whiskey on the rocks at the bar and brought his drink to Rudy's table. He sat down and leaned forward. "How'd you know?"

Rudy shrugged. "I have my sources. How long have you been working with them?"

Freddy fidgeted. "I can't talk to you. Understand? I just *can't.*"

"You know I'm not going to let go of this."

"Sorry. You have to." His neck started to shine from perspiration. "I told you, I *can't talk. I just can't,*" he said in a hushed tone. He downed the whiskey, stood up, and left.

Chapter 5

Rudy sat in his office thinking. He had done a thorough search on his copy of the flash drive when he got home last night. He couldn't find Todd's name anywhere, even with different spellings, and that made him nervous. He began to wonder if the flash drive was complete.

The doorbell rang.

Rudy shook Roy's hand, and Georgia offered Roy a cup of coffee.

"Thanks, but I'll pass. I've had two cups already."

Rudy led the way. "We can talk in my office. I've got a rough idea of what we'll look for on Kurt."

As he followed him, Roy inhaled deeply and let it out slowly.

After Rudy shut the door, he motioned for Roy to sit in the chair in front of his desk.

Roy looked around before sitting down. "Looks like a real office. I see you still have this — what do I want to call it? Electric chair? Gotta say, it's intimidating. Is that why you keep it?

"Yup. Georgia hates it, but it serves me well. There isn't nearly as much room in here as I had in my old office, so I had to archive a lot of records and get rid of a lot of furniture — just not that piece. But this is adequate, considering I don't work much anymore. By the way, it's okay to say we're working together researching Kurt, but we still need to keep it under wraps on anything else."

"Well that's what we agreed on. I'm thinking of the family, like you said." He shifted his weight as he looked at the arms of the chair.

Rudy leaned forward with his elbows on the desk and grinned.

Roy looked at him suspiciously. "Okay, what've you got?"

"You'll never guess."

Roy crossed his arms. "Well, then you'd better tell me."

"Remember how I bugged Pierre's house?"

"Yeah. The captain still doesn't know where they came from. That was …."

"I don't mean Pierre's hideout."

"What?"

"I'm not talking about the house where he was arrested. I'm talking about the house he lived in for a while when he got out of that halfway house."

Roy's eyes got big. "Are you saying you bugged it, too?"

"Yup. I went there last night to remove the bugs. But I changed my mind."

"Why in the world would you do that?!"

"Three hoods were there when I arrived."

"They didn't see you, did they?"

Rudy shook his head slowly.

"Quit teasing me and tell me what you heard."

Rudy put his hands behind his head and leaned back in his swivel chair. "Remember that blonde guy Pierre met on the bus?"

"Yeah."

"He was there, and two others. They were searching the place."

"And?"

"Don't worry. They didn't find any of my bugs. They were looking to see if Pierre had made a copy of that flash drive. You know, like the copy I handed you."

"Did he? Make a copy, that is?"

"Nope. At least, if he did, he didn't leave it there." He sat up straight and put his hands on his armrests. "It's what they talked about that concerns me."

Roy waited silently.

"Remember last year I asked you to check out that license plate?"

Roy frowned. "Yeah, what of it?"

"You said someone caught you when you were looking it up."

"Yeah."

"Did you do your own search or did you ask Todd to do it?"

"I did it."

"Phew. That's good." He paused and then leaned forward. "Todd's one of the dirty cops."

Roy's eyebrows shot up. "No way!"

"Thing is, when I first got the flash drive, I looked it over and never saw his name."

"Look it up by Oscar. He hates the name. That's why we call him by his middle name, Todd."

"No wonder." Rudy frowned. "How come you didn't warn me that it was on there?" He eyed him. "You didn't check out the flash drive, did you?"

Roy shifted in his seat again. "Sorry. I scanned over it to get a general idea; but I've been so busy with work, and then there's Callie …." He cowered. "Well, you know," he said sheepishly.

"Just bring it back next time you come over. I'll check it out."

"Sure." He folded his hands in his lap. "What's your plan for Kurt?"

"Well, like I said at dinner last night, we need to track his whereabouts since he and Charlotte split. If he wound up out of state, then you could search for any warrants or arrests. We'll need to research any previous addresses, jobs, money trails, and so on. I can do a lot of searching on the Internet. Then, when we find out what cities he's been in, I've got a lot of connections around the country that can dig up details for us."

"Sounds like you've got a pretty good network."

"Well, after forty or so years investigating, you're bound to develop good connections. And then I help them out whenever they need me. It saves a lot on time and travel expenses."

Rudy reached for a notepad and handed it to Roy. "Here, I've already written down a few things you can do. You can add whatever notes you want to."

Roy looked it over. "Looks pretty comprehensive."

"There's always the chance that Kurt never broke the law. If that's the case, we'll have to figure out some other way to take care of him."

Roy held up his hands. "I hope you're not talking about what I think you're talking about."

Rudy folded his arms. "And what do you think I'm talking about?"

Roy paused. "I'm not doing anything illegal. You know I couldn't do that."

"Roy, what am I going to do with you? You know I'd never involve you in anything like that."

Roy leaned forward with his elbows on the arms of the chair. "Does that mean that you'll be on your own when you do? Or does it mean that you aren't going to do anything illegal?"

Rudy looked insulted. "That doesn't even deserve an answer."

Roy eyed him suspiciously.

"Oh, since you're here, I'd like to talk about a couple of things I can't talk about with anyone else." He paused. "You know that Georgia had a stepdad."

"Yeah, I was there when she told us last year."

"She gets all weird when the subject comes up, so I think there's more to it than she's letting on. I did some research and found out he was married before, twice. Both the ex-wives are dead, so I looked up the kids. He doesn't have any of his own, just step-daughters — some from each wife. Since it was so long ago, only a few of them are still alive. I could only talk with one of them. But that one said the weirdest thing — she said she was sorry for Georgia."

Roy cocked an eyebrow. "Are you sure that's what she said?" He flinched when Rudy glared at him.

"Of course I'm sure! Then she shut the door in my face. I knocked again, but she wouldn't answer." He frowned. "Oh, one other thing. When I first asked her about him, she wanted to know if it was because he'd been arrested."

Roy pressed his lips together, folded his hands and tapped his thumbs together.

Rudy waited.

"Give me what information you have on him. I'll see if I can find any arrests or complaints." After Rudy handed him the information, he fidgeted for a while. "Rudy?"

"Yeah."

He shifted his weight. "Remember when I said I didn't want to know what was in Pierre's box?"

"Yeah. Do you want to know now?"

"Yeah. Uh, no. Well, kinda. But not if it's money."

"It's not money."

Roy exhaled with pursed lips. "Okay, so tell me what's in it then?"

"I'm not sure."

"Huh? Seriously? You don't know?"

"Well, I know what the stuff is. I'm just not positive what it means yet."

"You're not making any sense."

"Do you want to see it?"

"Well, if I can help figure it out, then yeah."

"How much time do you have?"

Roy looked at his watch, "I've got to check in about twenty minutes."

"Okay, then let's meet after you get off work."

"So, about that flash drive. There are an awful lot of files that go back a lot of years. That's why I didn't check it out extensively. Anyway, I'm pretty sure it's a record of payoffs." He frowned. "It's possible there are more than a few dirty cops."

"All right, I'll make sure to look into it and make a complete list. Then we'll call in the Feds."

Roy looked at his watch again. "Hey, I gotta go."

"Okay. I know you're busy, but we really do need to get going on that." Rudy got up and opened the office door.

When they came into the living room, Roy was wearing a poker face. Georgia came up and gave Roy a hug. "Bye now." After she shut the front door, she turned to Rudy. "What was that all about?"

"What do you mean?"

"The tension between you and Roy?"

"What makes you think there was tension?"

She stared at him. "I know tension when I see it."

He shrugged. "Well, we were talking about Kurt."

"You're sure that's all?" She said slowly.

"Wouldn't I tell you if there was more?"

When he gave her a hug, she pressed her worried face into his chest.

That night, Rudy watched as Roy carefully looked at each item. Roy turned the first piece over in his hands, looking at each side. It was wrapped in old plastic that had turned opaque and brittle with time. Old masking tape had been reattached to the bag with new tape. The writing on the old tape was faded, almost unreadable. He put it down and picked up a second bag and gasped.

"You see it, huh?"

"Yeah, I almost missed it. The plastic was so stiff and clouded that I almost didn't notice there's another bag inside of each one." He looked more carefully. "Have you inventoried all this?"

"Yup. There was a strip of microfilm that already had everything listed. Even so, I put everything in a spreadsheet and brought it with me." He pulled it out of his pocket. "Look, each piece has a date, a name and a number assigned to it."

Roy's hand dropped to his side and he stared at him. "Why make *me* go through all this?"

"I have my suspicions. I just want to know what *you* think."

Roy huffed and picked it up again. "You're the one that reattached the tape?"

"Every one. Feel free to open the outside bags." Then he pulled a box of large, zippered plastic pouches out of his knapsack and opened it.

Roy opened the outer bag of the second piece and examined the inside bag. He looked up at Rudy. "This looks like an old evidence bag."

Rudy nodded with a smile.

"And this stuff was in Pierre's box?"

"Yup."

Roy placed the evidence bag into the pouch along with the outer bag and zipped it closed. He repeated the process until he had looked at everything and placed them in the zippered pouches. When he was done, he shook his head. "If these really are pieces of evidence from old cases, it's a lot of casework gone missing. I can't help wondering, how did Pierre get all this stuff? Most of these things are hand weapons, gun barrels, bullets, and documents. These are probably connected to criminal cases."

"When I first started looking at this, I had trouble deciphering everything. Well, you saw the condition. But when I compared the microfilm, it was pretty easy to match up the loose pieces of tape to the items they belonged to. The film was pretty comprehensive." He paused.

Roy leaned back. "Do you think this is crucial evidence?"

Rudy nodded slowly. "I'm pretty sure this stuff never went to trial."

"But how would Pierre have gotten hold of this stuff?" He scratched his head. "And if the dates are right, this stuff is almost twenty years old. I suppose I could look up unsolved cases, maybe dismissed cases, to see if any dates or names match up."

"I think you'd better look up *all* court cases, even ones that had a sentence. With missing evidence, innocent persons could have been convicted."

Roy's eyes got big, "Whoa, that's a tall order. You realize those records won't even be in the computer — they're too old. I'll have to physically look at every file. Do you know how much time that's going to take?"

"Believe me; I know how slow that is. Remember, I was doing this before computers became popular."

"Well, don't expect anything too soon."

"Remember, don't talk to *anyone* down there."

Roy frowned. "Do you think this could have anything to do with the flash drive?"

"Well, the flash drive is a record of paid bribes and payoffs. And to get this stuff out of the evidence box, someone was probably paid to remove it. And I'm pretty sure whoever paid him is going to keep their foot in the door. If the person who removed *this* stuff isn't there anymore, we'll have the name of the person who does it now."

Roy let out a low whistle as he folded the list and put it in his pocket.

They put everything back in the box.

Roy picked up the box so they could leave, and Rudy put his hand on Roy's shoulder. "Did you bring the flash drive?"

"Sorry, I was so focused on seeing what was in this box, I forgot. Next time, though."

Chapter 6

Josh yelled from outside, "Mom!" Other than the faint freckles, he looked like a young Kurt with shorter, brown hair. As soon as Josh noticed this resemblance, he made a mental note to ask his mom for a haircut as soon as possible. He hated the thought of looking like *him*.

Charlotte and Hal rushed outside as Kurt was getting up off the ground just outside the front door. Kurt moaned as he wiped blood from his nose.

Hal's jaw dropped. "Josh! What happened?" His brown eyes opened wide behind his wire-rimmed glasses. He was a little younger than Charlotte but the same height. He enjoyed spending time with his new family instead of working out at the gym, and having a desk job meant that he was relatively soft. His brown hair had a traditional cut because he worked in an office.

Kurt held up his bloody hand as if to stop them and shook his head. "It's okay. He had to let it out. Josh, that's a pretty good right hook for a fifteen-year-old."

Josh glared at him. "Sixteen. But how would you know? You've *never* been interested in us!"

Hal grabbed a tissue and handed it to Kurt. "I'm sorry. We didn't know it was you. Let's go inside."

"Oh, I knew it was him all right. I should've broke his face!" Josh clenched his jaw.

"I mean, we didn't know it was you at the door." Then he looked at Josh. "Josh, why *did* you do that?"

"You're kidding, *right*?" Then he leaned forward with fire in his eyes. "I'll never go anywhere with *him*! I don't even want to be *near* him!"

Charlotte reached for Hal's hand for support. Then she took a slow breath. "But your dad came to see you."

Josh yelled at his mother as he pointed at Kurt behind him. "If he was my dad, he would've been here all these years." Still pointing, he spun around to face Kurt. "You deserted us, and I'm glad of it! I don't want you in my life!"

Kurt looked hurt. "I understand." Then he turned to Cal who was standing at the far end of the living room. "Well, I guess it's just you and me then."

Cal chewed his lip as he glanced around at everyone in the room.

Charlotte squeezed Hal's hand even tighter. "It's entirely up to you. Don't think that you're hurting anyone's feelings with whatever you choose. Just like you can't make anyone do what you want, Kurt or Josh can't make you do what they want either. It's your decision."

Cal looked at Josh as if pleading for forgiveness. "Sorry."

Josh slapped the wall hard as he stormed out of the room.

"We're going down to Marine Drive by the Columbia River. We'll only be a couple of hours; the fish probably won't be biting after that anyway," Kurt said.

"Hey, I just bought some great fishing equipment. Cal, you can use my gear," Hal offered.

"Thanks, but I've got everything we need," Kurt said quickly.

Hal shrugged his shoulders.

After Kurt and Cal left, Josh came back into the room. "I can't believe you let him go!"

"I'm sorry, Josh. It was his choice. He wants to reconnect with your dad."

Josh's nose flared. "He's not my dad. He deserted us. Cal doesn't remember what he was like, but I do. I'll never trust him again."

Charlotte held back the tears. "Honey, he could've changed. People do, you know."

"If I see it, I might believe it. But I seriously doubt it."

Hal walked over to Josh, who was slightly taller than he was. His smile pushed his glasses up a bit as he put his hand up on Josh's shoulder. "How about we shoot a few hoops? I'll meet you outside."

Josh turned around. "Okay. And you're the only dad I'll ever want or need." He grabbed his coat and went outside.

Hal gave Charlotte a long hug. "I'm proud of you. You did the right thing." Then he went out to join Josh.

After Hal shut the door, Charlotte closed her eyes. "I hope so." She moaned.

Cal was grinning when Kurt brought him back. "It was so cool! I even got a couple nibbles, but they got away. Oh, and I almost fell in once."

Charlotte grimaced.

"Can we go again? Please?"

Charlotte took a calming breath. "I guess so."

Kurt started to speak to Josh, "You can …."

Josh threw his hands up and stormed out of the room. "Nope, don't want to hear it!"

"How about we plan our next outing for two weeks from now?"

"Can I, Mom?"

"I can't think of any reason why not." *Unfortunately.*

"All right. Sounds good. Well, I guess I'd better go. See you, Cal."

Cal hugged him. "Thanks, Dad."

Kurt smiled and then left.

Then Cal turned around looking horrified. "I'm sorry. I didn't mean anything against you, Hal."

"Hey, no problem. He *is* your dad."

"Whew. Thanks. I don't want to hurt your feelings."

When Cal got to his room, Josh was waiting for him.

"I don't know what his agenda is. Just don't get too close to him. He'll hurt you soon enough."

"Josh, I think he's really trying."

"For your sake, I'd like to be wrong. But I know what he's like."

Josh went to the kitchen where Charlotte was making dinner. "Mom?"

"Yes, Josh?"

"I'll protect you."

She turned around. "You mean from Kurt?"

"Yeah. I don't trust him." He gave her a hug.

"Well, you never know. He may have changed."

"We'll see."

She hugged him tight so he wouldn't see the worry in her eyes.

After dinner, the boys took the basketball outside to play horse in the driveway.

Hal rolled up his sleeves and helped Charlotte with the dishes. Concerned, he stopped for a moment to push his glasses up and look at her. "How are you handling this?"

She dried a plate, placed it into the cupboard, and paused for a moment. "At first, I was terrified. I'm so glad you're here." She looked at him. "I know I wouldn't have been able to face him alone. I thought he was going to do something awful. But now, I wonder if I should give him the benefit of the doubt. I guess I want it to be true so the boys can have some kind of relationship with him. And if he really means it, I hope Josh comes around. I don't want him to be filled with all that anger and hate. It's not good for him. But I'm not letting my guard down yet. I don't know if I'll ever be able to."

"I feel the same way — hopeful."

"I guess I'm feeling a little safer with all of you guys around." Then she quickly looked at him. "Listen, if he does turn out to have an ulterior motive, please don't tangle with him. Okay?"

"And what am I supposed to do if he starts something? Just let him have at it?"

Charlotte closed her eyes as she cringed. "I just don't want you to get hurt. He's really strong." Realizing what she'd just said, she blurted out. "I'm sorry. I didn't mean to make it sound like you're weak." She grimaced. "He's been known to use weapons to get his point across."

Hal's eyebrows shot up. "Weapons! Like what!?"

Charlotte took a cleansing breath as she looked up at the ceiling. Then she chewed on her left pinkie nail. "It was just once in a while at first. He'd use a crowbar to punch a hole in a wall, or stab the table with a fork. Sometimes he would use a hammer or a butcher knife for emphasis. He always acted like he was using restraint in not using them on me." She shuddered. "I was such a coward." Her voice was weak. "I didn't know it at the time, but he used scare tactics on Josh, too. He told me about some things after Kurt was forced to leave." She wiped a tear. "Poor Josh — Kurt always told him it was his fault. You know that Josh was nine when he ran away. Josh thought that if he wasn't there anymore, Kurt wouldn't have an excuse to threaten us anymore." Charlotte paused. "What I didn't tell you was that the night Josh ran away, Kurt was cleaning his shotgun and he blew a hole in the storage shed wall. He told Josh that 'accidents happen.'" She wiped away a tear running down her cheek. "And not to be surprised if there was another accident."

Hal pulled her into a hug. "Oh, Charlotte, why didn't you tell me before?"

"I just couldn't. I thought you'd hate me for being a neglectful mother."

"No! No! I'd never think that." He held her tight.

She leaned on his shoulder. "Kurt always told me that's what I was. He said anyone would be able to see it. He always pointed to accidents the boys had and said if I'd watch them better, they wouldn't happen." She started to sob.

"Oh, honey. I never knew." His face hardened. "Those accidents with the kids that you just mentioned — do you think Kurt could've been responsible?"

She breathed hard as she pondered that thought. She stood up straight. "I don't know. It's possible." Her eyes got big. "Oh, Hal! Some of those accidents were really serious." She turned red and her nose flared. "If he did that, I ... I don't know ... what ...." She put her head on Hal's shoulder again and hugged him as she trembled.

Hal looked up and saw Josh standing in the hallway listening.

"Dad, I'm pretty sure you're right."

Charlotte jumped up straight, wiped the tears away, and put on a desperate smile.

"Mom, you don't have to be brave." He walked up and hugged her.

She hugged back. "Oh, Josh. I didn't know."

"I was afraid to tell you. I didn't tell anyone else about that part — in the shed. Mom — he said that you might be the one to have that accident." His face contorted. "I'm sorry."

"Oh, Josh, you have nothing to be sorry about. None of it was your fault." She squeezed him tight.

Hal was pale. "Now what do we do? Cal's going to be seeing him. What now?"

Josh turned red. "I told you! I told you not to let him go! But you wouldn't listen!"

Hal took Charlotte's hand. "Didn't you say that Sharon's uncle is a private investigator?"

She nodded weakly.

"I'm guessing he'll find something on him. Surely he's done something that the authorities could put him away for."

"I'll ask."

"Do that — as soon as possible."

Just then Cal came in from outside. "What's taking so long, Josh? Don't you want to play anymore?"

"Oh, sorry. I decided to get a drink of water too. Let's go."

Chapter 7

"Sweetie, here's your supply of snacks. There are three dozen hot wings and dip, paper plates, and extra napkins." Sharon gave Jack a hug as he put on his jacket. "Anything else?"

"Naw. We'll be fine. I can hardly wait to see John's TV. When I called him yesterday, that was all he could talk about." He chuckled. "Bye, Pookie." He kissed her on the cheek.

"Bye, Sweetie."

Sharon had already set the table, so she went back to the kitchen to make the finishing touches on the cheese tray. She hummed as she placed loose red and green grapes among the four kinds of cheese. Then she opened three kinds of crackers and arranged them on another tray.

The doorbell rang.

She opened the door to find Bonnie holding a bottle of champagne, an empty crystal tray, and a small white sack.

"Hi, Sharon. I decided to get out of there before everyone arrived and John started asking for things. Where do you want me to put this?"

"Oh, I was expecting wine. Uh, let me put that in the fridge. Come on in and make yourself at home. Just put whatever you have on the table."

"Well, it didn't cost that much more, so I thought, why not champagne?" After she hung up her coat, she looked around. "Nice house. I love the fireplace. Did Jack build a fire before he left?"

"Yeah, it must be a guy thing."

"Where do you want me to put my purse?"

Sharon turned around. "Wow, Callie was right."

"Right about what?"

"Your purse is gorgeous. Did you make that?

"Yeah. How'd you know?"

"She told me that you made Charlotte's purse. I just assumed you made that one, too."

"Oh. That's pretty clever of you to figure that out. Actually, I made a lot of them. But they're all different. I like variety."

"You're going to think this is pushy, but would you show us how to make one?"

"Really? Of course. But I don't use a pattern, I just think about what I'd like and then I just make it. If it's okay with you, you can watch while I make one. If you know what you want, maybe you could draw something. I could do it."

"But we're not very artistic. Anything you'd like to make — I'm sure it would be great. And would you let us watch?"

"Why don't you come over, and I'll show you what I have already. Maybe you'd like one of them."

"Really?! I'll have to check with Callie on when she'd be available."

"Okay, just let me know."

Bonnie followed her into the kitchen and did a 360-degree turn. "Wow! I never would've guessed you'd have such an elegant kitchen. This is awesome."

"Well, when Jack took those high-end appliances from Alice's mansion, he remodeled the kitchen to make room for them. Besides, he wanted it to look like they belonged in here. There used to be a pantry over here, so he just took out the wall and made it part of the kitchen."

"I just might have to do that — you know, remodel our kitchen. But then, maybe we should just buy a new house. With John's giant TV and all those cool clothes I brought home, a bigger house would just make better sense. Don't you think?"

"Whatever works for you and John."

"Can I help you with something?

"Sure. I just finished the cheese plate, would you put it on the table?"

When she got to the table, she paused. "Where'd you buy this tablecloth? I'd like to get one, too."

"Georgia gave it to us for our last wedding anniversary," Sharon called out from the kitchen. "She said she made it years ago."

Bonnie put the platter down and then fingered the tablecloth as she bent over to look at it more carefully. "How'd she do that?"

"Do what?"

"Dye those flowers. They're perfect."

Sharon walked into the dining room. "Dye them?" She looked at where she was pointing and smiled. "Bonnie, the flowers were crocheted with different colored thread."

"Oh." Bonnie pinched her eyebrows together as she frowned. "But, I can't see how she sewed them in there."

Sharon turned to go back into the kitchen so Bonnie wouldn't see her grinning. "I'll have to ask her."

The doorbell rang again.

Bonnie stood up straight. "I'll get it."

When Arlene and Karen came in, Arlene frowned. "Bonnie? I should've known you'd be the first one here." After hanging her coat, she set her bottle of wine on the table.

Sharon waved from the kitchen. "Hi. So Mel and Grant didn't mind, eh?"

"Are you kidding? With all the food over there, he won't even miss me," Arlene huffed.

Karen smiled politely. "They'll be fine."

Sharon looked up from her preparations. "Karen, didn't you say you all play canasta? Maybe we can get in a few hands."

Before Karen could answer, Arlene raised an eyebrow above her bifocals and butted in. "A glutton for punishment, eh?"

"I've been known to hold my own."

Karen sighed.

Charlotte arrived after a few more minutes. "The boys were so excited to go over there with Hal. Mom, this was a great idea."

"Thanks. I manage to have one once in a while."

After everyone filled their plates, they sat in front of the fireplace. The wine and champagne lightened their mood as they sat talking for a couple of hours. Even Arlene seemed a little calmer.

Feeling relaxed, Sharon took a sip of wine and looked at Charlotte. "How was Kurt's visit with the boys?"

Arlene choked on her cracker and coughed a few times.

Charlotte's eyes got big as she shot an anxious glance at Sharon.

"What?! He's back?!" Arlene blurted out when she could breathe again.

Charlotte cowered and fingered her locket.

Sharon jumped when Arlene jerked her head around to glare at her.

"And you! You knew about it?" Arlene growled at her while pointing with an accusing finger.

Karen held her hand over her mouth.

"Just what were you thinking?" Arlene snapped at Charlotte.

Charlotte meekly hung her head. "He showed up and wanted to see the boys. I can't stop him. The restraining order expired a long time ago."

Arlene jumped to her feet. "It doesn't matter! That maniac has no rights. He deserted them for — for what — six years?"

"They just went fishing. At least Cal did."

"And what did Josh do?"

Charlotte cringed. "He punched him. Then he stayed home and spent time with Hal."

"Good for him!"

Bonnie reached for another slice of cheese.

"At least Josh has good sense!" Arlene's face turned red. "How come you could tell Sharon all about this and not one of us?"

Cringing, Charlotte closed her eyes and took in a shaky breath. "Callie was there when he showed up. She's the one who called Sharon over and told her, okay? And I didn't rush to call you because I knew you'd do this," she said weakly.

"Do what?! You know I want to help you. But no-o, you always shut me out." She huffed. "I can't believe this," she growled under her breath. She sat down with a thud.

Bonnie sat up with a smile. "Oh, I brought truffles, the good ones. They'll melt in your mouth. I figured chocolates are a girl's best friend. You know, PMS and all. I'll go get them."

After Bonnie got up to get the chocolates, Arlene rolled her eyes. "She has to be the most clueless person on the planet," she whispered loudly.

Karen patted her arm. "Now, now. Let's be kind."

"Mom — that *was* kind."

"Kind of mean," Charlotte mumbled.

"I heard that!"

Bonnie returned with the chocolates arranged on her crystal tray. "Here, I brought enough for each of us to pig out." She grinned as she passed the tray around.

They each took one and Bonnie put the tray on the small table in front of them. She tucked her feet under her and closed her eyes as she relished every bite of her truffle.

Breathing hard, Arlene increasingly gave Charlotte, and especially Sharon, accusing glares.

Sharon didn't say anything. *Me and my big mouth. I should have known better. I'm going to have to do something for Charlotte to make up for this.*

Arlene shot up to her feet, startling everyone. She glared at Sharon. "I just *knew* you were going to do this!" she shouted. "You just *had* to weasel your way into our family, didn't you? I *knew* I should've trusted my instincts. The only reason I was quiet all this time was because Mom asked me to. But I can't do it anymore! If it wasn't for your rotten mother, we wouldn't have to put up with you at all, and Mom would be okay, and we'd have our real dad!" She narrowed her eyes, leaned forward and pointed menacingly. "You're just like your mother! Using your charm to get what you want! I know what you're like — and I don't trust you!" she snarled.

Everyone gaped.

"And I know why Dad named you Sharon!"

Sharon's eye widened. "Huh?"

Arlene sneered. "Don't you get it?! It was his way to remember Mom! Think about it! 'Sharon' sounds like 'Karen'? He loved *her*, not *Alice*."

Sharon swallowed hard.

"What are you doing, Arlene?" Karen begged.

Arlene looked down at her mother. "You just don't *get* it, do you?" She turned and wagged her finger at Sharon, "What your mother did was despicable! She robbed us of our father! You *know* all that. But what you *don't* know is that Mom had a mental breakdown when he left!"

Sharon cringed.

"And I — I was only six!" She pointed at herself, then to her mother. "*I* had to take care of *everyone*," she pointed to her mother, "because *she* couldn't. I didn't have a childhood," she pointed to her sisters, "because *they* depended on me! Now, here *you* come — waltzing in, scheming to take them away from me with your *charming* façade! Well, you haven't fooled me!" She looked at each of her sisters as she warned them, "Watch out for her. Don't let her in!" She set her glass down with a clunk. "I'm leaving!" She grabbed her purse and coat and slammed the door behind her.

Everyone sat stunned and speechless — except for Bonnie. She seemed oblivious as she picked up another chocolate.

Karen fidgeted for a few uncomfortable moments. "I'm sorry," she mumbled. She put her hand on Bonnie's arm. "Will you take me home?"

Bonnie frowned. "But why? We've hardly begun."

"Please, I have to go," Karen urged quietly. "Arlene was my ride, and I have to leave. Please?"

Bonnie shrugged. "Okay." She turned to Sharon with a smile. "Thanks for having us. I had a nice time."

Karen's face was red as she got up to get her coat. "I'm sorry. And I want you to know that none of the rest of us think those things about you," she said with tears in her eyes.

"Thanks," Sharon replied quietly.

After they left, Charlotte closed her eyes and shook her head. "I don't know what to say. I knew something was bothering her, but I had no idea. I'm sorry you had to see that. And I'm sorry she's blaming you."

"Why are you apologizing? When you told me about your sisters and Karen, I should have realized not to say anything about Kurt. It was my fault for not remembering that. And for not picking up on Arlene's feelings about me. Please forgive me."

"Really, it's not your fault. None of us knew. I could see she'd been stewing for several months, but I just didn't know why. She's just very good at hiding her feelings from people — at least until she blows up. Really, you couldn't have known." Charlotte sighed and hung her head. "But those things she said, I'm sure she didn't mean it. She couldn't have."

"Nobody knows that. And she shouldn't have treated *you* that way."

"You're the one she treated badly. I don't know why she hates you so much. None of that stuff was your fault."

"I get it. Even though I didn't personally do anything — to her, I represent the whole mess." She shook her head. "I wish I knew what to do."

They collected some glasses and napkins to bring into the kitchen. "Let's talk about something we can do? You know, I think we can find out Kurt's true intentions. You'd like to know, right?"

Charlotte cringed. "Yeah, about that. Hal and I talked after Kurt and Cal got back from fishing. Kurt's too dangerous for us to cross him. I made Hal promise not to do anything. It doesn't look promising."

"I was referring to my uncle checking out Kurt's background. Maybe we can figure out what he's up to. Remember, I told you about him. He knows what he's doing. Please let me ask him."

"Yeah, I was afraid to ask you."

"Oh, Charlotte. Don't be afraid to ask me anything." Sharon laughed nervously. "I have a confession. We've already talked, and he's checking on Kurt now. Forgive me?"

"Forgive you? I'm relieved! Thank you!" She gave Sharon a hug.

"You're welcome. But there's one other thing."

"What's that?"

"You've got to stop letting Arlene bully you."

"Huh?" She stood back.

"You heard me. She's bullying you." She paused. "Has she always been so — forceful?"

Charlotte mulled that over for a while. "I guess. As long as I can remember." She bowed her head. "But I can't blame her. It's like she said — when she had to take charge after Dad left. Even after Mom married Grant, she kinda just let Arlene keep handling me and Bonnie. Grant was some help, but he didn't know what to do with all of us." She looked up again. "I can't blame her."

Sharon shook her head. "I'll bet that allowing her to boss you around made you a prime target for Kurt. He could see you were easily dominated, and it opened the door for him to do it, too."

Charlotte's mouth dropped open, and she shrank back. "Seriously? You really think so?"

"I've seen it before. But I don't know if you could learn how to stand up without help. I think you should talk to Dr. Reed; he's an incredible counselor. He helped my mother-in-law learn how to handle a bully. I'm sure he can help you, too. I'll get his phone number."

Looking down, Charlotte started to put on her coat.

"Wait a minute. Here's Dr. Reed's phone number." When Charlotte didn't respond, Sharon pressed the point. "Promise me you'll call? Please?" She stuffed the paper into Charlotte's coat pocket.

Charlotte smiled at her, nodded, and gave her a hug. "Thank you. Thank you."

When Bonnie got home, she waved. "Hi, John. I'm back."

"How'd it go?"

"Arlene ruined everything by yelling."

"Again?"

"Uh-huh. But other than that, we had a great time — mostly. How about you?"

"Okay. We had plenty to eat, but I lost a couple bucks on the game."

"That's okay. I'm glad you had fun. I saved a few chocolates, would you like some?"

John shrugged, and she gave him the last few pieces.

"Thanks."

She started to pick up the dishes and trash as he turned up the volume on the TV.

Chapter 8

Jack and Rudy stood talking in front of the fireplace with a glass of wine. Georgia was helping Sharon in the kitchen. When Roy and Callie arrived, she headed for the kitchen. Roy shook hands with Rudy and then Jack. Jack handed him a glass of wine.

Jack thought it was odd that Rudy's face showed no expression when they arrived. Rudy put his hand in his pocket just before they sat down. The men talked for a while until dinner was ready, and they all sat down at the table.

"How'd you like watching the game on that giant TV?" Callie asked her dad.

Jack's face lit up. "It was awesome! We're going to do it every Sunday — as long as the wives still agree." His face dropped as he looked at Sharon. "Fill them in on what you told me."

Sharon sighed. "We got a little distracted. But I called everyone the next night, so, yes we're still on — except for Arlene."

"What do you mean distracted?" Georgia asked.

After Sharon explained what happened, she added, "Arlene's been tense ever since I met her, so I just thought that's how she was. So this blowup was a total surprise. I had no idea she felt that way."

"I guess there's probably nothing you can do to change her mind. At least Charlotte and Bonnie are okay with you."

Sharon smiled briefly. "Yeah. But the worst part is that I feel so bad for Charlotte, because Arlene really let her have it. It seems like I'm the only one Charlotte can talk to without being told to be quiet or something. After everyone else left, I gave her Dr. Reed's phone number."

Georgia frowned. "Isn't he that shrink?"

"Yeah."

"From what you said, she's not unstable. Why would you do that?"

"I want her to learn how to be assertive, because Arlene's been acting like a bully. I thought that since Jack's mother learned how to deal with that kind of behavior, then Charlotte could, too. Besides, Kurt was a bully, and I figured she could learn how to handle him, too. I didn't tell her that, though." She cautiously gave a pleading look to Rudy. "Is it okay that I told her you'd investigate Kurt?"

"Of course. I already told you that. She's family, so it's no problem."

"Oh, good. Thanks again, Rudy."

Jack looked at Rudy. "I know it's only been a week or so, but how's that going?"

Rudy shook his head. "I haven't been able to find anything on him in the recent past — anywhere. It's like Kurt Morris disappeared off the planet for the last four years."

Roy leaned forward. "Does that mean you think he's been using an alias?"

"You see, this is why I took you under my wing. Yesterday, I checked out his rental agreement on the trailer; he uses the name Tom Rance. So I tracked that name back and found some activity for the last two years.

"Then I dug a little farther back and found out that a Tom Rance died four years ago in Reno, Nevada. Kurt was living there at that time. It's my guess he figured he could use that name and not get caught. But I don't understand why he'd wait two years before using it. For *that* two-year gap, I'm guessing Kurt was probably using one or more other aliases."

Roy leaned forward. "Do you think there's a connection between Kurt and that Rance guy that died there?"

Rudy shrugged. "I suppose it's possible that it could be a coincidence."

"That's just too close to be coincidental. I'll do a search from the station on that name. If you give me some more information, I'll be able to find out a lot that you can't." Roy frowned. "How come you haven't been telling me what you found?"

"Hey, I just learned it today. I knew you couldn't do anything before we sat down to dinner. Besides, I'm telling you now."

"Rudy, are we really working on this together?"

Rudy rolled his eyes and sighed. "Okay, I see what you mean. I'll work harder to keep you informed. I'm sorry."

56

"If Kurt had anything to do with this guy's death, then that would be what we'd need to put him away."

"That would be ideal."

Roy wrote down the details. "I want to nail this guy!"

From the corner of his eye, Rudy saw a satisfied smile on Georgia's face. "I'm glad to see you have that bulldog determination. You're going to make a good detective."

Roy grinned. "Thanks."

"Did you find out anything?"

"No, not really. There were some local traffic tickets right after they split. But that was all I could find. Now that we have an alias to check out and more cities to check, I'll get on it tomorrow."

When they got home, Rudy went to his office and decided to examine the flash drive Roy had slipped to him before dinner. Although he still had the one he originally copied from Pierre's flash drive last year, there was no point in opening the safe to get it when he had this one ready. He pulled it out of his pocket and plugged it into the computer.

Years ago, he would've been a bulldog to extract every detail from it right away. Now with Georgia in the picture and everything else that came up, he'd been distracted. He had only done a superficial scan of the files. Letting Roy take home this copy for a while seemed like a good solution at the time. He sighed, thinking how much time Roy had wasted. But then he shook his head knowing he was just as guilty of procrastination.

Since he had originally looked at the more recent files, he decided to look at the oldest, from 1999. As he checked the files up to the present, the entries increased each year, indicating that this operation was growing. He made a list of the men paying bribes; only half a dozen names were used at any one time. He leaned back and chuckled. *These have got to be nicknames or code names — nobody would name their kids like that. That means 'Frankie' is probably a code name. We'll have to let the Feds figure that out.*

He examined the names of men taking bribes or payoffs, with emphasis on finding "Oscar." He shook his head after counting dozens of entries for him over the last ten years. He leaned back, dragging his hands through his short hair. *Since Todd's a nickname, others could be, too.* He thought about different ways to research that. He made a couple of notes and returned to the flash drive.

Besides Todd, there were several names that were repeatedly paid, several occasional ones and a few one-timers. One vaguely familiar name, Barry West, came up a few times since the '90s with large payoffs. He became distracted whenever he saw the name, trying to remember where he'd heard it. When it clicked, he jumped up to retrieve the research he'd done last year on Pierre's relatives. Since he had an extensive family tree, the list was long. *I was right — there it is.* He scratched his head. *Wait a minute. it can't* be. *If I remember right, West died before the payoffs started. It's gotta be someone else with the same name.*

He returned his notes to the safe and went back to the menu on the computer and changed the view to full screen. *What?* He leaned forward to make sure he hadn't misread it. *Why was that one saved a week ago? I copied all of them at the same time.* The conflicting file had data from three years ago. When he opened it, he didn't recognize any names and scratched his head again. *That's weird. Roy must have done something to change it. I'll just compare it with mine.* He got up and retrieved his flash drive from the safe. *Probably just some innocent mistake.*

He checked one against the other and slumped down with a groan when he found the discrepancy. He leaned back in his chair with his hand cupped on his forehead. He closed his eyes and groaned again. It was several minutes before he could bring himself to look at it again. He wrote down the pertinent details and searched the Internet for anything about the case in the news. He found a couple of archived newspaper articles about it. When he read them, he shook his head. "I never would've guessed." He mumbled. "And that doesn't happen too often."

The following week, Rudy's phone rang. "Hey, Rudy, can I come over for a while?"

"Sure. I want to talk to you, too."

When Rudy opened the door, he was surprised to see that Roy didn't have the usual smile on his face. He decided to wait until they were in his office and they walked in together. Roy sat in the "electric" chair in front of Rudy's desk, and Rudy closed the door. "You look pretty serious, what's up?"

"You know that list you gave me — for the stuff in Pierre's box?"

Rudy nodded as he sat back in his chair.

"Remember how all the items in that box looked like evidence? Well, I've already found two court cases — for murder. The evidence, case numbers, and dates matched exactly.

And they were dismissed because the evidence went missing." He took a deep breath and continued. "The stuff in that trunk *was* key evidence. I'm going to check and see if, because of that, someone else took the rap."

"Good job, Roy." He paused, tapping his chin. "Since Pierre's dead, we're going to have to figure out how he got that evidence. It's pretty obvious he was more deeply involved than we first suspected."

"I know." He shook his head. "What did you want to talk with me about?"

"Have you found anything on Mick yet?"

"Georgia's stepdad? A little. When you told me he was married twice before, I thought that was kind of strange because it wasn't as common back then. From the few records I found, there was very little evidence of him working at a job. It appears that he'd just marry a desperate woman and have her support him. At least that's how it looked to me. I figure the wives eventually figured him out and divorced him. Even Georgia's mom filed papers, but he died before it went through."

"Did you find out anything on the stepchildren?"

"Yeah. That's where it gets kind of weird. His first wife had a daughter before they got married. Too bad, though, the daughter committed suicide just before the divorce. Poor kid was only fifteen." Roy shook his head. "The second wife had three daughters; they didn't turn out so well either. One developed mental problems and eventually died of a drug overdose. The other two, well, they had some pretty rocky lives. The youngest one is the one you talked to last year."

"Yeah, she really made me wonder." He tapped his chin. "Go ahead."

"Well, the other one, she was pretty hard to find. She became kind of a recluse and never married. When I looked her up, the neighbors wanted to know if I was there to arrest her. Apparently, there are a lot of complaints about her being a hoarder and creating a health hazard." He squirmed in his seat. "Creepy. It's kind of like everyone whose lives he touched turned out tragic — except for Georgia, of course."

"Any arrest records?"

"There were a few petty charges against him, but nothing stuck."

"Any medical records?"

"Well, you know he died from diabetes complications, uh — actually insulin shock."

Rudy shook his head. "I wish I could get Georgia to talk about it. Thanks for investigating all that. You did good."

"Thanks, but I was wondering."

Rudy eyed him. "About what?"

Roy frowned. "Do you think he was abusive?"

"I wondered about it, too, but I didn't want to say it." Rudy folded his arms. "Even though I do it all the time, I hate jumping to conclusions without evidence."

"If he was, then his death was a stroke of luck. It got them out of that situation."

Rudy's expression turned hard. "If I was there, I'd have made sure of it. Somehow."

"I couldn't do that."

"Do what?"

"What you were thinking. That's illegal — and wrong."

Rudy stood up like a shot and pounded the desk with his fist.

Roy jumped.

Enraged, Rudy pointed at him. "That's the last straw! I can't put on this charade any longer. You've got a lotta gall telling me you can't do anything illegal!"

Roy stared in shock.

"I know what you did!" Rudy bellowed with a red face. "Why'd you do it?!"

Roy stopped breathing for a moment. "What are you talking about?" He managed weakly.

"Three years ago, you delayed responding to a robbery. And the owner of that jewelry shop died because of it." Rudy took a slow, deliberate breath. His eyes seemed to bore into Roy's soul. "How much were you *paid* for it? And I want to know why you did it!" He stood up straight, crossed his arms and stared him down.

Roy's mouth was agape for several seconds. His voice was weak as he slowly shook his head. "I should've known." His energy seemed to evaporate. "I guess I'm glad you know."

Rudy leaned on the desk again. "Well! I'm waiting!"

He squeezed his eyes closed and started talking. "I — I was in a bind and I didn't know what to do. Grandpa was in the hospital from that heart attack. He didn't have the money to get the care he needed. Then when someone contacted me saying all his medical bills would be paid, it was like a miracle. All I could think of was to take it, to save him." He grimaced, put his hands over his eyes, and leaned forward with his elbows on his knees. "He promised me no one would get hurt. He promised." His voice cracked and he sobbed. Eventually, he looked up with tears running down his cheeks. "If I'd known that was going to happen, I never would've considered it! I tried to tell him I didn't like it, but I was on the hook. They said they'd make sure I'd go to prison if I tried anything." He shook his head slowly. "I'm so sorry," he whispered.

Rudy crossed his arms again. "So you sold out for fifty grand?"

Roy's mouth dropped open. "How'd you know? I de…." The air in his lungs escaped. He looked up at the ceiling, then down at his feet.

"What do we do now?"

"I guess you'll have to turn me in." His voice was dead.

"I considered it."

He cringed. Then he looked up at Rudy with wide eyes. "Wait, how'd you know?"

"Remember Pierre's flash drive that you borrowed?"

Roy's mouth dropped open. "You mean I'm in there?"

Rudy huffed. "Not in the copy I gave you. The original was in my safe. You changed the entry in the copy I gave you to a different name! I've been using computers since they first came out. It's apparent you don't know everything about them."

Roy hung his head.

"Is that why you were so anxious to borrow it?"

Roy stared at him for several seconds and hung his head again. "What are you going to do?"

Rudy sat down. "I have to think about that."

Roy shook his head and exhaled slowly. "I don't know what to say." He groaned. "What's Callie going to think?!"

"That's a good question." He looked at him sternly. "She'll have to hear it from you, you know."

He cringed. "I can't do that to her."

Rudy stared him down. "You have to!"

He sighed defeatedly. "Yeah, I guess you're right."

"As soon as possible."

He shook his head. "I guess I'll have to go to the station and turn myself in then, huh?"

Rudy tapped his chin. "I wonder …?"

"What?" His voice betrayed his uncertainty and dread.

"I think it'd be better to catch the whole kit and caboodle."

"Huh?"

"We were planning on exposing the whole lot of them — I still think we can. Since some of this stuff crosses state lines, that means the Feds will be involved. If we can show them that you're cooperating, that might give you a bargaining chip. You might be able to cut a deal."

"You're really gonna do that for me?"

"Look, I know you're not really a bad guy. You just made a really stupid decision. I'm willing to help you through this."

"I don't know what to say." Roy turned red and he squeezed back a tear. "That means a lot."

Rudy leaned forward pointing at him. "This is strictly so we can nail the traitors — mostly." His face softened a little. "Let's make our plan. The first thing you'll do is talk to Callie."

"Yeah," Roy croaked.

"Then *you'll* call the Feds. We just need to have all the information ready first."

Roy rubbed the back of his neck. "Thanks."

"Just how far did you look into those records — besides replacing your name?"

"I didn't." Roy looked away.

"I found something that doesn't make any sense."

"What do you mean?"

Rudy lifted the screen of his laptop, "Come here, I want you to see this for yourself." He turned the laptop so Roy could see when he came around the desk.

Roy bent over to see. "This one?" When Rudy nodded, Roy leaned closer. "Whoa! He's getting some serious money. Who's this Barry West?"

"Remember last year when I researched Pierre's family tree?"

"Yeah. What of it?"

"This is the name of one of his distant cousins."

Roy frowned. "If he's a relative, why would he be getting paid? I'd think it would be the other way around."

"I don't know. Gotta figure it out. There's another catch. This relative died 25 years ago."

"How is that possible?"

"Could be someone else with the same name. But for now, we've got to work on cleaning up the station."

Roy sat down, and Rudy got out his note pad and made notes as they talked.

They made a numbered list of things to do for each of them. As they outlined everything, Roy felt a glimmer of hope. After ten minutes, he looked up. "Say, how am I going to explain how I know all this?"

"First, you tell the Feds about your lapse in judgment and work a deal for telling them about the missing evidence. That'll get them into the station. Obviously, they'll want to make sure to catch any other dirty cops. Make sure it's part of the deal that they let you keep working so they can have your eyes and ears."

"Okay. But we'll have to make sure they catch all of them. How do we make sure of that? If they miss one, I'll have to give them our list."

"If necessary, you'll have to tell them about me."

"But you'd go to jail for how you got this stuff." He sat up straight. "Wouldn't you?"

"I guess you'll have to cut a deal for me, too." He leaned back in his chair. "You will, won't you?"

Roy looked stunned. "Of course! After all you're doing for me, why wouldn't I?"

"Only you can answer that."

"Huh? Oh, right." He looked down at his feet. "I guess I haven't proven myself, have I?" He took in a long steady breath and looked Rudy in the eye. "Well, I'll prove myself now! Even if I have to take the heat, you'll get a deal!"

Rudy's face softened. "I wouldn't expect you to, but it's nice to hear it." He brought his chair around the desk so he could sit next to Roy. "You'll need more than the flash drive or a list of names of the dirty cops."

"Are you talking about the box?"

"Not yet. I have another plan." He opened his notebook and pointed. "Here's what I have in mind. We both have to stay alert." Rudy explained the plan in detail. After thirty minutes, they shook hands, and Roy left with a satchel.

Chapter 9

Hal was taken aback when he answered the front door. "What are you doing here? You're not supposed to be here until next Saturday."

Kurt bowed his head. "Yeah, well I had such a good time with Cal that I had to see him again. Is he here?"

"Yes. But he has practice at two. You'll only be able to see him for a few hours."

"That's okay. I'll settle for whatever I can get."

"Cal, can you come here for a minute?" Hal called out.

After a few seconds, Cal came out of his room, and his face lit up. "Dad? What're you doing here?"

"What's the matter? Don't you want to see me?"

"Well, yeah — but I have plans for this afternoon."

"That's okay with me if it's okay with you. I thought we'd go out to Sandy to watch the bikers."

"We'll have to know where you're going," Hal butted in.

"Well, a few miles south of Sandy, there's this motorcycle track. I thought we'd go take a look." After Kurt described the location, Hal and Charlotte agreed. "As long as he's home by one so he can go to practice."

"Be sure to dress warm. We'll be outside most of the time," Kurt added.

Cal grabbed an extra sweater, gloves, and a knit cap. "Bye, Mom. Bye, Dad." Then he gave a quick look at Kurt. "Sorry — I didn't …."

Kurt patted him on the back. "That's okay."

After they left, Charlotte sat down on the couch and put her head in her hands.

Hal sat down beside her and rubbed her shoulder. "It's okay. It's weird, but Kurt doesn't seem to be at all like you said."

Charlotte took a deep breath. "He's been like this before. I don't know whether he's changed or if we need to watch out."

Out of sight, Josh frowned as he listened in the hallway. Then, he turned to go to his room. He closed the door quietly, picked up his phone and punched in one of his speed dials. "Hey, Al. It's Josh. He's back again, this time with no warning. What do you think? Should we call Smitty? … Yeah, they're supposed to be back by one. … I'll call Smitty to let him know you're coming. … Later." He folded his arms, took a deep breath. "We'll see what you're up to." he whispered.

After five minutes of driving, Kurt said, "Man, I wish I could take you to a ball game or something. But I'm strapped right now. I don't have two nickels to rub together. And it doesn't look promising for later on either."

Cal's brow furrowed. "It's okay. We get to spend time together. That's what counts."

Kurt patted Cal's knee. "You're a pretty smart kid. I'm proud of you."

Cal beamed.

About five miles short of Damascus, they ran out of gas, and Kurt coasted to the side of the rural road. "Doggone! I was hoping I had enough gas for this." He set the emergency brake. "Now what are we going to do?"

"There was a gas station about a mile back."

Kurt sighed. "Well that would be great if I had any money to buy some gas."

"I've got five bucks. We can walk back. Do you have a gas can?"

"Yeah. But I really hate to tap you out." He paused for a moment. "Is it okay if I pay you back later, when I can get some cash?"

"Of course, Dad. And you don't have to hurry; I get a regular allowance now."

They got out and started walking back to the gas station.

"Hal must make some good money then."

"No, he doesn't earn that much; it's Mom's money."

"When did she get money? Did she hit the lottery?"

"Well, kinda. Turns out that her dad passed away and left her some money."

Kurt's eyebrows raised. "Grant died?"

"Oh no, Grant's her stepdad. It was her real dad that left her the money. Well, he died fifteen years ago, but we just found out. It's kinda complicated."

"Really? Good for her. When did that happen?"

"Last year. And it came just in time. Our car was broke down, and we almost got evicted. Mom was able to buy the house we live in now."

Kurt's eyebrows raised even more. "She musta got quite a chunk."

"I don't know how much, but we have a new car, and I'm getting an allowance now. I never had that before. Mom says we might even go to Disneyland next year!"

"Well, good for you. That'll be fun. But I'm still going to pay you back when I can. I'll just have to earn some money."

"What kind of work do you do?" Cal shivered and put his hands deep into his pockets.

"Just odd jobs. But it doesn't pay much, and I can't count on it either."

"Can't you get a regular job?"

"Nah. My job history's a little sketchy."

"What are we going to do next week?" Cal asked after a few minutes of silence.

"I thought we'd go birding. It's not that expensive. Just a little gas, and I have the ammunition. Like I said, if I had the money, I could get some tickets, but they're pretty expensive, you know. Besides, with birding, we'd get something to eat out of it."

"I don't think Mom would let me go out with guns."

"Well, then, let's not tell her. We'll just say we're goin' to the motorcycle track again."

Cal bowed his head.

"What's the matter, Cal? Aw, you're worried about what your mom will say, huh?"

"Yeah."

"You don't have to tell her. Like I said, we'll just tell her we're goin' to the track."

Cal frowned. "But I don't want to lie to her."

Kurt sighed. "Okay. We'll try to think of something else that doesn't cost anything."

Cal grimaced. "Aw, Dad. I really want to spend time with you. I don't want you to feel like I'll only be with you if it costs something. I just want to hang out with you."

"Yeah, me too." Kurt hung his head. "I know! We could …. Uh, no. That won't work; that's money too."

Cal knitted his eyebrows together. "Dad, I need to know. How come you took so long to come see us?"

"I've been out of state. And with so little money, I just couldn't get back until recently. Just getting here took every penny I had."

"I wish I could help."

"Yeah, me, too. But you're only thirteen. There's nothing you can do. It's too bad your mom wouldn't want to help out."

Kurt told Cal about the hardships he went through while he was away. He put on a sad face. "When your mom made me leave, I felt real bad. I really wanted to spend time with you, but she wouldn't allow it."

Cal's voice went up a notch. "Why!? What happened?"

"Aw, I don't want to say anything bad. Your mom probably taught you that."

Cal nodded as he pressed his lips together.

Kurt pointed ahead. "Hey, look. There's the station."

Cal took the five out of his wallet and paid for the gas.

"Hey Mom, I'm going over to Al's for a while," Josh said.

"Okay, but be home before dinner."

"All right."

"Bye, honey."

Josh shut the door and ran down the street to where Al and Smitty were waiting in the car. He hopped into the passenger seat. "What did you bring?"

Smitty leaned forward from the back seat and grinned, showing his braces. "My hobby isn't so dumb after all, huh?" The high pitch in his voice matched the excitement in his eyes.

Josh waved him off. "Yeah, it's a cool hobby. What'd you bring?"

"Well, you said to bring everything. So it's all here in a box."

"Hey, Al, before we get started, can you park around the corner so he won't see us if he comes in on Park Street?"

"Sure thing." Lately, Al was almost glad he had freckles; they provided a distraction from the recent emergence of zits. Even so, he had also started to grow out his blonde hair to cover some of the ones on his forehead and neck. He drove around the block and parked with just enough room to see when Kurt parked in front of the house.

"Okay, Smitty. What've you got?" Josh twisted around in his seat to make sure he could see everything.

Smitty grinned proudly as he started to show them his treasures. He pulled out two watches.

Al laughed. "I knew it! Really? Watches? For what? So we can all have the same time? Look, I've got a watch, and it has all the options out there. How is that going to help?"

Smitty lowered his eyebrows and set his jaw. "They aren't *just* watches, they're a set of long-range walkie-talkies. Now, does that meet your approval?"

Al put his hands up. "Hey, I'm sorry. I didn't know."

"Are you still going to help me?" Josh begged.

Smitty was silent for a moment.

The corners of Josh's mouth dropped. "Please? I need your help."

Smitty exhaled. "Yeah, I'll help." He reached into the box. "I have several recording devices that look like ordinary things. This one's a lighter-camera, and here's a camera pen. Oh, this is my favorite." He put on a pair of sunglasses with ear buds.

Josh frowned. "Sunglasses with hearing aids?"

Smitty laughed. "See this cell phone? It's really a camera."

Al groaned. "Oh come on, almost every phone has a camera now."

"But not like this. I point it any direction and I see the image in the glasses. I don't even have to be facing the perp. And it has a directional microphone that transmits to my ear buds. Cool, huh? And I just put in fresh batteries."

Al's jaw dropped. "Whoa! That is totally cool! Hey, Smitty, I'm sorry I made fun of you."

"Hey, it's okay. I'm just glad we can put these to use. There's only so much spying on my sister that I can do."

As Smitty reached into the box for his next prize, Al twisted around in his seat to get a better look and accidentally honked the horn.

Josh glared at him. "You better not do that when Kurt gets back. I'm telling you, he'll do you in."

Al cringed. "Then why are we doing this? Shouldn't you call the police?"

"'Cause he hasn't done anything illegal yet. Don't you watch the cop shows?"

Al grimaced. "I don't know about this. You didn't tell me he was dangerous."

"We have to get evidence. Al, you've got the car. And, Smitty, you have the means."

Smitty sat up straight. "I'm in."

Josh looked at Al. "And what about you?"

Al swallowed hard. "I guess so. But I gotta tell you, this makes me nervous."

Josh put his hand on Al's arm. "Thanks, pal. This means a lot." He smiled as he turned to Smitty. "What else you got?"

Smitty pulled out a headset wired to what looked like a medical dog collar attached to a pistol. "This is my long-range bionic ear. But it's a whole lot more than that. When you look in here, you can see the perp, too. And it records just like a video camera!"

Al reached back to hold it. "Wow, this looks like the real thing."

Smitty's jaw clenched. "It *is* real! Look, if you're going to diss my stuff, I'm going home," he huffed.

Josh panicked. "No! He didn't mean it! I mean, isn't this stuff really expensive? How can you afford all of it?"

"Yeah, at first they were really expensive, and big. When I was eleven — remember teasing me?"

Josh closed his eyes and nodded.

"Dad really grumbled when I first started my collection. He thought I was going to flake out and lose interest like I did with baseball. Back then, I only got the toys and cheap stuff. But now everything's digital, so they're getting really small. And you can get some pretty good deals online. Besides, everyone in the family is giving me stuff." He snickered. "I even keep a wish list. But there's so many cool things out there, and more is always getting invented. I don't think I'll ever get tired of this." Then he glared and pointed at Al. "Don't ever diss my stuff again."

Al quickly shook his head. "Oh no! You convinced me. I'm impressed."

They spent the next half hour examining Smitty's collection of spyware.

On the way back to the truck, Kurt said, "Oh, man, I just happened to think. This is only just over a gallon. It won't be enough to get to the track and back. I'm sorry, Cal. I didn't mean to get your hopes up." Kurt hung his head. "And then I took your money, and now I can't even give you anything for it. Sorry, man."

"Please don't blame yourself, Dad. I know you meant well. But we still get to spend some time together."

"But when I bring you back so soon, your mom and Hal are going to think I'm a loser."

"Dad! No! Let's just be together, and we can just say we went to the track."

"You'd do that for me?"

"Yeah! Besides, they might not let me go next time if we told them what happened."

"Like I said, you're a smart kid. When we get back to the truck, let me see what I've got in the camper. Maybe there'll be something in there we can do."

Cal grinned. "Okay."

After Kurt put the gas in the tank, he opened the door of the camper. "Let's see. I've got my fishing gear. I've got my rifles and ammo. Traps, nah. Tools, that's no help." He turned around to face Cal, "It's either fishing or hunting. That's all I've got. And there aren't any streams around here." He reached in and pulled out a rifle, "The only thing I can offer is birds, squirrels, or rabbits."

Cal fidgeted. "Can't we just go for a walk or something?"

Kurt looked hurt. "Aw. I really wanted to impress you." He put everything back and said, "Okay." He shook his head as he grimaced. "Please don't tell your mom or Hal how lame I am."

"Aw, Dad, I'm sorry. I didn't want you to feel bad. But really, you didn't disappoint me. Really!"

Kurt hung his head as they started walking.

"Da-ad."

Kurt hung his head even lower. "Yeah?"

Cal sighed. "Okay. Let's go hunting."

Kurt looked up at him. "Really?"

"Yeah, really." Then he cringed. "But please don't tell. Okay?"

"Never."

They headed back to the truck. "I know a great place, just about a mile down the road."

Kurt showed Cal how to load the rifle and sight it, and they did a little target practice.

After a couple of hours, Kurt looked at his watch. "Looks like it's time to head back."

"Already?"

"Hey, I don't want to get in trouble for you missing practice."

"Oh, yeah. I forgot!"

They hurried back to the truck.

On the way back to Cal's house, Kurt said, "I'm real proud of you. For somebody that has no experience, you did real good."

Cal beamed. "Thanks."

"Oh, by the way, I read that the motorcycle tracks are kind of slow this time of year, not too many turn out. So if anyone asks, say they weren't crowded."

"Oh. Okay." Cal looked somber.

"Here we are. See you next week."

"Do you think we could go hunting next week?"

"I was hoping you'd ask. But let's just say we're going fishing. We know that's okay."

Kurt walked Cal to the door and gave his boy a hug.

Cal smiled. "Thanks, Dad. Bye."

"See you next week, son." Kurt waved as he headed back towards his truck. His grin grew with every step.

Josh pointed to Kurt's truck. "There he is. He just drove up."

Smitty used his bionic ear and set it to record.

When Kurt drove off, Josh turned around anxiously. "Well, what'd they say?!"

Smitty pressed a couple of buttons and turned on the recording, and Josh put the buds in his ears.

Josh's eyes got big. "No way! Mom's gonna freak!"

Al's eyes got big. "About what?"

"Is it 'cause he's gonna lie?" Smitty asked.

"Well, that and the fact that Kurt's putting a gun in his hands!"

Al gasped. "What? A gun?! And Cal's okay with that?!"

Smitty raised a finger. "Wait a minute, there's something fishy here. You gotta ask yourself — why is he doing that? We've gotta find out what he's up to."

Josh narrowed his eyes. "What do you have in mind?"

"We need more evidence. We've got to follow them and find out what they're doing. And find out where he's living. He might have something there that could give us a clue."

Al grimaced again. "Does this mean we have to follow them?"

Smitty nodded. "Well, *you* have the car."

Al pressed his head back against the headrest and moaned. "What did I get myself into?"

Josh thought for a moment. "Yeah. That's what we've got to do. But we have to be careful. Breaking into his house is going to be pretty risky. I know what he's like."

Al moaned. "I don't suppose you're going to tell us what he's like."

Josh put his hand on Al's shoulder and shook his head. "Sorry, I don't want to scare you."

"Too late," Al croaked as he dropped his head forward.

Debbie Kruse was only twenty. She had a slight build and would be attractive with some care. But she had given up trying, convinced it was useless. Her blue eyes displayed a profound sadness of late, and worry lines had already formed. No matter how she tried, nothing was good enough.

As she prepared lunch for Kurt, she hurried to get it ready, knowing what would happen if it was late again. She gasped when she heard the truck door slam shut. When Kurt came in and shut the trailer door, she cringed. "Lunch is ready, really." She looked up from the stove, saw his smile and relaxed a little. It looked like she would be safe this time.

He sat down and drummed his fingers on the edge of the small table, his smile growing with each beat.

She felt uneasy as she served him his lunch. It would be risky to disturb his train of thought, so she was careful not to say anything. She flinched when he snapped his fingers and jumped up from his seat. She barely got out of the way as he grabbed his coat on his way out the door. She heard his wheels spinning in the gravel, some of it clattering against the trailer as he took off. She closed her eyes and took some cleansing breaths. Since Kurt didn't eat his lunch, she took a couple of bites because she knew her body needed something to eat, but she couldn't get down much. She scraped everything else into the garbage. She wasn't going to take any chances on serving leftovers again. Then she pushed up the sleeves of her sweater and busied herself cleaning.

When she went into the bedroom, she caught a glimpse of herself in the mirror. She let out a defeated groan. She fussed with her straggly hair for a minute and let out a sigh as she gave up the futile attempt. She used a headband to try to tame some short stray hairs and scowled at her reflection. "He's right. You look awful."

Rudy had been distracted, but this just didn't make sense. He already had an idea of what kind of person Kurt was, so this was out of character. This was the last place he thought Kurt would go. As he waited outside the library, he wrote down everything he'd seen since he'd started tailing Kurt that day.

When Kurt came out and drove off, Rudy went inside and questioned the librarian.

"He was looking around for a while. Finally, he asked me where he should look to find some public records."

"Do you know what he was looking for?"

"He said he was trying to find the lawyer and executor for his uncle's estate. I told him to go to the Oregon State Bar office out in Tigard."

He got the address. "Thanks, you've been a big help."

Rudy sprinted out to the car and headed for Tigard. When he arrived, Kurt's truck was in the parking lot. Rudy put on a panama hat and sunglasses, and then he walked in with his attaché case. After asking the clerk where to find inheritance records, he followed her directions to the second floor.

When Rudy walked into the large room full of computers and microfiche machines, he made a note of where Kurt sat. The row of tables behind Kurt was empty so Rudy sat behind him, one seat to the left. Rudy opened his case and removed a telescopic high-resolution camera. As Kurt scanned records, Rudy took pictures of each screen that he seemed interested in. This went on for over an hour. Finally, Kurt perked up as he examined something, made notes, and printed a few pages. It was apparent that the angle was not right to get pictures of his notes, and Rudy shook his head in frustration.

"Whoa! I can't believe it. Cal said she got a lot of money, but this is the mother lode," Kurt whispered suddenly. He started writing furiously and printed several more pages.

At one point, Kurt's head was partly blocking the screen. Rudy leaned a little more to the left, but not too far. He didn't want to chance making a noise or moving into Kurt's peripheral vision and getting caught.

When Kurt closed down the computer, Rudy pretended to be working on his own research. After Kurt left, Rudy put his equipment away and then he scampered down the stairway to the main floor. He always did this ever since he'd learned his lesson early in his career. It was risky and too slow to wait for the elevator when following someone who'd just taken it.

Rudy reached for his sunglasses as he walked out the door, but he put them away when he realized it was already getting dark. He watched Kurt from the corner of his eye as he headed to his car.

Kurt climbed into his truck and drove off smiling.

Rudy followed him for a few miles, but when it appeared that Kurt was going home, Rudy headed toward home. His police scanner chirped. "Silent alarm at Hallberg Jewelers on Fifth and Wilson Avenue. Novak? You near there?"

"On my way, Captain." came the reply. "ETA about three minutes."

Rudy smiled and took off, knowing he'd get there first. As soon as he could see the storefront, he started filming, thankful he had invested in night vision. Making sure his panoramic camera didn't miss anything, he slowly parked a block away.

When Novak pulled up half a block from the store, Rudy watched him carefully. Rudy noted that even without the bulk of the bulletproof vest, Novak's broad shoulders, bulging biceps, and thick thighs were evidence that he regularly put time in at the gym. He could only get the profile, but Novak's Greek nose and strong chin were clear as he rushed into the store. *Now why would he just run in there like that and not even pull out his gun?* He clenched his jaw. *Of course! This is it.* A few seconds later, the same red-haired man that was in Pierre's house ran out the front door and down the alley. A few minutes later, Novak came out, reached in through the window of the squad car and picked up his mike. The scanner chirped. "Novak here. We've got a 187, code 4. Send the detectives."

"See anything?"

"Nope, it was all over when I got here."

Rudy smirked. *Gotcha!* Within five minutes, the detective team arrived with their equipment.

Rudy called Roy. "I got it."

Roy waited until the last person left the evidence room and out of hearing range. He walked up to Jerry, the locker guard, who was almost a permanent fixture at this post. The lack of exercise, boredom, and a fully stocked snack drawer in his desk had enlarged his gut, putting a strain on the buttons of his shirt. His neck bulged at the collar, and his eyes seemed to disappear above his rotund cheeks. Sweat trickled down from his temples, staining his collar.

"I know you've been as concerned as I have. You willing to help me?" Roy whispered.

"Exactly what are you referring to?" He squinted, almost completely closing his eyes.

"The strange 'misplacement' of evidence?"

"What are you saying?"

"Look, I know I can trust you. There have been cases — important cases — that have been dismissed because of missing evidence. I think we can figure out what's been happening."

Jerry eyeballed him. "How?"

Roy opened his satchel to let Jerry look inside.

Jerry's eyebrows lifted. He folded his arms and stared at him. "And why do you trust me?"

"I just do. You with me?"

Jerry clenched his jaw for a moment and leaned forward. "You got your phone on you?"

"Right here."

"Let's connect right now and if anybody comes around, I'll get them in a conversation about, say, the weather. That way you'll know to tidy up so they won't catch you."

They shook hands.

Jerry unlocked the gate and Roy hurried inside.

He was connecting the first camera when he heard Jerry's voice over the phone. "I can't stand being cooped up in here when the weather is so nice." Roy pushed the wires behind a box and picked up the evidence folder he'd brought in with him. The gate opened and shut.

Novak came in, waved at him, walked down an aisle, and opened a locker. He examined a piece of evidence for several seconds before he put it back. "See you later, Roy."

"Yeah. Later, Novak."

When Roy heard the outer gate clang shut, he went back to setting up the camera the way Rudy had taught him. "At least he didn't have time to remove anything — I hope." He cringed, thinking he might have missed catching him in the act, but he kept working. He'd just finished the second camera and started on the third when Jerry's voice came over the phone again. "Hey, Captain. What brings you here on a fine night like tonight? I hear it's so clear outside, you can see the stars."

"Yeah, well, I can't be outside, so I gotta keep things going in here."

Roy pushed the wires of the third camera behind a box and opened his evidence folder again just before the gate opened.

"Hey, Jackson, aren't you off duty?" The captain was in his late fifties and about an inch shorter than Roy. He had thin lips and hollow cheeks, and his hooded eyes drooped down at the sides.

Roy recalled having seen that face show many different expressions — sadness, exhaustion, sincerity, concern — just about every emotion he could think of. And now, knowing how the captain had worked the system, he wondered just how much of that was an act in order to attain a goal.

"Yeah. But I had to look into something that didn't seem to make sense."

"Really. Anything I can help with?"

"Well, I'm not sure, just checking some details."

"If you find anything, give me a report on it."

"You know I will."

"I'll look forward to it." The captain walked over to the next aisle where Roy heard him access another evidence box. He seemed to take a long time and Roy rolled his eyes impatiently. Finally, he heard footsteps coming up behind him and he intently examined the contents of the evidence box in front of him. "Find what you're looking for yet?"

"Not yet, still looking. Gotta make sure."

"Just keep me filled in."

"Sure thing."

Roy turned his eyes back to his folder as the captain walked towards the gate. He closed his eyes and exhaled slowly. When he heard the gate clang shut, he paused. He thought he heard Jerry's voice faintly say "weather," and almost immediately afterwards the captain tapped him on the shoulder. Roy jumped.

"Whoa. You're way too tense. Maybe you're working too hard. You need a day off or something?"

Roy turned around. "I guess I was just focused and didn't hear you come back. But thanks for the concern."

"I just happened to think. Maybe you can work with a seasoned detective. He might be able to help you sort out your dilemma. You know, help you to figure out what doesn't fit."

"Thanks."

"I'll look at the schedule and get back to you."

"Okay. See you tomorrow."

"And keep that focus. That's what being a detective is all about." He waved as he left.

Roy turned back to the box, inhaled deeply, and let it out slowly. *That was close. I almost went back to work on that camera.* The gate clanged shut.

This time, he waited for a couple of minutes before returning to his installation. When he reached the gate ten minutes later, he thanked Jerry.

"Hey, I was concerned for you in there."

"You're not the only one. I'm just glad we had that phone connection. Thanks again for the idea."

Chapter 10

John shut the front door as usual. He was taken by surprise when Bonnie wasn't there to greet him, and then he realized he didn't smell dinner either. "Oh, that's right. We're going over to Jack and Sharon's tonight." He looked around. "Bonnie?" When there was no answer, he took off his overcoat and went to the bedroom.

Bonnie was sitting at the vanity putting on her makeup. She looked up and smiled. "Oh, hi, John. We should leave in about twenty minutes. I laid out your clothes."

"I'm dressed."

"You're going to wear your suit?"

"I'll just take off the jacket and tie. I'll be fine."

She smiled again. "Oh, okay."

He went to the den and checked his emails while she got ready.

They were early; he always insisted on it.

When Jack let them in, he took their coats.

Bonnie giggled. "Thanks, Jack. You're such a gentleman." She headed for the kitchen with the wine and waved when she saw Sharon.

Jack shook John's hand. "I'm glad you two could come for dinner. We really need to get together more often."

"Yeah, thanks for inviting us." He sat on the rocker. "It's better than being home alone with *her*," he mumbled under his breath.

Jack tried to control the frown as he changed the subject. "How's your job doing?"

John filled him in on the latest layoffs and his concern that he could be next.

Jack shook his head. "I'm sorry to hear that. But you should be okay, shouldn't you? Haven't you been there for fifteen years?"

"Nobody's safe, especially the high seniority. Since we earn the most, we have the biggest target on our backs. The bank will save the most by letting us go."

"I don't get it. With your seniority, you really know the job. If they give the responsibility to a newer person, won't there be more mistakes? That's pretty important with approving loans isn't it?"

"You'd think so, but the dollar is always the bottom line. I've already updated my resume. At least the house is paid for, and Bonnie's inheritance will keep us afloat if I do get the ax."

"Glad to hear you're looking at the positive side."

"I have to."

Sharon called out from the kitchen. "We're putting dinner on the table. Come on in."

The men came in as the women brought in the hot dishes.

Jack smiled. "You're going to love Sharon's spaghetti. But you'll never guess how our first dinner played out."

Sharon pointed at him. "Are you going to wear out that story again?"

He laughed. "Come on. Even *you* thought it was funny."

"Okay, but you've got to let me tell it."

He made an exaggerated, sweeping bow. "Be my guest."

John grinned. "I can hardly wait to hear this."

Bonnie giggled. "I already heard it. It's a hoot!"

John glared at her. "Well don't spoil it for me. Make sure you let *her* tell it!"

She grinned as she sat down. "Okay."

Sharon glanced at John from the corner of her eye. Not sure of what to expect from him, she started slowly. "It was the first meal I made after we were married. Alice never showed me how to cook, so the only things I knew about cooking was what I'd learned in home economics in high school. And that wasn't much."

Jack started passing the dishes around as she talked.

"I was so desperate to impress him. The spaghetti itself was okay, but I really blew it on the garlic bread. I was going to make it from scratch, well almost. I'd bought a loaf of French bread and I sliced it and sautéed the garlic in butter. I didn't want to make a mess so I strained the garlic butter over the sink. By the time I realized I'd forgotten to put a bowl down to catch the butter, it had gone down the drain. I didn't have any more garlic, so I buttered the French bread to broil it. I didn't realize how quickly it would brown and the smoke alarm was going off when Jack got home from work." She rolled her eyes. "There was no saving it so I made toast."

Jack grinned. "It gets better."

Sharon smiled as she shook her finger at him. "We didn't have much furniture, and we were using the ironing board as a table. When we sat down to eat, I bumped my knee against the leg of the ironing board and we almost dumped the whole dinner on the floor."

"Yeah, but we saved it."

"I thought for sure he was going to chew me out, but he said the sweetest thing. He said, 'Even if we have to warm up a can of soup, it'll be great, because it's with you.' I cried right there, and he held me. I knew right then that I'd made the right move marrying him." She blew Jack a kiss and he winked at her.

Bonnie cooed. "Aw, and they're still in love."

Sharon blushed.

John poured himself some wine and then handed the bottle to Jack.

Bonnie frowned. "Isn't an ironing board awfully high to eat from? I mean, it must have been up to your chins."

John shook his head as he picked up his wine glass to take a drink.

Sharon did a double-take before she responded. "I just adjusted it before I put everything on it. You do know that you can set it for different heights?"

Bonnie frowned again as she thought about it. "Oh." Then she sat up straight and chirped, "Oh, yeah! Right." Then she picked up her fork and took a bite.

John lowered his head as he took a bite of garlic bread.

Bonnie hummed. "Mmm. You've got to give me your recipe for this spaghetti. It's kind of spicy. I like that."

"I'm glad you like it. I'd be glad to."

John chimed in. "You'd better write it down. And be specific, spell *everything* out for her."

Bonnie giggled. "Yeah. You know those big T's and little t's. I get them all mixed up. Sometimes recipes and me just don't get along. One time I was making this recipe that called for maraschino cherries. It musta been labeled wrong, 'cause when I poured it out onto the scale to weigh it, there wasn't enough. I had to go back to the store for another jar!"

"Did the recipe call for two ounces or two fluid ounces?"

Bonnie frowned. "What's the difference? Two ounces is two ounces, right?"

Sharon smiled. "Ounces mean weight, but fluid ounces refer to volume. They aren't the same."

Bonnie's face went blank. "Huh?"

"When we're done eating, I'll show you."

John drained his glass and then refilled it.

Sharon brought out dessert. "Lately, I haven't been making as many desserts, so I hope you like this."

Bonnie eagerly sat up. "What is it?"

"It's chocolate mousse."

Bonnie cringed and stared as Sharon passed around the dessert glasses.

Jack smiled. "Thanks, Pookie."

John picked up his spoon and took a bite. "It's really good, Sharon."

Bonnie stared at the dish in front of her. "It looks like pudding. Are you sure it's meat?"

Jack snorted. "Uh, sorry."

John turned red, closed his eyes, and slowly shook his head.

Sharon laughed. "It's not made of moose, it's a thick pudding. It's just called mousse."

"Well, that's just silly. They should think of calling it something more appetizing." She looked at it more closely. "Are you sure there's no moose in it?"

"I'm sure. We have some whipped cream if you'd like to have some with it."

"Let me try it first. I wouldn't want to waste it if I didn't care for it." She scooped a pea-sized bit onto the end of her spoon and tasted it. "Okay, I'll have some whipped cream."

"Hey, I understand you guys play canasta." Jack said.

John smiled. "Yeah. Bonnie's parents host a big canasta party once a month."

"How about a game or two?"

Sharon noticed John rolling his eyes. "Hey, Bonnie? How about you and I pair up against the guys?"

"Hey John, I'll bet we could skunk 'em," Jack said before Bonnie could answer.

Bonnie smiled. "Count me in."

Jack got the cards, paper, and pencil as the women cleared the table.

John dealt the first hand as they talked. "You'd better be good, Jack."

"Don't worry, I won't hold back."

Sharon picked up her cards to sort them. "So, Bonnie, what have you been doing with yourself?"

"Well, I volunteer at the hospital a couple days a week. That's pretty cool."

Sharon perked up. "Really, what do you do there?"

"When gifts, flowers, or cards come in, I deliver them to the patients. I just love seeing their eyes light up, especially the kids. Then I talk with them for a while. Did you know that there are some people who never get visitors?"

"That's just not right." Jack piped up. "When you're sick, that's when you need people the most. I don't know how people can just desert their loved ones." He frowned.

"Well, some people just don't have anyone. I try to do what I can."

Sharon smiled. "Bonnie, that's wonderful. I think you're doing something priceless."

John's face softened as he looked at Bonnie.

Sharon drew a card, sorted her hand, and discarded.

Bonnie told them about some of her experiences at the hospital. "When I go home at night, sometimes I'm sad, but mostly I feel good."

Sharon smiled. "I wondered what keeps you so happy."

John mumbled to himself but nobody understood what he said.

"What was that, John?" Jack asked.

Surprised, he looked up. "Huh? Oh, nothing. Just thinking out loud."

About an hour later, Jack laid his cards down. "See, John, I told you we'd beat 'em."

John gave a weak smile.

The men went into the living room to talk as the women tidied up.

"Oh, that's right. You've got to give me that recipe." Bonnie said.

"I really don't have it written down, but you can write it as I tell it to you." She tore off a sheet of paper from the tablet they used for the game and gave it to her. As she listed the ingredients, she added, "You have beautiful handwriting."

"Oh, thanks. I really try. I wouldn't want to be confused with a doctor. Then I'd have to know something."

Smiling, she recited the rest of the recipe, making sure Bonnie wrote down the measurements with complete words. "Oh, is next Saturday still okay for us to come over for a purse?" Sharon asked when they were finished.

"Sure, but I still don't know why you're making such a fuss over them."

"Because they're so cute and unique."

Bonnie shrugged. "I have way more than I use. I'm just glad someone can take some off my hands."

"You've shown them to me and I can tell you, they're good, all of them. You should be proud of them."

"Really?" she asked in disbelief.

"Really, really." Sharon didn't know how else to show her sincerity, so she gave her a big hug.

Chapter 11

Roy had built a roaring fire, and he stood there for a few minutes admiring his work. The scent of burning pine mingled with the aroma of Sharon's full-course turkey dinner.

When Sharon called everyone to dinner, they took their usual seats at the table. Multiple conversations were punctuated with frequent laughter.

Callie announced, "Georgia, you're never going to believe this. Mom and I went over to Bonnie's last night. She actually let me pick out three of her purses. They are *so* cute. I was going to ask her to show me how to make one myself, but she just gave them to me."

"Is that one of them on the coffee table?"

"Yeah. Isn't it great?"

"I admired it when we came in. And you say that Bonnie makes them?"

Callie nodded enthusiastically.

"It takes a special kind of person to do that kind of work. I do crafts, but I'd never be able to do anything like that."

Jack picked up the carving knife and attacked the turkey. "Roy, did you learn anything when you looked up Kurt or his alias?"

"A little. Seven years ago, Kurt was living in Las Vegas at the same time as Tom Rance, like Rudy said. Rance was working at a construction site when he was killed in a drive-by shooting. Nobody was arrested, but the police there are pretty sure it was related to a drug gang. The report says he was just an innocent bystander. There's nothing to connect Kurt to the shooting, but he disappeared a few months after that shooting. That looks suspicious. And there aren't any records of Kurt Morris anywhere after that. That's about all I could find."

Rudy nodded. "Good work, Roy. We just have to find out what the connection is. But I've got an update, too. I've been following Kurt, and I found something interesting."

Everyone leaned in to hear.

"Yesterday Kurt looked up the public probate records. When he found out how much Charlotte inherited, he looked like he'd won the lottery. I heard him talking to himself as he was checking it out. He said that Cal told him about Charlotte inheriting money." He paused. "I think he's here trying to get some of it."

Everyone at the table scowled as they made unintelligible comments.

Jack glared as he emphasized his point by waving the carving knife. "I knew it! I hope I never run into that rat!"

"Hey, be careful with that thing!"

Jack looked at the knife in his hand. "Oh, right." He continued carving. "I'm just saying …."

"I did a little more research on his past, too. He doesn't stay in one place for very long. With about six years to check out, it's taking a while to piece it together. Considering what I've learned, I'm guessing he didn't want child support to catch up with him. You know, work just up until the first garnishment hits, then he'd quit. There's a long series of jobs like that." Rudy shook his head. "A real deadbeat! And from what I can tell, he has a new girlfriend every few months. And that was just for the first two years." Rudy rubbed his chin, "Roy, I want you to do a search for any outstanding arrest warrants in all states, not just the ones we know he was in. Hopefully, there'll be something out there. That'd be the easy way. If not, I'll bet we can come up with something else."

Roy nodded. "You bet. I'll do a search tomorrow. By the way, if you can get his prints, I can run them."

"I'll see what I can do."

Georgia scooped some mashed potatoes. "Jack, how are the games with you and the guys?"

"We have a good time. But I wish Mel could relax a little more."

"What do you mean? Do you know what's bothering him?"

"*Do* I? Oh yeah! And everyone else, too. First thing in the door, it's always something about Arlene. I really feel bad for him."

"What's wrong between them?"

"Arlene's always in his face. She accuses him of everything that goes wrong; always says he's doing something wrong, accuses him of bad motives, and treats him with disrespect. And then she says he's at fault for starting the argument. The last couple times we talked, he said it's getting even worse. I guess you really don't know what goes on in other people's lives."

Rudy's mind shot back to Sharon's mother, Alice, and all the drama she created.

Georgia frowned. "Well, when I asked about the games, I didn't think I'd stir up such a hornet's nest."

"You didn't. It's all on Arlene."

Sharon grimaced. "I wish I knew what to do, but she refuses to talk to me. And she's mad at Charlotte. Bonnie doesn't think anything's wrong, and Karen just wants to cover up everything. It's like she can't handle it."

Jack shook his head. "Yeah, I don't know either. Mel said he's about to call it quits."

Sharon moaned.

After dinner, Sharon, Callie, and Georgia went to the kitchen to clean up. Jack watched as Rudy took Roy aside to the hallway for a few minutes. He could still see them just at the corner. Rudy was animated and had that intense countenance he always had in serious matters. Roy nodded sullenly and slouched a bit.

When they came back to the living room, Roy continued into the kitchen and put his hand on Callie's shoulder. "Can we talk privately?"

"Sure. Let's go to the family room."

Rudy sat down on the couch next to Jack and whispered, "This is going to be hard for everyone, but please, don't interfere. Callie will tell you when she's ready."

Jack frowned. "You're not going to tell me what it is?"

"That's up to Callie. I thought Roy would do this a lot sooner. And you'd better tell Sharon so she won't barge in there."

"Okay." He went into the kitchen to tell Sharon and Georgia what Rudy said.

The muffled conversation in the family room was barely audible through the closed door. Sharon anxiously looked at Jack when Callie started yelling.

"What?! How could you?! All this time I thought you were solving the problems, and now you're saying you're part of it! You should be ashamed!" they heard Callie yell.

As the volume went down, their voices were muffled again. But it was clear that Callie was angry. The sound of breaking glass and more yelling made Sharon jump.

Jack grabbed Sharon's arm. "I know. I want to go in there, too. But Rudy said no."

"But why?!"

"I don't know, but we've got to trust him."

Eventually, Roy came out with a red face, walked past them, and put Callie's ring on the table by the door before he walked out.

Sharon rushed after him and pulled the door open. "Roy?"

He didn't turn around but kept walking to his car.

She looked at Rudy. "What happened?" Then, she slowly closed the door and turned around to Jack. "What was that all about?" She picked up the ring. "Does this mean the wedding is off?"

He'd barely shrugged when they heard Callie sobbing. Sharon grabbed Jack. "Oh, Sweetie, what are we going to do?"

He held her. "Whatever it is, she's got to let it out. She'll come to us when she's ready."

"But I want to go to her now!"

Rudy stood up. "Sharon, she'll tell you when she's ready. I'm pretty sure that won't be now."

Georgia shook her head and started to tear up. "Sharon, do you want us to stay?"

"I don't know." She leaned her head on Jack's shoulder. "Maybe not." She squeezed her eyes closed and started to cry.

Rudy and Georgia went home.

Chapter 12

Josh stood in the doorway with his arms crossed. His jaw was clenched, and he glared as he watched Cal change his clothes. "You're really still seeing him?"

"You don't know him. In fact, right now, you're acting more like a bully than anyone. I don't believe you. And even if he was like that back then, he's changed." Cal picked up his coat. "As soon as he gets here, I'm gone. It's better than having *you* in my face." He pushed Josh out of the way as he walked past him.

Josh frowned and then snuck out the back door.

A few minutes later, the doorbell rang, and Cal ran to open it. "Bye, Mom. Bye, Hal."

Before they could say good-bye, Cal slammed the door behind him.

Charlotte groaned, "Oh, Hal, I'm so sorry." She gave him a hug.

"Don't worry about it. It's not your fault. I knew I wouldn't be 'Dad' after Kurt arrived." He frowned as she put her head on his shoulder.

Josh jumped into the front seat of Al's car. "Thanks for coming on such short notice, guys. I called as soon as I found out he was coming."

Smitty got his bionic ear ready. He grinned. "Ready to go."

"Right," Al mouthed.

"I can't thank you enough for doing this, guys. I don't know what I'd do without you. Look, there they go. Make sure to keep a couple blocks behind. We don't want him to get suspicious."

Al started the car. "Yeah, we don't want that," he mumbled.

Smitty frowned. "I'm not sure how much reception we'll get from two blocks behind. We might not be able to get anything until we get closer."

Josh shook his head. "Naw, we'd better play it safe. There's bound to be something said when we get closer. Besides, I want to find out where he's going and what they're doing."

Smitty shook his head. "Nope. I can't get anything from back here. We'll have to wait until they park."

Cal fastened his seat belt. "Are we going to go practice?"

"I think you're good enough we can actually go for a rabbit or something."

Cal smiled. "Really?"

"You bet. You took to it like a real man."

Grinning, Cal folded his arms as he daydreamed.

Kurt saw him from the corner of his eye. "Thinking about showing off your prize?"

Cal came to attention. "Yeah. Uh, no. Mom would kill me."

"But I'd be real proud of you, son."

He grinned again. "Thanks, Dad."

"You know, this is about the only way I can get enough to eat."

Cal looked worried. "Aw, Dad. Is there anything I can do?"

"Naw. There's nothin' you can do. You're still a kid. But your mom could if she wanted to."

"What do you mean?"

"Well, you said she got all that money from her dad." Kurt dropped his shoulders a little and made sure his voice had a sad tone. "I raised you guys for the first ten years, and what did I get? Nothin'." Kurt patted Cal's arm. "But that's not your concern. It's not like it's your money or anything. I know you'd help if you could."

When they got to the woods, Kurt turned up an old lumberman's access road. The entrance was almost overgrown, and within a few feet, they were well out of sight from the main road. The brush and tree branches slapped and swept the truck as Kurt drove up the dirt road. Cal flinched each time a branch came at them. "Are you sure this is a road?"

"Oh yeah. When it's overgrown like this, it means nobody comes out here. We should be able to find a lot of game out here."

They got out of the truck and walked back to the camper doors. "I've got everything we need." He pulled out the gear and gave Cal an orange vest as he put on his own.

"Now, remember the signals I taught you. We can't make any sounds out here, or the animals will run off before we can see them."

Cal nodded, but he wasn't as enthusiastic as he was at first.

As they hiked further into the woods, Kurt watched him from behind and noted that he hung his head. He smiled smugly as he tapped Cal's shoulder. He put his finger up to his lips. Then he took aim and shot a squirrel.

Cal jumped. "Dad! Why'd you do that?"

"Dinner. Can't be too picky when you can't buy what you need."

Cal grimaced.

"A couple more and I'm set for a few meals." He stuffed it in his bag.

They continued to prowl the woods, and Kurt took a few more shots.

Kurt signaled to their left and pointed out a rabbit. He motioned for Cal to take the shot.

Cal missed. "Aw, Dad. I'm sorry. That would've been a lot of food."

"Hey, it's okay. You'll get better."

"Well, this should be enough for the week," Kurt said after about two hours. "Are you sure you don't want to bring some home?"

"Dad, you know what Mom would say. You keep it. Besides, you need it more than I do."

"Well, then, we should head back."

Smitty held up his hand. "They're coming back. We've got to hide in the brush or they'll see us."

They all stumbled into the bushes and squatted down behind a tree until Kurt and Cal went by.

"Dad, are you really going to cook those squirrels?"

"Yup. There isn't much on them, that's why I need so many. I just put in a couple potatoes and a few greens and I'm set."

"Uh, guys, I think we might be in some poison oak," Josh whispered after the voices faded down the trail.

Al jumped up. "You're kidding, right?"

Smitty slapped his hand over Al's mouth. "Shh, they're still within hearing distance. You want to blow our cover?"

Al's eyes became big as he shook his head. "You just put your hand on my face! Just how are we going to explain how we got poison oak?" He whispered firmly.

Smitty rolled his eyes. "Look, I'm sorry. I didn't mean to. It was a reaction. What's worse? A little poison oak or Kurt coming back for us?"

Al's pupils got big. "And that's supposed to make me feel better?" he whispered loudly.

"Hey, they're getting out of range. We gotta go if we want to keep recording."

About halfway back to the car, Smitty said, "They just shut the doors to the truck. They're gonna be out of range when we get to the car."

Josh slapped his forehead. "We should've waited at the house. Then we could've followed him home." Then he looked at Al. "Do you think we'd have time to get there before he leaves?"

Al grunted. "Yeah. If he doesn't see us."

"They just drove off. Let's go." Smitty said.

They ran to the car and jumped in.

Al turned to Josh when he shut the door. "Do you think they saw the car?"

Josh turned pale. "Probably. There was nowhere to hide it."

Al moaned as he turned the ignition.

As Al took off, Smitty groaned. "Well, the recording we got was useless."

Josh shook his finger at him. "Nothing is useless." Then he turned to Al. "Pick it up. We don't want to lose him. We've got to get home so we can follow him to his house."

"Look, there's only one road out of here, and I don't want to come up on his bumper. Don't tell me how to drive! All right?!" Al snapped.

Josh held his hand up. "Okay, you're the driver. Sorry."

"If you two don't stop arguing, this isn't going to work. We have to be a team. Right?" Smitty sighed.

Josh reluctantly nodded. "I'm sorry, guys. I just want this so bad."

"Yeah, well, you make me nervous." Al huffed.

"Hey, they're in range. We need to back off a little. We don't want him to see us in his rear view mirror if we come across a straight patch of road." Smitty said.

Al let up on the gas. "Thanks, Smitty. At least someone's thinking ahead."

Josh frowned. "Look, I said I was sorry. Okay."

Smitty shook his head. "Just calm down. I've got this under control."

"Okay, how about this? Next time we'll just wait until they get back, and we'll follow Kurt home to see where he lives." Josh sighed.

Al glanced at him. "And?"

"And when Kurt isn't home, we can snoop."

Al frowned. "You're saying we're going to break into his house? That's just great. Didn't you say your cousin is marrying a cop? That's a pretty dumb idea."

"But we aren't going to get caught. We'll wait until Kurt's out with Cal again. We know he won't be back for a long time. Smart, huh?"

Al shook his head.

"Hey, Pookie. I'm home."

Sharon came out of the kitchen. "It's only two-thirty. What happened?"

"There was a power outage at work. A tree shorted out a power line, and the whole area's without power. The power company is going to take a while fixing it. We all got sent home, so here I am."

"Well, welcome, Sweetie." She wrapped her arms around his neck and gave him a long kiss.

"Mmm, I should do this more often." He held her as he gave her a nuzzling bite on the neck, and she wriggled with glee.

"Ja-a-ack. You know what that does. Come on! Ha-ha-ha!" She collapsed in laughter, and then struggled to get away.

"Oh, no you don't! I've got you now." He stopped and sniffed. "Do I smell something burning?"

She jumped out of his arms, ran to the kitchen and grabbed the pan from the burner. "Yup. It's burnt." She dumped the contents into the garbage.

"Aw, I'm sorry."

"It's okay. I'll just start over." Then she looked at him with a cocked eyebrow as she turned off the burner. "You know, I don't have to restart it right away."

"Hmm … that sounds like an invitation."

"Well, that's probably because it is."

Just after four o'clock, Sharon brought out some cheese, crackers, and wine while Jack built a fire in the fireplace. They sat on the rug in front of the couch. Jack spread out his arm and waved her toward him. "Come on Pookie, into your nook."

She leaned against him and snuggled under his arm. "Oh, guess who called me today."

"I wouldn't even try. Who called?"

"Bonnie. She and John have put money on another house."

"Already?"

"Yeah, I was surprised, too. They must have been looking for a while before telling us about it. She said they think it'll close in a few weeks. She called because she wanted to know if we'd be able to help them move. Do you have any plans?"

"I don't think so."

"They're actually hiring a moving company, but they'll need help with putting things where they want them. She said John wants his man cave to be done first."

"Sometimes I wonder about them."

"How's that?"

"Well, neither one seems to care much about the other. They just pursue their own interests without considering the other, especially after they got the inheritance."

"Yeah, I noticed it, too. A couple months ago, before she blew up, Arlene said it's because Bonnie's so clueless." She leaned closer. "I wonder. Do you think we could make a difference? By talking to them, I mean."

"I don't know. I guess we could try. Go ahead, call her back, and say we'll help them move. Who knows, maybe we can find a way to get through to them."

"If you talk to John, I'll talk to Bonnie." She took a bite of cheese. "Oh, and Charlotte called, too. During the move, the giant TV will be over at their house. That way you guys won't miss out on any games."

"That's cool. I'll bet Hal's excited about it."

"I know the boys are."

Jack put his glass down. "Has Callie told you what happened yet?"

Sharon slowly shook her head. "No. With her living with your parents, I don't see her as much. And I don't get as many calls from her since they broke up. I know I'm not supposed to press her, so I don't call more than usual. I know she's really upset, and it kills me that I can't comfort her. I can't figure out why they'd call it off so suddenly. I thought they were such a good match." She looked up at him.

"It's weird, but it almost looked like Rudy forced Roy's hand."

"What do you mean?"

"Just before Roy took her into the family room, Rudy talked with him quietly in the hallway. He looked really firm, like a father chastising his son."

"That's weird."

When Callie got off work after eleven, she set the alarm and locked the door behind her. She was still smarting from the breakup with Roy, and she knew she was prone to break down at any moment. To have some quiet time to herself, she had insisted that everyone else leave early, saying that she'd finish up the cleaning on her own.

Her car was at the other end of the lot because employees had to take the farthest spots so the customers could park close by. She took a tissue out of her purse, wiped her eyes, and blew her nose. She reached for her keys but she couldn't focus. She blew her nose again.

She was halfway across the parking lot when she felt a sharp pain on the back of her head, and everything went black.

The phone woke Sharon just after midnight. She rolled over and groped for the phone. Still groggy, she mumbled, "Hello." After a few seconds, she sat up with a gasp. "Cora, are you sure? ... Did you try to call her? … Did you call her work? … Okay, okay. I'll call you as soon as I find out anything." She hung up, turned to Jack with tears running down her cheeks, and shook him. "Jack! Your mom called and said Callie hasn't come home yet!"

He rubbed his eyes, got up, pulled out his phone, and called Callie's work. "I'm just getting the off-hours message. I'll go over there to see if I can find out anything." He started to get dressed.

"I'm going with you."

When Jack pulled into the parking lot, he saw Callie's car under the lot light.

Sharon moaned. "Where is she?"

Jack parked next to her car, got out his flashlight, and scanned the pavement as he walked towards the employees' entrance. His heart rate picked up when he saw the used tissue on the ground halfway to the door. He bent over to pick it up and he flinched. He could feel the blood pounding in his ears.

Sharon came up next to him. "Did you see something?"

He put his arm around her, put the tissue in his pocket and led her to the employee's entrance.

Even though he didn't say anything, she knew something was wrong.

Jack pounded on the locked door, but no one came to answer it. Reluctantly, he led her back to their car.

"What did you see?" she asked.

He didn't look at her. "I'm going to call some of her friends."

None of them had seen her. He paced as he called Rudy. "Hey, I'm sorry to wake you, but we have an emergency. We think something happened to Callie. Mom called Sharon to tell us that she never came home after work, so we came down here. Her car is here but she's not. … I've already called her closest friends, none of them have heard from her tonight. What do we do now? … Yeah, we'll come over. … Thanks. Bye." He closed his eyes for a moment then looked over at Sharon. "Breathe. Just breathe."

"What did he say?" Her voice was shaky.

"He's going to call the police to see if there have been any calls or reports that could possibly be related. Then he's going to call the hospitals for —" He bit his lip.

"For what?"

His lips turned down and his jaw tightened. He put his hand on her arm. "He's going to call for Jane Does."

"Oh!" She started to sob.

"That doesn't mean anything. Come on. We'd better get going." His hand shook a little as he started the engine.

When they arrived, Georgia opened the door, grabbed Sharon, and led her into the kitchen. Rudy clicked his phone off. "I've already called the City, County, and State Police. Nothing there. I was just about to call the hospitals."

Jack pulled Rudy to the side. "Can we talk privately?" he whispered.

Rudy nodded and led Jack to his office.

When Rudy shut the door, Jack fidgeted. "I didn't tell Sharon what I saw in that parking lot. I knew it would freak her out. Callie's been crying a lot lately because of the blowout between her and Roy. When I saw a tissue on the pavement, I had this awful, sinking feeling. I bent over to pick it up. Rudy, there was blood on the ground nearby." He stopped breathing.

Rudy usually controlled his emotions, but his eyes gave it away as he reached out to steady Jack. "Don't worry. I'll do everything in my power to help find her."

Rudy searched for a list of hospitals near Callie's work. After the first call, he shook his head. "I should've known. The HIPAA laws won't allow them to say anything — not even if there's someone there answering her description." He stopped to think for a moment. He smiled. "I'll call the ambulance companies to see if there were any calls tonight." On the second call, he frowned. "What hospital? ... Thanks." He hung up. "Come on. They brought a woman to City Memorial tonight."

Jack headed for the door. "What was her condition?"

"They wouldn't say."

Sharon and Georgia grabbed their coats and joined them when they came out.

When they entered the emergency room, and Jack asked to see the patient, the doctor looked at him solemnly. "She's downstairs. I'll take you there."

When Rudy took Georgia's hand, she looked up at him with her hand over her mouth.

Sharon stopped. "Wait a minute. Did you put her in a room already?"

"Follow me."

Jack turned pale. "What are you saying?"

"Just follow me." The doctor led them to the elevator and pushed the button for the basement.

Jack's heart pounded.

Rudy forced himself to put on his poker face.

When they reached the lower level, the doctor led them around a corner and headed for a swinging double door.

Sharon gasped and let out a loud cry. "No! I don't believe it! It can't be!"

Jack put his arm around her to hold her steady, and he tried to breathe.

Rudy stepped up. "Jack, I'll go in and make sure it's not Callie."

The doctor led Rudy into the morgue.

Sharon trembled as Jack held her. When he saw Georgia tearing up, he put his arm around her, too.

Rudy came out and sighed with relief. "It's not her. I'll have to call more ambulance companies." He stopped in his tracks. "But even if we get another hospital, they won't let us see her."

"What do you mean? This one did!" Jack's face was red.

Rudy pulled him aside so the women couldn't hear. "That's because they were hoping to get an ID on the corpse," he whispered.

Georgia held Sharon. "We'll find her. And she'll be okay."

Jack turned away in a huff. After pacing a couple of minutes, he turned to Rudy. "Do you suppose — "

"What?"

"Since Roy's a cop, would he be able to get access? I know Callie made it pretty clear she doesn't want to see him, but this is urgent."

Rudy tapped his chin for a moment. "Yeah, I think that might work. There are only two more hospitals in the area; I'll have him go check them out."

When they went outside, they split up. Rudy went to the side to make the call, and Jack brought Sharon and Georgia back to the car. Jack explained what they planned as they put on their seat belts.

Sharon's eyes widened in expectation.

Jack shook his head. "Don't get your hopes up on that."

"I just thought that if she saw him …."

"I know what you were thinking. And don't imagine that it hasn't crossed my mind, too."

Rudy came over with a smile. "Roy's off duty right now, so he's going to change into his old uniform and head over to the hospital on 85th. We'd better wait here; we don't know if he'll even find her."

Georgia took Sharon's hand when she started to cry.

Twenty minutes later, Rudy's phone buzzed. "Hi, Roy. … You did!? Awesome! Which hospital? Okay, we're about fifteen minutes away. Here, I'll give you to Jack while I drive." He started the engine as he handed his phone to Jack.

He snatched it and blurted out, "What's her condition?" He moaned. "Okay. Will the doctors say anything? Okay. Keep us posted."

Sharon leaned forward from the back seat. "Well, what's her condition!?"

"She's unconscious."

Sharon gasped and started to cry again.

He looked over to Rudy. "They won't tell him anything. But at least he was able to look in the room. That's when he could see she was unconscious." He paused. "They aren't going to talk to us either, are they?"

"Roy got in to see her because they probably thought it was related to a case. So until she wakes up and says we can see her, they won't say a thing."

"But we're her parents!" Sharon barked.

"Doesn't matter. It's the patient who decides. That's how the law is written."

When they arrived, they all rushed into the emergency lobby.

Roy was waiting for them. "She's still not awake yet."

Jack shook his hand. "Thanks for doing this. And I'm sorry."

Roy sighed. "It's okay. You know I'd do anything for her."

An hour later, a doctor came out with tired dark eyes and a smile. His hair was unkempt and there were several hours' growth of stubble. "Cooper? Jack Cooper?"

Jack jumped up. "Yes, right here."

"I'm Doctor Prichart." He shook hands with each one of them. "We did a scan, and she has a concussion. She's given permission for us to let Jack and Sharon Cooper, and Rudy and Georgia Burke see her. Although she woke up right after you got here, she's still very foggy and can't tell us what happened. We'll keep her overnight for observation. We'll be moving her to a private room where you're more than welcome to sit with her."

Roy waited outside the door, just out of sight. Georgia and Rudy stood in the corner while Sharon hugged Callie carefully. "How do you feel?"

Callie put her hand on her head. "My head hurts."

"Oh, my baby. I'm sorry." She stroked her cheek.

Jack looked down at her. "What happened?"

She paused. "I was walking to the car after work. I heard a noise behind me, something hit my head, and everything went black. I guess somebody knocked me out."

"Didn't any of your co-workers see what happened?"

She cringed. "I told everyone else to leave, that I'd handle locking up. I didn't want them to see me crying, and I didn't want to have to answer all their questions. I was about halfway to the car when it happened. Whoever it was must've been after my purse, because it's gone." She quickly looked up at her mother. "Bonnie's going to be so mad at me!"

"She'll understand." Sharon held her hand.

Jack shook his head. "Thank goodness you're going to be okay." He looked at her a little more sternly. "But I am a bit disappointed. We've had this talk before."

"I know, Dad," she said with remorse. "It was really stupid. I just wasn't thinking. Usually we all leave at the same time, and I didn't think about safety." She closed her eyes. "I was pretty distracted."

He swallowed hard, walked out of the bay, and found the doctor. "I have to know. Did anything else happen to her? You know, besides the hit on the head?"

The doctor put his hand on Jack's shoulder. "No, nothing else. You can rest easy."

Jack put his hand over his eyes. "Thanks," he croaked. He pulled out his phone to call his mother to tell her that Callie would be okay, but an orderly tapped him on the shoulder. "Sorry, you'll have to go outside to use your phone. The signal will interfere with our equipment." Jack poked his head into the bay and told them he would be right back.

Ten minutes later, the doctor came into the room. "Since this is probably a crime, the police have to take a statement."

Roy walked in with a notepad. "Hello, I'm Officer Jackson. This should only take about ten minutes."

Callie looked up, bit her lip, and turned away. Her blood pressure monitor started to beep.

When Sharon saw the pained look in her eye, she picked up Callie's hand and held it. "I'm here, honey."

The nurse rushed in and checked the monitor. "Officer, this might be too much for her. You only have a couple minutes."

Callie moaned softly, and her lip trembled.

Sharon looked up at Roy and shrugged.

As Roy questioned her, she answered with mostly one-word answers, refusing to look at him.

He closed his notepad. "I guess that should be it for now. If I have any more questions, I've got your number." He left.

When he was out of sight, Callie rolled onto her side, curled into a fetal position, and cried into the pillow.

Sharon stroked her hair as her own tears ran down her cheeks.

Rudy looked at his watch. "Hey, Georgia," he whispered. "Do you want to stay here or go with me? Now that everything is settled down, I've got some things I need to take care of."

"You go ahead. I'll stay here." She kissed him goodbye, turned around, and held Callie's hand.

Chapter 13

Cal ran to the door when the doorbell rang. "Hi, Dad! I'm ready!" He slammed the door behind him without a wave good-bye.

With his hands in his pockets, Josh fidgeted as he came into the living room where Charlotte and Hal were talking.

Charlotte looked up. "What's up, honey?"

"How do we get Cal to see what Kurt's like?"

"We can't do that, honey. He's got to figure it out for himself."

"He hasn't done anything, and the law says that Kurt has the right to see you boys. And we have to consider the possibility that he's changed," Hal said.

Josh crossed his arms. "I don't believe that for a second." He sat down next to Hal. "Dad, I was listening when Cal left. He didn't mean it."

"Mean what?"

"*You're* our dad. Even though Kurt donated the sperm, he'll never be a dad to me."

Hal hugged him. "Thanks, son."

Josh hugged tighter as he smiled. "I love you."

Cal's face glowed with anticipation. "What are we doing today?"

"I thought we'd do some tracking. I'll teach you all about what signs to look for and how to maneuver without leaving a trail."

Cal grinned as he fastened his seat belt.

"Oh, and I caught a couple trout so you'd be able to take one home for dinner."

"You mean so I'll be able to say we were fishing?"

Kurt winked at him. "I always knew you were a smart one."

Cal folded his arms and smiled as he looked out the window.

After 30 minutes of driving, Kurt turned off onto an old access road. "You know, these roads were built by lumberjacks so they could transport their vehicles to where they cut the trees. But nobody hardly ever uses them anymore; that's why they're so good for hunting. You can get deep in the woods without bothering anyone. We'll just go about a mile in and we're set."

Cal sat up straight and flinched a few times as branches unexpectedly slapped the windshield.

After ten minutes, Kurt stopped the truck and they went around to the camper. He unlocked the door and pulled out his gear. "Here, you take the compass, and I'll get everything else."

Kurt showed him how to read the compass and showed him where the sun was in the sky compared to the time. "Let's go off in that direction. It's not so dense."

After fifteen minutes of walking, Kurt grabbed his chest and sank down to his knees. He gasped and grunted.

Cal jumped to his side. "Dad! What's wrong, Dad!?"

"It's my heart."

Cal became hysterical. "What do I do?!"

"My meds. I left them in the glove box. You'll have to go get them and bring them back to me. I'm not going to be able to walk." He sat on a log, and then he grimaced as he bent over.

"I don't know if I can do that!"

"You have to. Use the compass." Kurt's breath was quick and shallow.

Cal's lips curled into a horrid grimace as he hurried back to the truck, reaching it in ten minutes. He rifled through the glove box and retrieved the bottle. He slammed the truck door and almost panicked. "Which way did we go?" After a moment, he remembered. "Oh yeah, we went that way."

He used the compass to guide him back. Eight minutes after he left the truck, he started to call out as he went, "Dad, tell me which way to go!" "Dad, talk to me!" "I'm coming, Dad, hold on. Tell me you're okay!"

Finally, he heard a faint voice. "I'm over here."

Cal ran to him and pulled the bottle out of his pocket.

"I just need one under my tongue." Kurt grimaced again.

Squatting down, Cal took one out and placed it under his tongue. "You're gonna be okay. Please be okay," he said desperately.

After a couple of minutes, Kurt started to breathe more naturally. "Thanks. I think you just saved my life."

Cal plopped down on the log, wrapped his arms around his knees, placed his forehead on them and started to sob.

"I don't know what I'd have done if you hadn't been here." Kurt patted him on his back. "Thanks again."

Cal put his arm around him and held tight. "Why didn't you tell me you had a bad heart?"

"I didn't want to worry you. But I should've known better. I should've had my meds with me."

"Does this happen a lot?"

"No. Just when I get low."

"What do you mean?"

"Well, when I don't have the money, I try to make them last longer by not taking them so often. Sometimes I run out."

Cal's eyes got big. "Run out?!"

Kurt nodded.

He cringed. "But — but what could happen then?"

"I don't know how bad it would be, but I'd probably go to the hospital."

"No-o-o!"

"I really need surgery. But there's no way I could afford that. I just make do."

Cal frowned. "But I'm just getting to know you. I don't want to lose you now!"

"Unless somebody offered to pay for it, it won't happen."

Cal sobbed on his shoulder again.

Kurt put his arm around Cal and patted his shoulder.

"I think I can get up again," Kurt said after a few minutes.

Cal jumped up and reached out to help him up. Then he wiped the tears away with his sleeve. He supported him all the way back to the truck.

When Cal climbed in, his eyes widened. "Are you okay to drive?"

"If we wait for a while, I'll be okay. Thanks again, son."

Cal smiled weakly.

They talked for an hour, mostly about Cal's plans for the future, what the family was going to do, and Kurt's chronic unemployment.

When Kurt dropped Cal home, he climbed out, too. "Cal, don't forget the trout." He got it out of the cooler and handed it to him.

"Bye, Dad." He held his dad as if he might never get to again.

"I'm real proud of you, son." Kurt patted him on the back before he let go.

Rudy heard the noise of someone running through the woods toward him. He slipped out of the truck just a few seconds before someone rushed out of the brush and fumbled with the passenger door. He rolled under the truck as the door was yanked open, and he waited. He heard rummaging noises and things falling on the floor of the cab. The door slammed shut and then he saw the feet of someone running back into the woods.

Rudy waited until he couldn't hear the sounds anymore, then he quickly went back to his car and drove away. About a mile down the main road, he pulled over to the side of the road to start up the new app on his phone. Then he drove over to the trailer park and parked around the corner from the entrance. He got his tool kit from the trunk, put on his fake glasses, and went to the third trailer and knocked.

The young woman called out from inside, "Who is it?"

"The manager sent me. There's a problem with the electric line."

She cautiously opened the door a crack. "What are you going to do?"

He pushed up his fake bifocals. "I need to inspect the electrical connections out here."

She looked him over for a few seconds. "Okay." She quickly shut the door.

Rudy walked around to the electrical connection, and during some perfunctory checks, he placed a small device underneath the trailer. When he was done, he knocked on the door again.

"What do you want?" She called out from inside again.

"Just wanted to let you know everything checks out okay. I'm all done. Thanks."

As he turned to leave, he noticed her peeking out through a slit in the curtains. He waved and she quickly closed the curtains. He walked out to the street and around the corner to his car. On the way, his cell phone buzzed. He quickly put an ear bud in his ear and turned it on. Rudy's face contorted and he mumbled, "Huh? Why wouldn't he be okay to drive?" He climbed into his car and listened. As he put the pieces together, his jaw tightened.

On his way back home, the hair raised on the back of his neck. Kurt's truck was coming from the other way. *Good thing I still have my disguise on. Hope he doesn't recognize the car.... No way! Is that Josh in the next car?*

He made a U-turn at the next corner and followed them to the trailer park. Kurt pulled into the trailer park, and the other car pulled over on the side of the road well beyond the entrance. He pulled up right behind them and got out. He walked up to the driver and tapped on the window.

Al practically jumped out of his skin. He stared up at Rudy with his mouth open.

Rudy motioned for him to roll the window down. "Just *what* do you think you're doing?" he scolded them with a loud whisper.

Josh cringed. "Rudy? What are you doing here?"

Rudy bent down. "That's my question! Spill it."

"It was his idea!" Al blurted out, pointing to Josh.

"To do what? Get yourselves in more trouble than you could possibly handle? You will NOT do another thing. You will leave Kurt alone. He's too dangerous. I am handling this. Now go home and don't ever try this again. Got it?!"

Three heads quickly nodded as Al started the car.

Rudy pointed forward. "Leave that way. No point in tempting fate any more than you have already."

Al drove up to Josh's house and turned off the engine. "Oh, man, that was close."

Josh frowned.

Smitty leaned forward from the back seat. "Josh? If you want to continue, I'm game."

Al jerked around to glare at him. "Are you kidding? Didn't you hear what Josh's uncle said? That guy's dangerous. And I don't want to cross his uncle either; he gives me the creeps!"

Josh turned to look at Smitty. "Do you have something I could sneak into Cal's clothes or something?"

Al grimaced. "Are you serious? You're gonna do it anyway? You're nuts!"

Josh held up his hand. "I've gotta hear what they're saying. If Smitty had some recording device, we could do that."

Smitty smiled. "Is Cal a Ducks fan?"

Josh rolled his eyes. "Is he?! Totally! Why, do you have something?"

Smitty grinned. "Yup. Look at this." He pulled out a small pin with the Duck's green and yellow O. "It has a small battery and it lasts for a week. It bounces a signal off a satellite, and we can record it. We don't even have to be close."

Josh reached his hand out. "Can we use it, please?"

Al socked Josh in the arm. "You just won't listen, will you? Your uncle said to let him handle it."

Josh glared at him. "You don't understand how much I hate Kurt. You don't know what he's done. He's evil."

"And that's my point." Al spoke slowly and firmly. "If he finds out — well, you know him better than we do." Then he shrank back. "What *would* he do?"

"I don't know. I never had the courage to do anything before."

"Well, I'm guessing that whatever he's done, this will be ten times worse." Al eyeballed him. "Right?"

Josh was silent for a moment. "I just have to. I have to protect my baby brother." Then he turned to Smitty. "So can we use it?"

Smitty bit his lip. "You better make sure nothing happens to it."

"Hey, I know how important it is to you."

Smitty looked at it. "Okay."

Josh closed his hand over it. "Thanks, buddy."

Smitty reached out quickly. "Hey, don't squeeze it. It's delicate."

"Oh, sorry. I'll be careful. I'm going to go do it right now. Bye guys. And thanks again."

Al went limp. "I knew it," he mumbled. We're gonna die."

Chapter 14

Cal paced.

Charlotte chewed her pinky nail as she fussed in the kitchen. "Hal, I've got your nachos ready. Everyone should be here in about fifteen minutes."

Hal walked into the kitchen. "Are you okay with this?"

She leaned against him as she put her arms around his waist. "I don't know," she whispered in his ear. "Are you sure you're okay with this?"

"Cal wants it really bad. And I've got Rudy's phone number. We'll be okay. Besides, what's he going to do with everyone here?"

She groaned as she fingered her locket.

Josh called out as he headed to the garage. "I'm gonna punch the bag until the game starts."

Charlotte looked Hal in the eye. "Do you think it was a good idea getting that punching bag?"

"Well, it helps him blow off some steam."

"Yeah, but won't it train him to lash out?"

"We have to trust him." He squeezed her again. "Muffin, you'd better leave now. I don't think you want to see him."

She nodded, put on her coat, and picked up the bottle of wine and her purse. "Thanks, Hal. See you later." She kissed him on the cheek and left.

Hal brought the nachos out and put them on the coffee table. Then he moved the cooler again. "Hey, Cal, do you think it's better over here or over there? Cal?"

Cal looked away from the picture window. "Huh?"

Hal shook his head. "Never mind. On second thought, would you bring in some more chips?"

"Okay."

Cal had just put the bag of chips down when the doorbell rang. He practically tripped as he jumped for the door. His face dropped. "Oh, it's you, Uncle John." He held the door as John walked in with a bucket of fried chicken and a plate of brownies.

John looked at Cal. "Thanks. I love you, too."

Cal's shoulders dropped. "I didn't mean it that way, Uncle John. I was expecting Dad."

John placed the food on the coffee table. "I get it. It's okay." Then he patted Cal on the back and smiled. He looked at Hal. "Are you sure we want Kurt to be drinking?"

"Remember? We all agreed we'd carry on as usual. Besides, I'm gonna want a couple just because he'll be here."

After the next arrival, Cal was visibly disappointed again. This time, it was Jack and Mel. Jack brought hot wings, sauce, and a case of beer, and Mel came in carrying bags filled with chips, dips, and doughnuts. But when he was ready to shut the door after them, Mel saw the TV and shot his arms straight up — like goal posts — almost dropping his offerings. "Woohoo! It's here!" He was acting like a kid with a new toy; his thick eyebrows shot up and his brown eyes turned to the ceiling as he let out a giant guffaw. On the way down, his bulky arms almost knocked John over. "Sorry, man. Oh, and thanks for letting us use your TV here!"

"Sure."

Standing at the front window, Cal saw Kurt park right after Grant drove up. He jumped up and ran to the door to hold it open for Kurt. "Hi, Dad! I'm so glad you could make it!" Cal left the door open as he gave Kurt a bear hug.

Grant squeezed past them, loaded down with a tray of sliders and a twelve-pack of sodas. He usually had a pleasant demeanor, and although he prided himself on self-control, Kurt's insincere display of sentiment galled him. He clenched his jaw. No matter what Kurt said or did, Grant would never forgive him for what he'd done to Charlotte. He put his food down, then put his hat and coat on the bed. As he walked to the living room, he kept pulling his fingers through his graying sandy hair, as if to release some of the anger.

Hal busied himself with arranging the food on the coffee table while John made sure the TV was on the right channel.

Josh walked in from the garage and through the kitchen. When he saw Kurt, he stopped and crossed his arms. "I promised Dad. Just suck it up," he mumbled to himself.

Grant sat in the easy chair. John, Mel and Jack sat on the couch. Hal and Kurt sat on dinette chairs. Josh and Cal sat on the floor, with Cal right in front of Kurt and Josh on the other side of the room.

The usual chatter was gone. As the game progressed, the tension lessened, and enthusiasm finally escalated to the usual cheers, boos, whoops and hollers.

At half time, Grant looked at Kurt. "What are you doing nowadays?"

"Well, I'm looking for a job, but the market doesn't look too promising."

"You used to fix cars out of your own garage. Why don't you do that? Cars always need something fixed."

"Well, I don't have a garage anymore. And I had to sell some of my tools, so there isn't much I can do being self-employed anymore."

Jack wore an ambiguous smile. "There's an opening down where I work. We need a gofer. It doesn't pay much, but it's something. And it would be a foot in the door. At least you'd be able to pay your bills."

"That'd be great — if I could. My health isn't what it used to be," Kurt said. After a pause, he sat up straight and smiled. "Yeah, I'll come over. Just tell me where to go and who to ask for."

Cal smiled with pride as he gazed at Kurt.

Jack and Kurt exchanged information, and the mood seemed to lighten a bit.

Josh's face softened.

Within a few minutes, Kurt grimaced as he caught his breath. He pulled out his pill bottle and placed a tiny pill under his tongue.

Cal's jumped up as his eyes widened. "Dad! Are you okay?"

Kurt nodded quickly. "I will be in a couple of minutes."

Josh squinted at him.

Everyone's attention was now on Kurt.

Grant leaned forward. "What's wrong!?"

Hal stood up quickly and pulled out his phone. "I'll call 911!"

Kurt waved them off. "No, no. I'll be okay. Honest. I've got my meds this time."

Mel frowned. "What do you mean, this time?"

Cal was almost in tears. "He's got a bad heart. He needs surgery, but he can't afford it. I didn't want to tell you, Hal. I thought you wouldn't let me go out with him anymore."

Mel asked more firmly. "What do you mean this time?"

"He had an attack last time we were out," Cal said with a shaky voice.

Hal grimaced. "You've got to be checked out, man."

"I've been checked out. My meds keep me going. Don't worry about me." He slumped back, closed his eyes, and leaned his head against the back of the chair.

"Dad! Are you okay?"

"Yeah. Just gotta rest up a bit."

Jack went to the kitchen and motioned for Hal to follow.

"What is it?" Hal whispered.

"I think the timing was awfully convenient for him to have to take a pill right then."

Hal's eyes widened, then narrowed. "You think he's playing us?"

Jack nodded. "He's already got Cal convinced."

Hal glowered. "How can we know for sure? I don't want Cal going out with him if there's any chance .... If he really does have a heart condition, how *dare* he take a chance like that when he's out with my son!? *His* son?!"

"Whether or not he really has a heart condition, I couldn't care less. Personally, I wouldn't want my kids around the guy at all, but he's their father, so that makes things tough. But to make sure, I'll ask Rudy to see if he can find out anything."

Hal slowly shook his head. "If he's ...," he growled.

Jack put his hand on Hal's shoulder. "Look, we can't do anything." He looked him in the eyes. "Absolutely nothing. Rudy'll take care of him. But don't tell anyone what we suspect. Okay?"

Hal took a deep breath and blew it out. "Okay. But you tell me as soon as you find out *anything* from Rudy." Hal glared at Kurt from the kitchen. He took another deep breath, shook his hands at his sides and blew a silent whistle. "Okay. I trust you. But this better work!"

Jack nodded again. "We'd better go back in, or somebody might get suspicious."

"Here, you take in some beer and sodas, and I'll get the next round of food."

They walked in just as the second half was ready to begin.

Like a scared little boy, Cal put his arm around Kurt's calf as he leaned on him. He smiled weakly when Kurt put his hand on his shoulder and then he laid his head against Kurt's knee.

Josh was so disgusted that he got up and went back to the garage and slammed the door.

Even over the sound of the game, everyone could hear the punching bag getting hammered.

Kurt reached for a beer.

Jack leaned forward with the most concerned look he could muster. "Are you sure you want to drink beer right after taking your meds?"

Kurt glared at him with a hint of contempt. Then he put on a smile, displaying his dimples. "You're probably right." He returned it to the cooler.

"Here, let me open a soda for you."

Kurt's pupils became pinpoints as he leaned back, and he tightened his jaw. "Thanks."

John and Grant put five dollars each on the home team, and Mel, Jack and Hal had their money on the away team. The last few minutes of the game increased the tension between the opposing fans. They all, except Kurt, were on their feet either cheering or booing. He remained seated. When the game was finally over, the cacophony of cheers and jeers drowned out the announcers and crowd on TV.

"What a crock! I can't believe they won!" John yelled.

"Well, it's about time! They couldn't lose forever!" Mel shouted back.

"If it wasn't for their quarterback, they wouldn't have had a chance. And what's with him anyway? His performance through the year has been pretty spotty. Why's he playin' so great now?"

"Aw, you're just mad 'cause you lost." Mel stretched out his open hand, "Pay up!"

John huffed and pulled out his wallet. "Here! I hope you choke."

"Thanks, man." Mel grinned as he put the money in his wallet. "Hey, let's do this again next week!"

John glowered at him.

Mel laughed. "At least you're a good loser. Arlene woulda …." He huffed, set his jaw, and waved it off. "How long will it be until we help you move?"

"We get the keys in about a week, so it should be a week from Saturday. The moving company will be there first thing in the morning, but we'll need help moving little things, too. Bonnie's got a lot of clothes, you know."

"Just let us know when to be there."

Hal whistled to get everyone's attention. "Hey, guys. Charlotte agreed to let us meet here only if we pick up after ourselves." Hal brought out a heavy-duty trash bag, and everyone pitched in to fill it.

Cal jumped up. "No, Dad, I'll do it. You just sit."

After the flurry of activity, Kurt put his hand out to shake hands with Hal. "Thanks for letting me come. That was real hospitable of you."

"You're welcome. It's what Cal wanted. Cal said he wants you to come next week, too."

Cal noticed them talking and joined them. "What's up?"

Kurt put his arm around him. "Well, I guess I'm invited next week, too."

Cal gave Kurt a big hug. He turned around. "Thanks, Hal." Then he looked up at Kurt and grinned. "See, I told you it would be great."

Kurt went around to everyone and shook their hands before he left.

After shaking, Grant wiped his hand on his jeans. He started to say something, saw that Cal was watching, and then stopped himself.

Everyone sorted out and collected the dishes they brought.

Jack was careful not to let anyone notice as he put Kurt's soda can in a baggie. Then he placed it in his sack to take home.

Grant walked out the door with Mel. "I can't help thinking he's up to something." Grant said.

"Yeah. I don't trust him either. Do you know anything about that heart trouble he's talking about?"

"No. But Karen would say I'm vindictive if she knew I was glad about it. It would be a favor to everyone if he croaked."

Mel nodded with a smile. "Only you would say that."

"Don't tell me you weren't thinking the same thing?"

"Yeah. But I wouldn't say it."

They got in their respective cars and drove off.

Jack followed John out the door.

"Hey, John. Can we talk for a moment?"

"Sure. What's up?"

"I couldn't help but notice that you and Bonnie don't seem to get along very well. I was thinking that if you laid off the derogatory comments about her, well, it might help you two to get along better."

"*You've* seen her! She's an absolute ditz! And I'm not telling you anything you don't already know!"

Jack put his free hand on John's shoulder. "What I'm saying is that the bad attitude you have about her will rub off on others. And besides, those comments usually come around, and she'll hear about them. Do you really want her to think you despise her?"

John frowned. "I can't help how I feel, Jack."

"I'm not saying you have to act like newlyweds; just show her a little respect. You'll be surprised. She'll respond."

"That isn't going to make her smart, Jack."

Jack unlocked his truck and placed his sack on the floor of the cab. "What was she like when you met her?"

"What do you mean?"

"Is she any different now from then?" Jack locked the door as he waited for John to respond.

As they headed for John's car, John bowed his head as he slowed his pace. "No. She hasn't changed."

"Then why'd you marry her?"

John stopped short to look him in the eye and paused. "Well, I thought it was cute at the time, and I loved her."

"Anything else?"

John opened the trunk of his car, placed his sack inside, and then looked down at his feet. "Well, she was always happy."

"I'd say that's pretty good."

"I guess I've started to think that she's happy because she's so oblivious. You know — ignorance is bliss." He slowly closed the trunk.

"But she must see the good in others if she's so happy."

"I guess so." John sighed. "But every time I try to talk with her, it always goes over her head."

Jack frowned. "You'd rather have an intelligent grouch?"

John flinched. "No! Of course not!"

"Well, if she's always seeing the good, then isn't that to your benefit?"

John fidgeted. "I never thought of that."

"So she hasn't changed. Why have you?"

John looked him in the eye and sighed again. "I'll have to think about that." He walked to the driver's door and turned around. "See you later, Jack."

Chapter 15

"Are you sure you're okay?" Sharon's face showed her worry.

"Well, the doctor released me, so I guess so."

"I mean how are you handling all of this?"

Callie frowned.

"Oh, honey." Sharon hugged her. "You know I'm here if you want to talk about it."

"I know."

"I got you your favorite ice cream."

"Thanks, Mom. And thanks for picking me up for dinner. I really didn't feel like driving anyway."

"It was my pleasure."

Rudy held the door open for Georgia to enter. As she walked in with this week's dessert, he called out, "We're here. I think it's gonna snow."

When he shut the front door behind them, Rudy shivered off the chill. Then he helped Georgia with her coat. His phone started to beep, so he tapped his touch screen a few times and put it back in his pocket.

"Thanks, Rudy. But I think I'll keep my sweater on for a while — at least until I warm up again." When Georgia got to the kitchen, she placed the container on the counter. "Hi, Callie. Hi, Sharon," she said with a shudder.

Sharon looked at her carefully. "Are you okay?"

"I'm just cold from being outside."

Sharon placed the back of her hand to Georgia's forehead. "I think you have a fever."

"I guess that would explain it." Her eyes were listless.

"Come on. You're going to lie down in Mark's old bedroom."

"Okay." She didn't resist.

"Callie, would you put on some tea?" Sharon called out over her shoulder.

"Sure, Mom."

Georgia lay down on the bed, shivering.

Sharon pulled a comforter out of the closet and wrapped it around her. "After I get you something for that fever, do you want me to stay?" She stroked her hair.

Georgia slowly shook her head as she pulled the covers up around her neck.

Rudy walked into the kitchen just as Sharon came out of the bedroom. "Where's Georgia?"

"Rudy, she's sick."

His eyes popped. "What?! She was fine when we left home! Where is she!?"

Sharon pointed the way. "She's lying down. Callie's making some tea for her."

Rudy hurried into the bedroom. "Hey, Sweet Cheeks," he said softly. "I heard you're sick." He sat on the edge of the bed and smiled tenderly as he stroked her hair. He leaned over her and placed his cheek on her shoulder and put his arm behind her. "I wish it was me instead."

Georgia smiled weakly. "Aren't you just the sweetest."

Sharon came in with the tea and medication. "Here you go, Georgia."

Rudy helped her sit up so she could take the pills.

Georgia looked at them with droopy eyes. "Thanks. But I want all of you to go in there and have dinner. You won't be able to help me in here, and I'll just feel worse if you don't eat."

Sharon smiled at her. "Okay. But I'm going to check on you." She walked out.

Rudy grimaced and then kissed her on the cheek. "I love you, Sweet Cheeks," he whispered.

She smiled weakly, poked her hand out and blew an air kiss. "I love you, too."

When Rudy reluctantly went back to the kitchen, Callie pulled him aside. "How is she?"

"I don't know. I've never seen her sick before." He blew out a quick breath. "I don't know what to do."

As Sharon hugged him, she signaled Callie to set up a distraction. "You're not alone. We're all here to help you get through this." When she stepped back, she saw a look of vulnerability and desperation that she'd never seen on his face before. "Rudy, I know you're worried. We've all gone through it before. Don't worry, you'll survive." She picked up his hand and patted it. "She'll be fine. Really."

"Hey, can I get some help putting the food on the table?" Callie interrupted.

Sharon winked at her. "Okay. Rudy, you bring in the pot roast. It'll help to be busy."

As Rudy carried it to the dining room, Sharon went into the living room. "Distract him," she whispered to Jack.

When they started to pass the dishes around the table, Jack started the conversation. "Say, Rudy, what have you found out about Kurt? Anything new?"

Rudy just turned his glass around and around.

Jack stood up. "Oh yeah. I almost forgot. I got the soda can Kurt used at the game. His prints should be all over it." He retrieved the zippered plastic bag and held it up. "Where do you want it?"

Rudy looked up. "Huh?"

"Are you up to this?" Jack asked.

"Up to what?"

He waved the bag. "The can? Where do you want it?'

"What would I want with a can?"

Jack shook his head. "It has Kurt's fingerprints all over it," he said slowly.

"Oh. Okay. Just put it in my coat pocket."

Jack did as he said. But when he got back to the table, Jack put his hand on Rudy's shoulder. "It looks like we need to talk about something else. Rudy, did you bring chains?"

"Chains? Why chains?"

"Because you were right. It started to snow. On second thought, I insist that everybody stay here tonight."

Rudy smiled halfheartedly. "Thanks, Jack. I wouldn't want to take Georgia out while she's sick, anyway."

"No problem."

Rudy stood up. "Excuse me."

Sharon followed him to Georgia's room. They tiptoed into the bedroom. "See, she's fine. Just let her sleep. That's what she needs right now," Sharon whispered.

Rudy lingered at the door and sighed.

As Sharon urged him to come back to the dining room, Georgia started mumbling in her sleep. "I think he's asleep. Are you sure it'll work? … It better. … Yeah, he's snoring, so he's definitely asleep. …." There was silence for a moment and she mumbled again. "Lissy, I'm scared. … No. I know it's got to be. … but still …." More silence, then she started to sob in her sleep.

He ran his fingers over his hair. "I wish I could help her." He shook his head and pulled the door so that it was ajar.

Sharon sighed. "She's probably just hallucinating from the fever."

Rudy frowned as they sat down at the table. "Do you know who Lissy is?"

"No, I was hoping you'd know."

Jack looked up. "Lissy?"

Sharon smiled half-heartedly. "Georgia was mumbling as she slept. She was talking to someone named Lissy about some guy being asleep. There was something she wasn't sure would work. She sounded scared about something that had to be. That's all."

"That's weird."

"We can ask when she's feeling better. But it's probably nothing. She might not even remember. After all, it's only a dream."

Rudy sighed and picked up his fork. This time, he actually took a bite.

"Callie, you've been awfully quiet. Are you okay?" Sharon put her hand on Callie's shoulder.

"I guess." She looked down and shook her head. "Not really."

"What's the matter?"

She looked up at her mother. "I've been thinking more about that night."

Sharon held her tongue. She didn't want to interrupt.

"I guess I never thought about it before because Roy made me feel safe. But now that he's not — not around anymore — well, I feel vulnerable. Especially after getting mugged. I just can't shake being scared."

Rudy put his fork down. "You're only scared because you don't know what to do if something happens again. What you need is to be prepared. Then you won't feel helpless."

"What do you mean? Do you want me to carry a gun?"

"I was thinking about you learning how to defend yourself."

"Oh. Well, I guess I could take a class."

"Pshh, nonsense. When Georgia's back on her feet, she can teach you everything you need to know." He gave a sly smile. "Believe me, I know."

Jack looked at him curiously.

"Seriously? She could do that?" Callie looked surprised.

"Definitely!"

"I think I'll take you up on that."

"And I've been thinking. How would you like to help *me* out a little?"

"Me? Help you? How?"

"I want you to do some research. Since I don't have much extra time, it'd help me out a lot. It's kind of labor intensive, but I'll tell you what to look for."

"Sure. When?"

"I'll go with you on Monday to get you started."

"Okay."

Sharon sighed with relief when she saw Callie perk up a little.

Jack looked at Rudy as he picked up a slice of bread. "Have you learned anything new about Kurt?"

"Huh? Oh, yeah. I put a bug in his truck while he and Cal were in the woods. They aren't going fishing or to the motorcycle track; I know that. I just don't know what they're doing yet. But I heard the weirdest thing when they came back to the truck last time. Cal asked him if he was okay to drive."

"Could it have anything to do with a bad heart?" Jack interrupted.

"Yeah, how'd you know that?"

"Well, you know he was invited to watch the game with us."

"Why'd you do that anyway?" Callie blurted out.

"Apparently, Cal talked Hal and John into it. Since Cal was so adamant about it, they said okay. Anyway, at half-time, we were all talking, and Grant asked him about his work. Kurt made it sound like he was really trying to get a job but couldn't find one. I told him to come over to where I work; they're looking for some help. You know, start-up positions."

Sharon grimaced.

"He sounded like he was going to apply for the job, and right then he had an *episode*," Jack said with air quotes. "Cal explained to us about Kurt's *heart problem* and how he needs surgery and can't afford it. I took Hal out to the kitchen and told him it sounded pretty convenient."

Callie leaned forward. "You think it's a scam?"

"Absolutely!"

Rudy put his fork down. "The way Kurt was talking to Cal in the truck, I could tell he was playing the sympathy card. Besides, I've seen him when he's alone. The way he moves when he doesn't think anyone's looking — he does *not* have a bad heart. Poor Cal, he's just green and gullible." He frowned. "When this snowstorm passes, I'm going to tail the scumbag and find out how he's paying for rent, food, and gas. Oh, I bugged his trailer, too. But I haven't heard anything between him and Debbie yet. They don't talk much." He paused and looked at Sharon. "Are you sure Georgia's going to be okay?"

She nodded. "Yes, Rudy."

Jack leaned back. "So-o-o, with the snowstorm, it's a good thing John and Bonnie won't be moving for a while. They'd never be able to pull it off in the snow. Well, not very easily anyway."

Callie raised her eyebrows. "Rudy, are you going to be able to help with the move?"

"I'm pretty sure I won't. If Georgia's still sick, I'll be taking care of her. And then when she's better, I'll be tailing Kurt." He was careful not to let on about the investigation at the police station.

Sharon waved him off. "I think Jack will agree with me. You need to keep Georgia here until she's well. We can't have her travelling in cold weather like this. Whatever you need to do, we've got your back. We'll take care of her."

Jack nodded. "Yup, you two stay here as long as you need to."

Rudy smiled with a tenderness they'd never seen before. "Georgia's right. Family really is priceless. Thanks, guys." He went back to eating still wearing that smile.

The phone rang and Sharon got up to answer it. "Hello." Her eyebrows shot up and her eyes got big. "What?!" She paced as she listened. She put her hand over the phone, and then she turned to everyone in the dining room. "Cal's still out with Kurt in this storm. They were supposed to be at the track, but when Hal called over there, the track was closed — has been all day."

Rudy clenched his jaw. "I knew it. Kurt took him somewhere else." He pulled out his phone. "I know how to find them."

"What do you mean?" Jack said.

Rudy sighed. "Well, there might be a GPS tracking device on Kurt's truck that I might be able to access from my phone here." He took out his phone and tapped on the app. A few moments later, a map appeared with a blip flashing in Clackamas County. "He's moving. I'm pretty sure it's towards Charlotte's house." He zoomed in a little. "He's moving slowly, probably because of the snow."

"I'll tell Charlotte he's coming," Sharon said.

Rudy jumped out of his seat. "No! Don't do that! She'll act different, and Kurt will know something's up. Cal should be okay. We don't need to do anything. Not now anyway. Tell her to call you back when she hears anything."

Sharon went back to the phone.

Jack watched over Rudy's shoulder as he started typing. "Hey, that's pretty clever."

"Don't tell anyone, okay? It looks like they took another trip to the woods." Rudy tapped his chin. "I wonder what they're doing out there all the time." Then he slapped his forehead. "Well, duh." He accessed another app from his phone. "Anyone want to hear what they've been saying?"

Jack stepped back. "Well, yeah!"

"My phone started to beep when I got here. That was the cue they started talking, so I set my phone to record it."

Everyone leaned in to listen.

"Here goes…."

"Hey, Dad, do you think it's gonna snow? The weatherman said it's gonna be a doozy."

"Aw, those weathermen only make guesses anyway. We'll be fine."

"But Mom and Hal didn't look too okay with it."

"They worry too much. Besides, I've got chains, and if we need 'em, we'll just put those on."

"But your heart. Won't that be too much strain?"

"Well, it's about time for you to learn some self-sufficiency. I'll just tell you how to do it."

"Okay. Where we going this time?"

"We're going to get some game for dinner. Just like last time. You're getting pretty good, you know."

"Well, you're a good teacher."

There was silence for two minutes.

"What's the matter, Cal? You look down."

"Yeah. I just can't convince Josh that you're okay. He's still yellin' at me …."

"What else?"

"I, uh … I feel guilty."

"How come?"

"It's 'cause I can't get over having to lie to Mom."

"Sometimes it's okay to lie when you're doing it to save somebody's feelings. Didn't you say she'd feel bad if she knew you were learning how to shoot?"

"Yeah. But …."

"No buts about it. You're doing a good thing here."

"How's that?"

"Isn't a man supposed to know how to support a family?"

"Yeah."

"Well, I'm showing you how to do that."

"Yeah! I never thought of that! Yeah."

"Well, well. It looks like the weatherman was right this time. It's starting to snow."

"Aw, does that mean we have to go back?"

"Afraid so."

There was a long silence.

"Cal."

"Yeah, Dad?"

"I've gotta ask …. Aw, this just kills me."

"What?"

"I really need your help."

"Anything, Dad. What is it?"

"This is embarrassing."

"Tell me, Dad."

"Cal — I talked with the doctor yesterday. It's pretty bad."

"Dad?! What is it? Are you gonna be okay?"

"No. He said my condition is worse. There's no way around it. I've gotta have surgery. And the best team is in Mexico. But it might as well be on the moon. There's no way I can get the money to get there, let alone pay for the surgery. If only your mom was willing …. No, I couldn't ask her."

"Dad! I'm sure she'd want to help if she knew!"

"Naw, I couldn't ask her."

"Then I will! She has to help!" He started to cry.

"Hey. I don't want you crying, okay? You've gotta man up. But I gotta tell you, you're the best son a man could ever want. I love you, Cal."

"Aw, Dad! I don't want to lose you! She's gotta help!"

"It looks like we're here."

The engine turned off. "I'll see you next week … if I make it that long …."

"No!" Cal started to sob. "Dad, I don't want you to die. Please be okay, please!"

Everyone heard muffled moaning for a couple of minutes, and then Cal sniffed. "I'm gonna go ask mom right now. Bye, Dad."

The truck door opened and slammed shut. Then the engine started and the truck shifted into low gear. After a moment of driving, Kurt started to sing. "Money, Money, Money …."

Rudy turned off the recording. "Well, that pretty much cinches it. He's definitely scamming them for money."

"What are we going to do about it?" Sharon fretted.

"Aren't we going to tell Charlotte?" Callie said.

"I think this is where we step in." Rudy said.

Jack frowned. "Can we call the police on him?"

"That won't fly. Kurt's not blackmailing them or threatening them. If she decides to give him the money, they'd say it was of her own free will."

"And we're just supposed to let it happen?!" Jack blustered.

Rudy held his hand up. "I didn't say that. I just said the police can't be legally involved. I'll call Hal back, and we'll work out a plan."

Rudy went into the dining room to call Hal.

Charlotte waited by the front window. When she saw Kurt drive up, she yanked the door open and started to sob.

When Cal came in, she wrapped her arms around him. "Oh, honey, I'm so glad you're safe."

"Mom! You know I'm safe with Dad." He turned somber.

"Cal, what is it? Are you okay?"

"Mom, I've gotta tell you something awful."

She turned white as he led her to the couch. She chewed her nail as she sat down.

"Mom, I think Dad could die."

She stiffened. "What?"

"Dad told me he saw the doctor yesterday. He's worse. He needs surgery right now!"

Hal stood listening in the hallway behind Cal. When Charlotte noticed him, he put his finger to his lips.

"Mom, he doesn't have any money. He can't even get to where the doctor is that can operate on him." Cal's face pinched with anguish, "He's gonna die if he can't go. Please? You have more than enough money; you've *got* to help him." Cal doubled over crying.

Charlotte looked up at Hal and shrugged.

"It's up to you," Hal mouthed.

Just then, his phone rang.

Chapter 16

The men put their snacks on the kitchen counter.

"What do we want to start with?" Hal said.

John smiled. "I really don't care as long as there's enough beer on hand."

"Well, maybe you'd better stay here a while after the game. Alcohol and driving don't mix, especially in the snow." Grant glowered at him.

John frowned.

Jack put his hand on John's shoulder. "Hey, John, how about you and I go take a short walk before the game starts?"

"Yeah, sure." He glared at Grant on the way out the door. "Okay, so what do you want to talk about?" John asked before they got to the sidewalk.

"I was just wondering if you thought about our last conversation here."

John hung his head. "Yeah. I guess you made sense. I started thinking about what attracted me to her, and you're right. She hasn't changed. And I still like that girl I married — so positive and cheerful. I guess I forgot about that when I started concentrating on her not being so bright. I decided you're right. I've gotta change my attitude and focus on her good points. She's a good woman. She never flirts with other men, she's been a good mother to our kids, and she's fun."

"I'm glad to hear that. I was worried about you two. You know, it's easy to find faults in others, just like it's easy for them to find faults in us. We just can't let the little things get in the way. Man, I can't tell you how many times I've had to readjust *my* thinking."

John chuckled. "And I thought you and Sharon had a perfect marriage."

Jack stopped in his tracks. "Seriously? It's been a long road getting to where we are. We've both made a lot of mistakes. And it's not something you can just stop working on. If we didn't work hard, who knows where we'd have wound up."

"Well that's a revelation! Who would've known?"

"I'm just thankful that Sharon shares my values."

John thought for a moment and nodded. "Bonnie shares mine, too. …" He shrugged. "When I'm on the right track. I guess I just need to make sure I don't get sidetracked any more. I've decided that the clothes don't matter. We can afford it, and we'll have all the room we need after we move. I'll just have to let it go."

"Good man, John. I'm proud of you." He put his hand on John's shoulder.

John stopped and looked at him. "Really? That means a lot. Thanks." He shook Jack's hand and pulled him in for a bro hug.

"I'm not just feeding your ego — I mean it."

John wore a contented smile as they turned around to go back to the house.

"About what Grant said, do you intend to drink a lot? 'Cause, I think he's right."

"Nah. I think I've been drinking too much for so long that everyone kind of expects it."

"Then why?"

"Why drink too much?"

Jack nodded.

"I think I was feeling sorry for myself and trying to drown my sorrows. I was all caught up in thinking Bonnie was beneath me. But now that I'm coming around, I don't think I need to anymore. Thanks to you."

"And …."

John crossed his arms. "You're not going to let it go, are you?"

"Nope."

"Don't worry, I'll stop at three. I'll just fill up on the food."

Jack chuckled. "Me, too. But I'm going to fight you for Sharon's hot wings."

"And everyone else! Man, those are good!"

"Well, we'd better hurry, or they might be gone before the game starts."

When they walked in the door, they took their coats to the extra bedroom before helping carry food and drinks to the coffee table.

When the doorbell rang, Cal jumped up to answer it. He threw open the door and wrapped his arms around his dad.

Kurt whispered in his ear, and Cal nodded.

"Dad's here. Come on, you can sit here like last time. Do you want anything?"

"Just you by my side is all."

Cal beamed.

In the kitchen, Jack rolled his eyes. When he saw Hal fidgeting in the dining room, he waved for him to join him and then led him to a far corner of the kitchen to be out of sight. "Hey, I understand. We just have to play it cool for a while. Okay?"

Hal crossed his arms as he looked out the kitchen window. "Yeah, I know. I just can't stand seeing what he's doing to Cal."

"I get it. I'd be the same way. But Rudy's working on it — it's being handled. We just have to be patient."

Hal shook his head slowly. "It better work out."

"It will." *I hope.* "Come on. We don't want to bring any attention to ourselves."

Hal clenched his jaw. "Coming."

John was adjusting the sound when they went into the living room. They all sat in their usual places.

Grant sat with his arms crossed, and scorn slowly chiseled his face, deepening the lines in his forehead. He peered at Kurt. "I hear you're going to die."

Cal jumped to his feet. "Grandpa! How could you?! That's mean!"

Kurt patted Cal's back. "It's okay. He's entitled to say what he wants. You just sit down now and let it go."

"But, Dad, it was mean."

"No. Just sit down and let it go."

Cal scowled at his grandfather.

Grant stood up. "I won't be able to enjoy the game. I'm going home." He collected his coat, hat, and gloves from the bedroom and slammed the front door as he left.

"Good riddance," Cal grumbled.

Kurt looked down at him. "Hey, don't do that. Be a man."

Jack clenched his jaw. *Yeah, right! Just like you? Hah!*

Everyone filled their plates as the game started.

Chapter 17

Georgia blinked and slowly looked around. Eventually, she noticed the muffled chatter in the other room. "Oh, right. I'm at Sharon's." When she tried to sit up, her head throbbed. So she lay back down. "I must be dehydrated." She looked around, saw a water bottle on the nightstand, and picked it up. "Oh good, it's cold." She drank about half of it.

Just then, Rudy came in grinning. "Hey, how's my Sweet Cheeks?" He sat on the edge of the bed.

She put her hand on his and smiled. "How long have I been here?"

"Longer than I'd like." He winked. "Two days."

"Seriously? No wonder I'm dehydrated."

"We've all taken turns getting you to drink. Sharon said that if you weren't better by tomorrow, we were going to take you to the hospital." He leaned over her and held her. "I'm really glad you're okay." When he sat up again, a tear ran down his cheek.

She caressed his face, wiping away the tear. "I think I'll keep you."

"Would you like some tea? The girls have wine in there." He frowned. "Is wine a good thing for when you're sick?"

"Did you say the girls are in there?"

"This is Sunday, so yeah." He shrugged his shoulders. "Well, all of them except Arlene."

"Why? What happened?"

"Oh, I guess you missed what happened after her blowup. Arlene told her sisters that she doesn't want to be around Sharon anymore."

She rubbed her forehead. "Why? What could she have done to make Arlene so mad?"

"Sharon hasn't done anything. I'll tell you all about it when you feel better." He leaned over to kiss her. "Right now, you're the topic for all their gossip."

She covered her eyes. "Oh no! I've ruined their fun."

"They're all concerned about you, really! The guys were all going over for the game, and the girls came here anyway, except for Arlene, of course. Even though Sharon said you'd have plenty of caregivers, they couldn't chase me away."

She smiled. "Don't worry; I wouldn't think anything of it if you weren't here. Say, would you help me into the bathroom? I want to clean up. I must smell awful."

"Never." He must have realized how that sounded because he suddenly gasped before sputtering, "That's not what I mean! I meant that you don't smell awful …. I … I just …." He grimaced as his voice faded. "Of course I'll help," he said meekly.

She put her hand on his cheek again. "Rudy, you're so cute."

When they got home that night, he offered her his arm, because she was still weak. He led her to the kitchen table, put the teapot on the stove, and kissed her on the forehead. "Hey, I'm going to get the mail. I've kinda been neglecting it."

"You go right ahead. I'm just going to sit here for a while anyway."

When he opened the mailbox, it was almost full. He flipped through the envelopes on his way back into the house. A large envelope with block letters and no return address caught his attention. He put the rest of the mail on the kitchen table in front of Georgia. "Except for this, it's just the usual. I'm going into my office to look at it. Probably business related." He poured her tea, kissed her, and went to his office.

He shut the door, opening the envelope carefully in case he had to examine it for clues. When he saw who it was from, he smiled and started to read:

Rudy,

I put up the cameras like you told me to, all pointing where they should be. Jerry was happy to cover for me. He's been suspicious for a while and he was thinking about doing something like this anyway. But it wasn't Novak that went in there, though. It was Harrison. He signed in to access a different case, but he only went to Novak's case. He replaced the bullets with some he brought in, just like you said might happen.

That's when I contacted the Feds. Thanks for getting that video of Novak letting the culprit go. They really jumped on it. You were right; I was able to cut a deal. Not sure how good it'll be. Depends on where this goes. I still might have to go to prison. And, of course, I won't ever be able to work as a police officer again. But then, I guess I deserve that.

For now, to everyone at the precinct, it looks like nothing happened. But the Feds are tracking everything I do, even off hours. I can't blame them. That's why this letter. I don't want them to see I have any connection with you — other than being family. But I guess even that's ended now — with Callie anyway. I brought them all the names of the dirty cops from the flash drive. It looks like we'll be collecting evidence against all of them. The Feds have already started to follow the money. But the evidence box is first priority right now. They're making it look like an audit. That's why it'll be another week — paperwork, you know. But it's all undercover, so no one knows it's the Feds. They're pretty sure there's a link between the missing evidence and all those cases, even current ones.

I'm going to have to bring Pierre's box to them eventually, but I'm going to have to have a pretty good reason how I got it. Can you help me with that?

I opened a generic email account so we can talk more freely. It's listed at the end of this letter. I'll have to go to the library to use it, though. Even that's iffy; they're going to watch me pretty closely. When you get an email from Bernie Shaw, it isn't spam. If you never reply, I'll know you think it's too dangerous to use it.

It's been killing me. How is Callie? She said she doesn't ever want to see me again. And then at the hospital — seeing her like that, it just about killed me. I just hope I didn't break her spirit. I'd hate myself if that happened.

I hope to hear from you soon. I didn't realize how much I'd come to depend on you.

Roy

Rudy leaned back in his chair, shaking his head. *Poor kid.* He thought for a while, fingering a pencil in his left hand. Finally, he pulled open the bottom drawer of his file cabinet and addressed a pre-paid mailer. He printed a note and placed it, Kurt's soda can, and a small package inside of it.

He went into the kitchen and gave Georgia a hug, "I'm going to mail a package; you need anything while I'm out?"

"You're so thoughtful." She grinned and kissed him. "I think I'll keep you."

He laughed. "I *know* I'll keep *you*. I should be back pretty soon." He gave her a peck on the cheek. "There's more where that came from."

"I hope so."

The next morning at the library, Rudy pulled out a chair for Callie and placed her laptop on the table. He sat down, pulled out his notes, and smiled at her. "Now don't get all tense, thinking that this is going to be difficult. I just want you to learn what you can about the governor."

Callie recoiled. "Seriously? Why him?"

"Can't disclose that just yet. I want to see if there's anything — suspicious, let's say."

"That's pretty vague."

"Even go back to his childhood, maybe even his parents. Read every article available. Get into his head, how he thinks, feels, reacts. If you don't see anything, don't worry about it." He pulled out a flash drive. "I also want you to check out this list of names — just find out what you can about each of them." He chuckled.

"What's so funny?"

"I was just thinking. This is exactly how I started. Only back then, we didn't have computers. I guess I'm subconsciously grooming you to be a P.I."

"Why is that funny?"

"I was just thinking how you don't fit the mold." He leaned back and grinned. "You'd probably be able to get away with a whole lot more than I ever could. That'll work in your favor."

"Are you serious? You really think I could be a P.I.?"

"You bet! All it takes is being able to think, reason, and put things together. You know, being people-smart. You've already got that — you just need a little training. And the fact that you already know photography — well, that's just icing on the cake."

She looked aside, deep in thought.

He waited. When she looked up with that twinkle in her eye, he knew she was hooked. "Write down everything, even your feelings on things. Sometimes your gut will tell you more than the facts will."

"How come I have to work from here? The Internet should have everything I need."

"Well, a lot happened before the Internet took off. You'll need to access the microfiche, too. It's right over there." He pointed to the far end of the room. "I've got a few things to do, so I'll leave you to do your thing." He stood up.

"Okay. And thanks for the compliment."

"Compliment?"

"Yeah. You know, saying I'm smart."

"I thought you already knew that. Don't worry; I know you'll do a good job." He turned to leave.

She smiled and waved as he walked out of the room.

Chapter 18

Josh put the Ducks pin in his pocket and then went into Cal's room. "Hey, Cal."

"Yeah, what do *you* want?" He looked up suspiciously.

Josh looked down at the floor. "I wanted to say I'm sorry."

Cal eyed him warily.

"I've been pretty rough with you, and I don't want us to be enemies. I'm sorry."

"Do you really mean that?"

"Yeah. I got something for you." He pulled the pin out of his pocket. "I thought if you put it on your baseball cap — you know, for when you're out with Kurt — it'd be like you had me with you." He held it out in his open hand.

Cal looked at it. "Wow, a Ducks pin!" He grinned. "This is pretty cool. Thanks."

"Here, let me put it on your cap. I know just where to put it. I want it on the left of the bill so Kurt can see how much you mean to me."

"He knows that."

Josh sighed. "Is that okay with you?"

"Sure."

After Josh pinned it on, they hugged. Cal couldn't see the anxiety in Josh's face.

When Cal left with Kurt on Saturday, Josh called Smitty. "They just left. You got them on? ... Good, I'll be right out." He smiled and grabbed his coat.

"Hey Mom, I'm gonna go meet Smitty."

"Okay, call to let me know when to expect you."

"Sure, Mom."

He ran down the road and around the corner and jumped into the front seat of Al's car. "Are you sure we'll hear everything?"

"Yup."

"And does it have GPS?"

"Technically, no. But I can trace the signal if you want to."

"Good. That means we don't have to stay close enough for them to see us." Then he nudged Al. "Well, let's go."

Al held up his hand. "Whoa! Didn't you say we don't have to follow them?"

Josh closed his eyes and let out a slow breath. "Yes."

"Why are we following them?"

Smitty frowned. "Yeah, why are we?"

"'Cause if anything happens, I want to be there."

Al squinted at him. "And just what do you think we'd be able to do if something did happen?"

Josh pinched his lips together before his anxious response. "I don't know. But I have to be nearby."

Al let out a resigned sigh. "Okay!" He mumbled as he started the engine. "Well, Smitty, tell me where we're going."

Smitty pointed the way. "Sounds like they're going hunting again. From what they're saying, they're probably headed to where we were last time."

"I know the drill."

Josh leaned over to Al. "I really appreciate this. Thanks."

Al huffed as he shifted into first gear.

After parking in a turnout near the road Kurt took, Al gripped the steering wheel. "I'm not putting us in view of that road. And I'm not getting out of the car."

"Hey, that's okay," Josh said.

"Sounds like they're getting the guns and stuff from the truck now. Wait. Kurt said he knows of another spot. They're gonna walk," Smitty said.

Josh got antsy. "Is there any way we can all listen?"

Smitty smiled. "Yeah, I'll just hook it up to this speaker."

"Will that make it so it won't record? 'Cause I wanna make sure we have evidence."

"Oh, it'll still record." He dug into his box of equipment, pulled out another device, and made some connections. "Voila!"

The sound was low, but they could all hear.

Josh motioned to turn up the volume.

"It's already up. I think they're whispering."

"Watch out, Cal. The ground here is pretty uneven. This is a deer trail, but there's still a lot of underbrush and branches to trip on."

"Thanks, Dad. How'd you learn so much?"

"My dad taught me just like I'm teachin' you. Only we had a lot of game nearby. We didn't have to drive a long way to get to it."

The voices dropped so low that the boys had to strain to hear.

"Are they getting out of range?" Josh whispered.

"No, the signal's still strong. They must still be whispering." Smitty put his finger up to his lips.

"Cal, look over there. See the deer? Slowly take aim, slow now. Get your sight. Slowly squeeze the trigger."

Boom!

"Aw, Dad. I missed."

"That's okay. We'll just keep going."

For a couple of minutes, the only sound they heard was the faint movement of brush. Then, they heard a branch break and a thud.

"Cal, you've got to keep an eye on your feet."

"I'm sorry, Dad."

"Well, that does it! The game has been alerted, now. We'll have to go to another spot."

"Kurt sounds irritated," Josh whispered.

Smitty put his finger up to his mouth. "Shh."

Josh shook his head. "Can't you turn it up?"

"No. It's not the equipment, they're whispering."

"Ouch."

"Cal, I told you to watch out."

"I'm sorry, Dad. I didn't see it."

"With all this noise, all the game is going to disappear!"

Josh frowned. "I don't like this."

Another five minutes went by with Kurt sounding edgier. There was a moment of silence and a loud crack, like a branch breaking. *"Ahhh.h..h...h...."* The yell faded quickly.

Josh sat up straight. "That was Cal screaming! He must be hurt! We've got to go help him!"

Al was wide-eyed. "Are you nuts! Didn't you hear that noise before he yelled? That was probably Kurt hitting him with a branch! Don't you think he'll kill us too? And he's got a rifle! There's no way I'm goin' in there! I say we get outta here before he gets us, too," his voice squeaked.

Josh panicked. "No! I gotta help Cal!"

Smitty slowly shook his head. "I think Al's right. We gotta go tell your uncle."

Josh's face dropped. "After what he told us, he'd probably kill us."

"Yeah, but at least *he* could find out what happened without getting killed."

Josh's face contorted with dread and anxiety. "I knew it was bad, Cal going out with him. I just couldn't convince anyone."

Al folded his arms. "Look, if we wait too much longer, Kurt could drive down that old road and catch us. We need to leave!" he said carefully.

Josh was firm. "I have to look for him after Kurt leaves!"

Smitty shook his head. "If Kurt was teaching Cal how to hunt, they won't leave a trail. How are you going to know where they went?"

Josh's mouth turned down again. "Didn't you say you could find his coordinates? Where are they?"

Smitty cringed. "It's only a direction finder."

"Well, then let's wait until Kurt leaves and then go in to get Cal!"

Al closed his eyes. "And just how do you suppose we're going to find our way out? We aren't mountain men, and we don't know what we're doing."

Then Josh's eyes got big. "Do you have our coordinates?"

"I can get them." Smitty assured him.

"Does your direction finder have the distance?"

"Yeah! I'll just write it all down. Then we can tell that to the …. Who *are* we going to tell?"

"We can't go to the police 'cause what we're doing is *so* not legal. We'll get in big trouble," Al whined.

Josh frowned. "I can't believe you guys!"

Al looked at his watch. "Well, I think it's too late to leave before Kurt. We'll have to watch for when he leaves and then wait another ten minutes after that to leave. To be safe."

"I think Al's right. But what'll we do after that?"

"I don't know!" Josh growled.

Al pointed ahead. "I think I saw movement. Is that his truck leaving?"

Josh exhaled forcefully. "It must be. I wanna go."

Smitty grabbed his arm. "No, you don't. We're waiting for ten minutes, like Al said."

By the time Al drove up to Josh's house, Josh was fit to be tied.

"What're you gonna tell your Mom?" Smitty asked.

Josh hung his head. "I don't know. I still can't believe this."

Both Al and Smitty tried to comfort him, patting him on the shoulder.

"Bye, guys. Thanks for helping me." Josh got out of the car and walked slowly up the walk, not even waving good-bye when they drove off.

When he went in, Charlotte was in the kitchen. He didn't even stop to take off his coat. "Mom?"

"Oh, hi Josh. Did you have a good time?" Without turning to look at him, she reached into the freezer.

He squeezed his eyes closed and moaned.

She turned around. "Josh, what's wrong?"

Josh could feel the blood pulsing in his ears. "I … I have something awful to tell you."

Alarmed, she walked up to him. "Sit down, what's the matter?"

"I can't sit. It's too awful."

"Well, what is it?" Cal called from behind him.

Josh spun around. "Cal?!" He rushed over to grab him but the force knocked them both to the floor.

Cal moaned. "Oh, great. First a sprained ankle and now a bump on my head! What's the matter with you?!"

"I'm so happy to see you! What hap …." He stopped mid-sentence as he looked at his mom. Then he helped Cal to his feet. "A sprained ankle? What happened?"

"Uh, we went hiking. I wasn't paying attention, and I stumbled over a branch. Mom put an Ace bandage on it. She was getting the ice bag when you knocked me down. It's not bad." Then he glared at him. "And *you* didn't help it any!"

Josh bit his lip.

"Are you sure you're all right, Cal?" Charlotte helped him to a kitchen chair.

"Yeah, as long as Josh doesn't attack me again."

Then Charlotte stepped back and looked at Josh. "Okay, so what awful thing were you going to tell me?"

Josh's eyes widened. "Oh … I … uh …. It doesn't matter now." He rushed to his room.

Cal hobbled to the living room to sit on the couch. "He's weird."

Charlotte shook her head as she brought the ice pack to Cal.

Josh called Smitty when he got to his room. "He's okay. He just tripped and sprained his ankle. … No, I didn't ask him — I figured he might get suspicious. … Don't worry, I'll find out. … Would you call Al and tell him? … And thanks, buddy. I think we'd better leave this to Rudy after all. … Yeah, I know. Al will be thrilled. … Bye."

Chapter 19

Rudy and Georgia had Jack and Sharon over for a game of cards. As Rudy dealt the cards for pinochle, Georgia poured coffee for everyone. "I want to apologize about last week for being so sick. I didn't mean to ruin everyone's good time."

Sharon waved it off. "You didn't ruin anything. We were just fine." Then she put her hand over her mouth. "Not that we didn't care. We were all involved in caring for you."

Georgia chuckled. "Oh, for goodness sake, I never thought that for a moment. I know you care."

"When our kids were growing up, we had a lot of kids at our house," Jack piped in. "You know, with our two and all their friends coming over most of the time, Sharon developed a pretty good eye for what to look for when someone got sick. You were in good hands."

Georgia passed the lemon cookies and picked up her cards. "Sorry about these being store-bought — I'm still a little foggy."

"Don't apologize. We weren't expecting anything. We're just glad you're okay again." Sharon patted her hand.

"Thanks." She looked across the table. "I probably won't be much of a partner. Sorry, Rudy."

"Hey, that's okay."

Sharon sorted her cards. "I'll open. Are you sure you're okay with us being here?"

"Oh, yeah. I'm just a little slow on the uptake. I should be okay in a couple of days." She looked at her cards. "I'll pass."

Jack passed.

Rudy grinned. "Well, Sharon, I guess it's up to you and me to duke it out. Two-fifty."

Sharon rearranged her cards. "Georgia, who's Lissy?"

Rudy noticed a subtle flinch, so he watched her more closely.

"Where'd you hear that?" Georgia asked, a little too coolly.

"When you were sick, you mumbled a bit. You were talking to someone named Lissy."

"Oh. That's what I used to call Alice. You know, when you first learn to talk, things just come out a little off. And it just stuck."

"Well, you were talking to her about some guy being asleep. And then you said you were scared. What was that about?"

Georgia caught her breath. "Uh, I must have been hallucinating. I don't remember."

After Jack and Sharon left for the night, Rudy's phone rang. "Hello?" He held his hand over the mouthpiece. "Georgia, I'll take this in my office." He closed the door and resumed. "You got some news?"

"You bet!" Roy said. "Oh, by the way, thanks for sending the prepaid phone. Now I don't have to worry about anyone listening in. Anyway, there's nothing on that perp from the video you took, not even any arrests. But since Novak let him go, the Feds are looking at any cases in other states *he* might be involved in, so this is going to get interesting."

"Say, I just had an idea."

"What's that?"

"Talk with the Feds and suggest that they copy the video and send it in as an anonymous tip to the station. The captain will probably assign Todd to examine it and then the Feds can compare how it looks after he's done with it."

"Good idea!"

Rudy nodded when he heard the smile in his voice. "Oh, and you might want to give this bit of information to them — the captain specifically sent Novak to that call."

"Really?! I guess I shouldn't be surprised since his name is on the flash drive, too." There was a moment of silence before Roy continued. "What do I tell them when they ask me how I knew that?"

"Don't you hear the calls, too?"

"No. Since I'm a detective now, I'm on a different frequency."

"Just tell them that the guy who gave you the video heard it on the scanner."

"Okay, that should work. Oh, get this. Remember I told you the Feds are busy investigating financial records? Sure glad I already disclosed my end. Anyway, even though I gave them the information from the flash drive, they're looking at everyone."

"That's what I would expect. What about the evidence box?"

"Since they saw the video of Harrison tampering with the evidence, they installed more cameras so all the lockers are covered. So far, it looks like Harrison and Novak are the only two doing the tampering. But it's still pretty early. I'm pretty sure it's just them, since they're the only names on the flash drive besides Todd and the captain." There was silence.

"You okay?"

"Yeah. They want to know where I got it."

"Well, didn't you say you'd get me a deal?"

"I said I would. I just haven't yet. I gotta make sure you're okay with me telling them about you."

"We talked about that. Just make sure there's a deal for me."

"Okay, but I'm not sure I can make the deal with you not there."

Rudy tapped his chin. "Well, can you tell them your source doesn't want to be disclosed right now? I'll come forward later."

"I guess. Why?"

"I want to make sure this stuff with Kurt gets settled. I don't want to miss something on him because of being stuck in some interrogation room."

"I'll see what I can do."

"Say, did you run Kurt's prints from the can?"

"Oh, yeah. Nothing there, not from any states."

"Okay. Keep in touch."

"Will do."

Chapter 20

It was eleven-thirty Tuesday morning. Rudy pulled out slowly, making sure there were a couple of cars between him and Kurt. Kurt pulled into in the parking lot of a bank, and Rudy parked on the street. Rudy walked in the front door as Kurt approached the customer service counter in the corner. Rudy walked up to a brochure display which was about ten feet from Kurt. He selected a brochure and pretended to read it while listening.

"Box number 287."

The customer service rep had freckles and curly, red hair. Puffy pouches hung under his red eyes and the corner of a tissue stuck out of his breast pocket. His necktie was off-center and uneven at his belt. He looked like he was about to sneeze as he opened a file box and retrieved a card. "Sign here please." He sniffed.

Kurt signed it and handed it back to him.

After the customer service rep compared the signatures, he date-stamped it and returned it to the box. Then he placed the box back in the drawer and locked it. "Right this way, Mr. Rance."

Kurt followed him into the vault and Rudy noticed an empty looking gym bag in his hand.

The employee came back out, went behind the counter again to blow his nose, and pumped the nearby hand sanitizer.

Rudy returned the brochure back to the display and went out to his car. Kurt came out with a full gym bag. Rudy followed him back to the trailer park while keeping a safe distance between them. When he parked, he made sure that he could see Kurt's trailer. Instead of going to his trailer, Kurt went to the manager's office. After a few minutes, Kurt got back in his truck and drove away.

Rudy waited a few minutes before he got a couple things out of his trunk, put them in a briefcase, and went to the manager's office.

The man behind the desk looked about sixty and apparently shaved his head to hide the fact that he was balding. His sunken eyes looked up quickly when Rudy walked in. He wore loose, faded blue jeans and a denim jacket over a plaid shirt which had the top three buttons undone and a stain by the left lapel. "What can I do for you?"

Rudy flashed his fake detective badge. "I'm looking for any information I can get on Mr. Rance."

The man's eyebrows shot up. "I don't know. What can I tell you?"

"When did he move in?"

"I'll have to open the books for that." He flipped through a few pages. "He and his wife came and rented a furnished trailer on December 26th."

"What kind of rental agreement does he have?"

"It's month to month. The owner wasn't particular, just as long as somebody's renting it. It didn't matter to me."

"Does he always pay cash?"

"Yeah, how'd you know?"

"Sorry, can't divulge that information."

The manager's eyebrows shot up again as he looked at the safe. "Is he paying me with funny money?"

"Well, let me look at it, and I'll tell you."

The manager's hands started to shake as he opened the safe. "He was just here, so here's what he paid me."

Rudy looked at the hundreds carefully against the light. Then he opened his briefcase, opened a small bottle of liquid and then opened a sealed Q-tip. He dipped the Q-tip in the bottle and wiped it over both sides of the bill. Then he inserted it into an empty bottle and sealed it. Handing the bills back along with a card from his pocket, he said, "They're okay, but I want you to call me if he does anything different or suspicious."

The manager blew a silent "whew" as he returned the money to the safe.

Rudy closed his briefcase. "Have you noticed anything unusual about Mr. or Mrs. Rance?"

The manager thought for a moment. "I only talk to Tom when he comes to pay the rent. He doesn't say much, but he's always pleasant. Well, there was this one time he came to have me call the owner of the trailer to fix the heat in there. He was pretty mad then, but I couldn't blame him. It was during that bad cold snap. As for the missus, I don't ever see her. And I only got a glimpse of her when they moved in. It was cold that day, and she was all bundled up, so I didn't really see her." He shrugged. "They pay on time, so I don't worry about it."

"Be sure to call me if you see any change in his behavior."

"Sure. What are you looking for?"

Rudy put on a stern face before he left. "You know I can't tell you that." He turned to leave and then looked back. "Don't let him know I was here. We wouldn't want him to panic."

The manager inhaled quickly and shook his head.

When he got back to the car, he looked at his watch. "Whoa! It's almost time. I'd better get going."

Rudy pulled into the parking lot right after Kurt. He opened his tote bag and took out the camera. He made sure to get the business sign in the pictures of Kurt walking toward the gym and entering the building. He returned the camera to the bag, got out of the car and then followed him in.

He flashed his fake identification to the man behind the counter. It was apparent that the man worked out during his time off; his biceps and torso were well developed, and you could see the six-pack under his tight, black T-shirt bearing the company logo. His square face sat atop a short thick neck, making it appear as if there was a block of wood on his shoulders. The sweats were just tight enough to see the definition of his thighs.

"I'm a reporter doing a story on the benefits of exercise. I wonder if I can take a few shots of the equipment here. Of course, I'd be sure to put your name in the article, maybe even your picture."

He came to attention, thrusting out his chest. "Okay. Let me show you around. I'm Bruce Wiggins, two g's." He shook hands and led him to the main area. "Besides this big room, we have several classrooms, an Olympic-sized pool, sauna, juice bar, a gift shop, and just about any dietary supplement you can think of. Come this way, please."

Rudy took pictures of each piece of equipment as Wiggins pointed them out — until he saw Kurt come out of the locker room in sweats. Kurt did some stretches and stepped onto the treadmill, quickly going to a full run.

"Say. I'd like to take a few photos of the equipment in use. Is that okay?" Rudy asked Wiggins.

"Uh, I guess so."

Rudy took three scanning videos, making sure Kurt was always in view, as well as photos of several other areas so as not to alert Kurt. When Kurt went to the showers, he thanked Wiggins and left. When he got to the car, he called Hal.

Hal opened the door. "Wow, you're good. I can't believe you got them already. Come on in." He gestured for Rudy to sit down. "Hey, Charlotte, boys, would you come in here?"

"What's going on?" Josh asked.

"Rudy has something to show us."

Everyone came in and sat down.

Charlotte looked puzzled as Rudy pulled out the camera.

"Cal, I know about Kurt and what he's been telling you. I'm here to show you that he's been lying to you."

Cal glared at him.

He pulled up the videos to play in sequence, and handed the camera to Cal. "Cal, Kurt's been going to the gym every Tuesday. I just now took pictures of him on the equipment. You'll see from these pictures that if he had the heart condition he told you about, he'd never be able to do this. He would have collapsed or died with this much exertion. Here, look for yourself."

Josh stood behind Cal to watch over his shoulder.

As Cal scrolled through, his mouth dropped open and his eyes welled up. "Why? Why would he lie like that?"

Josh stood up straight and clapped his hand on Cal's shoulder. "You're kidding, right? He played you. Can't you see? He doesn't care about you. He's only here for the money. I *knew* it!" He started pacing and muttering to himself.

Cal slowly shook his head as his mouth turned downward.

"Oh, honey. I'm so sorry." Charlotte hugged him.

"Thanks for doing this, Rudy. I owe you big time. Not because of the money. I'm just glad the boys didn't get hurt more than they did. What do we do now?" Hal was eager.

"Did you make arrangements to give him the money?" Rudy asked.

Charlotte nodded.

"When?"

"Next Thursday. We took your suggestion; it's just inside the South entrance of the Rose Quarter. I'm supposed to have the money in a gym bag and give it to him before the game starts."

"Smart woman. You'll keep the appointment. But you'll tell him you know the truth and that he's not getting the money."

Charlotte's eyes widened as she stiffened. "I can't do that!"

"Why not?"

"I just can't." She fingered her locket.

"I'll be nearby. And we'll have a bug on you so we can record everything."

She shook her head quickly. "No. I can't face him like that. He'll go into a rage."

Cal slowly turned towards her. "I'll do it, Mom."

Josh put his hand on Cal's shoulder again. "I'll go, too."

Hal looked worried. "I'll go."

She gasped. "No! No! I can't allow any of you to go." She gulped some air and frantically waved her hands. "Okay, okay. I'll do it." She squeezed her eyes shut and her mouth trembled.

"I know you can do it." After reassuring her, Rudy discussed the plans with everyone. "I'll be here a couple of hours early to get you wired and go over every detail.

Chapter 21

The captain wanted to hurry to the IT department and had to remind himself to slow down so as not to be conspicuous. *Leave it to Novak to get himself caught on video,* he thought as he walked down the hall. He pulled the flash drive out of his pocket when he entered the room and approached Todd's desk. "Rush job on this, Todd. Some anonymous tipster sent in this video. Would you check it out to see if it's legit? Make sure nobody tampered with it." The captain's thin lips twitched when he winked at him. Todd nodded when he saw the signal. "Sure thing." Todd's clear, pale skin and lack of much facial hair made him look twenty years younger. He dressed the part to enhance that impression, and he worked out just enough to stay fit, yet not develop bulky muscles. Looking younger suited him just fine; he appeared less threatening, and women were attracted to him.

"I know you will." The captain patted him on the shoulder.

The next day, Novak closed the door behind him when he entered the captain's office. He chewed his lip as he sat down. "Can we talk?"

The captain looked up. "Sure, what's up?"

"Is it true there's a video of the job at the jewelry store?"

"Yeah. Some guy filmed the whole thing, from when you got there to when the detectives arrived."

Novak winced. "Then you know that when I got there, one of Frankie's guys was still inside. You were right to send me."

"I had no choice. I knew about the job going down, but I had no idea there'd be anyone still inside after hours. With neighbors hearing gunfire, I couldn't risk taking too long to get someone out there. Obviously, someone saw you let him get clear of the scene."

"Hey, I looked around, and the neighborhood looked all buttoned down. All I can say, is I'm glad Todd's taking care of that video."

The captain sighed. "I've told you before, don't worry. I've got your back."

"What can we do to be more proactive when we know something's going down in the future? What do you know about the upcoming jobs?"

"Well, you know about the big heist happening at the docks next spring, when the drugs come in, but the next job is at the bank in a couple days. We already went over the plans, but since it's a pretty big job, I've arranged for some distractions in other parts of town to give them more time, just in case someone sees something and reports it. They expect that they'll need at least ten minutes from the time they get in till they get out."

"Are there any guards on duty that might get in the way?"

"There is a guard, but the guys will have silencers this time when they take him out. You play your cards right on these, and I can guarantee a promotion for you after the job at the docks."

"Isn't this a bit risky having so many major robberies so close together? We can't risk the Feds getting involved."

"I don't think we need to worry about that, especially when we have friends in such high places — if you know what I mean."

"Well, I know about Todd and Harrison, but they don't count. Who're these friends in high places?"

"I guess you can be trusted. Governor Munson has been very supportive of Frankie's business. I don't ask why, but I was told that I could call him whenever I need help covering something up."

"The governor?" He let out a long whistle. "I never would've guessed. Well, I guess you've got it covered, all right."

"Like I said, don't worry." The captain looked at him carefully. "Just make sure that nervous tic doesn't give you away."

Novak swallowed hard. "Well, I've got to clock out. Thanks for the talk."

When Novak walked into the warehouse, a muscular guy in coveralls patted him down. Then he escorted Novak up the stairs, opened the door at the top, and pointed inside. "Right in there." When they entered, the two men inside stopped talking.

Novak looked at Agent Riley, who looked different than the last time they met. Now, Riley was sporting a mustache, probably fake, and a buzz cut. He still had the square jaw and a small scar on his left forearm. "Do you want me to take it off, or are you going to?"

"I'll do it, but take off your shirt first." When Novak was done, Riley meticulously removed the tape, wires, and mike. "Wait here until we hear what you got." He pointed to the chair in the corner and brought the equipment to the next room. Another agent crossed his arms and stood at the door.

In a few minutes, Riley came out with a straight face.

Novak's breath involuntarily escaped. "It wasn't good enough?"

Riley shook his head. "Oh, no! It's just what we wanted and more. Good job. Of course, you know you can't tell *anyone*?"

"Yeah." Novak rolled his eyes.

"Tell us about that bank job."

Novak spent several minutes describing every step as he understood it.

"That's how the captain told it to you. Now we're going to tell you how it's actually going down."

It was the middle of lunch hour at the bank. Because there were so few tellers, the line was long, and two of the customers looked worried that they might not get back to work on time. The woman at the head of the line was wearing a business suit, repeatedly looking at her watch, and tapping her high heel anxiously. The man at the end of the line wore a yellow construction hat and coveralls, shifting his weight constantly and sighing often.

Roy stood by the small counter between the placard showing interest rates and the large plate-glass window, pretending to fill out a deposit slip. He had a good view of the street without being obvious. Occasionally, he glanced over at Novak, who was filling out a loan application at the loan officer's desk. Novak's bulky jacket was unzipped almost to the waist and the heel of his tennis shoe drummed the floor as his leg bounced nervously. Roy took out his phone and sent him a text. Novak pulled his phone from his pocket, looked at it, and put his hand on his knee to stop it from bouncing. He shook his head as he returned the phone to his pocket.

After smiling briefly, Roy continued to casually glance up each time someone passed by on the sidewalk. When two men in trench coats and ski hats came to the door, he tried to type in a text to Novak to alert him, but it was too late.

Suddenly, the robbers pulled out guns and the taller one shouted "Hands up!" in a mechanical tone. Roy could see he was wearing a device around his neck that disguised his voice. The other robber shot the guard in the chest, and he went down.

A woman at the counter standing with her young daughter turned around, screamed and dropped to the floor trying to protect her child with her body.

The shorter man ran to the tellers holding a semi-automatic pistol. "Don't touch those alarms, or I start dropping customers! Put all the cash in here!" He threw a gym bag towards the first teller and told her to pass the bag down as they emptied the contents of their drawers into the bag.

The first man, who was holding an assault rifle, ordered Roy and the other customers to go to the wall opposite the counter, so that he could better control them.

Roy slowly started to put his phone into his inside pocket and the tall man whipped his rifle towards him. "Freeze!" Keeping his rifle aimed at him, he walked towards Roy. "Put the phone on the ground and kick it away from you — now!"

Roy dropped the phone on the floor and kicked it away from the crowd.

The robber hit him on the side of the head with his rifle. Before Roy could regain his balance, the man forced him to the floor. "Face down and don't move! Hey Brick, we've got a hero here. Hurry it up!" He frisked him, and when he found Roy's gun, he put it into his belt. Then he stood with his foot on Roy's lower back. "Don't be a hero!"

A woman's frantic crying distracted the robber. "You! Shut up!"

Another customer held her, trying to calm her down. "Please be quiet, and maybe he won't shoot," he whispered.

"Hurry up with that money!" the man at the counter shouted.

Roy looked over his shoulder at Novak and nodded. Novak, who was mixed among the customers, pulled out his gun and shot the man whose foot was on Roy's back, and he collapsed onto Roy's legs, partially trapping him.

The second robber, who was caught by surprise, turned and shot Novak, who spun around from the impact of the bullet and fell to the floor. The screaming from the customers added to the chaos as Roy struggled to take the rifle from under the robber that fell on him, and managed to shoot the second robber. Roy's position on the floor protected him from getting hit by the other bank robber, although it was unclear if he just didn't know that Roy was a threat or if he was just unwilling to shoot towards his partner.

Four Feds, responding to the gunfire, ran in the front door just as the robber at the counter tried to get up, holding his abdomen. Two of the agents pinned and cuffed him. A third agent ran over to Novak, and the other came over to cuff the other robber who was lying unconscious on Roy's legs. The Feds retrieved all of the weapons, including the one that Roy used to shoot the second robber at the counter.

The guard stood up and took off his bullet-proof vest just as paramedics came rushing in. Roy told them that he was fine and to tend to Novak.

When Roy was freed, he ran over to Novak, where a paramedic was treating him. He bent down to check him out. Novak's breathing was shallow and blood was oozing from his left shoulder where the bullet just missed his bullet-proof vest.

Novak looked up at him. "I figured this'd happen." He winced in pain. "I guess I deserved it."

"Nobody deserves this." Roy looked up and saw the first Fed calling for three ambulances. He looked back down at Novak. "I'm no doctor, but I think you're going to be okay. Shoulder wounds are rarely life-threatening."

Novak gritted his teeth. "That doesn't mean they don't hurt."

Chapter 22

The next morning, Rudy opened his large suitcase and looked at the choices.

Georgia walked in and cocked her head. "What's that?"

"This is my collection of disguises. What do you think of this wig?"

Georgia laughed. "If you wear that, I'm getting my camera. I haven't seen that style in years. You'd attract more attention than you bargained for."

"Yeah, I should get rid of it." He frowned. "I guess most of this stuff is outdated, too."

"Do you have a make-up kit in there?"

"Yeah. You feel artistic?"

"Sure. Let me see what you've got."

After about ten minutes, she giggled. "You could pass for your father."

He frowned. "You made me look older?"

"Well, yeah. I don't want women to fall at your feet, do I?"

He stood up to get a better look in the mirror. "Whoa! You're good! If I put gray in my hair, that'll cinch it."

She looked in the case. "Here, put these on, too."

He smiled. "You have a good eye; those are the good ones. Yup, that's a good touch all right." He looked in the mirror and grimaced when the old man with horn-rimmed glasses staring back at him. "Whoa! I sure look old."

"Well, isn't that the point?"

"I guess."

She grabbed a small pillow. "Here, stuff this in your shirt too. And I think I saw some suspenders in that case, didn't I? You don't want to look too fit. You're supposed to be an old geezer, you know."

"Old geezer, huh? We'll see about that."

She giggled as he chased her into the living room.

He grabbed her, and she giggled again.

She looked up at him with a twinkle in her eye. "You better watch out, Mister. You'll be late."

"Oh, yeah." He begrudgingly went back to the bedroom to make the finishing touches, and then he left with the glasses in his shirt pocket.

Rudy parked around the corner from the trailer park. Then he tapped the app on his phone to listen.

"What's this?! Can't you keep this little trailer clean? You're a pig! I should've let you stay in that dump you were living in. You're worse than a tramp! This place better be cleaned up by the time I get back! Got it?!"

"I'm sorry, Tom. It'll be clean. I promise."

Rudy heard some rattling and shuffling sounds.

"Come here!"

"No, please! Not again!"

"This'll help you remember!"

"No. Please, no." She started crying.

A moment later, he saw Kurt slam the door as he left the trailer. Kurt drove off with his tires spinning.

Rudy shook his head as he followed him to the parking lot of another bank. "Now what are you up to?" he wondered out loud.

With the disguise, Rudy knew Kurt wouldn't recognize him from the other bank lobby. He put the glasses on as he entered the bank right after Kurt. When Kurt approached the back counter, Rudy got in line behind him.

"Safety deposit box 390, please," Kurt said.

The short, pudgy man with glasses behind the counter retrieved his card. "Sign here, Mr. Baxter." Rudy was glad he wore the special glasses; he was able to see the full name on the card — "Gene Baxter".

After the card was returned to its box and locked away, the man behind the counter led Kurt into the vault.

Another alias, huh? I wonder where he got that one. Rudy took off his glasses and left to wait in the car.

Kurt came out in about five minutes and Rudy followed him to a sporting goods store.

Rudy decided not to wait; he made a couple of phone calls as he raced to Kurt's trailer.

He pounded on the trailer door.

"Who is it?"

"A friend."

The curtain parted in the window. "Who are you?"

"I know Kurt's ex. I'm here to help you."

"Who's Kurt?"

"Tom, I'm a friend of Tom's ex."

The curtain closed and Rudy waited through the silence. After a couple of minutes, she opened the door. "What do you want?" She frowned. "Hey, aren't you the guy that checked the electricity?"

"Yeah." Rudy got the first good look at her since he started this case. Her hair was cut to different lengths and she had dark circles under her sad eyes. *Kurt, what've you been doing to her?* "I'm here to rescue you."

Debbie's eyes got big. "What do you mean?"

"Do you really want to continue living like this?"

Her shoulders tightened and she slowly shook her head.

"Get your things, and I'll get you out of here."

"Are you serious?"

"Extremely! Get your things, *now!*"

When she turned around and hurried off, he called Georgia to let her know they were coming. Debbie rushed to the door with a stuffed duffel bag and stopped in her tracks. She dropped the bag, stared agape over Rudy's shoulder, and cringed.

Rudy turned around just as Kurt punched him. He fell to the ground just missing the steps to the trailer. Kurt picked him up by his shirtfront and hit him again. Rudy fumbled for his pocket and Kurt kicked him in the side with the toe of his right cowboy boot, knocking the wind out of him. With a vicious sneer, Kurt reached down to pick him up again. Rudy pulled out the Taser and gave him a jolt on his leg. Kurt shuddered for a couple of seconds. The Taser slipped, and Kurt fell to the ground. Rudy shakily got up on one elbow and gave him another jolt, this time longer.

"Grab your stuff, and let's get outta here! I don't think you want to be here when he gets up."

Frozen in horror, Debbie gaped for a moment before she obeyed.

Rudy got to his feet, and they hurried around the corner to his car.

He peeled rubber and took an indirect route that he'd never seen Kurt use. After they were out of sight, he held his side. "I think he broke a rib." He groaned and turned to look at her. "Are you okay?"

She nodded, looked down, and started to sob.

"At least I got you out of there in time. I'm pretty sure he would've done something to you. He's pretty mad."

During the ride, he explained everything to her and that "Tom Rance" was only an alias. They arrived home ten minutes later.

Georgia let them in and gave Debbie a hug. "You'll be safe here. And this is Sharon. Please sit down."

Rudy excused himself and went into the dining room to make a phone call.

Debbie sat on the couch and started to cry. "Why are you doing this?"

Sharon smiled weakly. "Kurt doesn't know about Rudy and Georgia. He's never met them or even seen a picture of them. That's why he brought you here — to keep you safe." Then she gave her a short description of what they knew.

Rudy walked back in to the room. "I've got to go. They're meeting pretty soon."

Rudy entered the arena ten minutes before the scheduled meeting. He made sure his earpiece was turned on as he walked over to wait near a food concession stand. Even with the crowd, he'd be able to see everything. Then he waited. *Ah, there you are, Kurt. Yup, looks like you're pretty mad now that Debbie's gone. I wonder if you know about your boxes yet.* He watched Kurt head over to the far pillar where he would meet Charlotte.

Then he saw Charlotte come in, and he wondered why she stuffed her locket inside her dress. *Don't look at me. Good, girl.* He adjusted his earpiece as he watched her approach Kurt from the corner of his eye.

"What's this? No money?" He scowled.

"How come you're demanding money? You know you left me broke."

"I heard you inherited money. But I had no idea how much until I looked into it. Be grateful I'm not asking for more. So try to get on with your life and maybe I'll stay out of it."

"But, how'd you even find out I *got* an inheritance?"

"I've been getting updates on you for a very long time, Chickie Baby."

She took a cleansing breath. "I know what you've been doing."

He glared at her. "What're you talking about?"

"You've been lying to everyone, especially Cal. There's nothing wrong with your heart."

Kurt turned red. "How would you know anything, you stupid tramp?"

Rudy clenched his fist. *Come on, Charlotte, you can do this.*

"I have proof. Look." Her hand shook as she handed him three good shots of him exercising in the gym.

His nose flared. "You had me followed?!" He growled.

"You lied to us."

He sneered and leaned in close to her face. She cringed as he reached out and stroked her hair with his right hand. He lowered his voice in a patronizing tone. "I see you've grown it out. But I liked it better when I cut it short!" At that, he grabbed a fistful of hair behind her left ear and pulled her face up to his.

Her eyes and mouth were wide open in terror.

He whispered slowly and firmly, emphasizing the last word of each sentence. "If I were you, I wouldn't be a chicken. 'Cause you *know* what happens to chickens." His eyes narrowed.

Unable to breathe, she closed her eyes and swallowed hard.

Don't cave now, Charlotte.

He jerked on the fistful of hair. "Look at me! You *will* give me that money! Or we'll see who squawks!" He pressed his forefinger into her belly and gave her a horrid grin.

Charlotte took a quick breath. "Okay, okay! But only if you promise to leave and never come back."

"Why would I want to stay? You and your pathetic little brats make me sick."

"But they're your kids, too."

"You think I care about them? They're just a means to an end — to get me that money."

"But Cal really cares about you."

"What's your point? This *father-son thing* is getting old, and I'm fed up with acting like I care." He held her face close as he jabbed her chest with his forefinger. "Don't tell him a thing — got it? We don't want to mess up our nice little arrangement, now, do we? You'll get that money to me tomorrow." He put on a sinister sneer. "Or there'll be more than one chicken getting plucked."

"I can't get it tomorrow. The money's in an annuity, and I have to make a request for it. It'll take several days. I can call you when I get it." Her voice quivered.

He leaned forward with a deliberate smirk. "I know you will. But next time, we won't be meeting here. Here's where we'll meet." He let her go and wrote an address on the back of one of the pictures. "And it won't be when you call me; it'll be Thursday night, at midnight. Sharp!" He chuckled. "Don't be late for dinner. *Chicken* dinner that is!" He gave her an evil laugh and stormed off.

Trembling, Charlotte looked for a bench. She shuddered as she sat down and then doubled over in heavy sobs.

When Kurt was out of sight, Rudy rushed over to her. He put his arm around her and she jumped with a sharp gasp.

"Oh, Rudy! It's you." She collapsed on his shoulder.

An armed security guard came over and glared at Rudy. "Are you okay, Ma'am?"

"Yeah, she'll be okay," Rudy said.

"I'm asking her."

Rudy patted her shoulder. "Charlotte? Charlotte, the guard wants to know if you're okay."

She nodded quickly.

The guard stepped away but he watched them from across the entry.

When she was able to stand, Rudy helped her out to the parking lot. "Do you want me to take you home? We can pick up your car later."

She nodded. Her eyebrows pinched together as her lips quivered. "Thanks for being here. I couldn't have done this without you."

"I know it was hard, but you did exactly right. And I got everything." He called Hal to tell him they were on their way.

They got into his car. "Where's this place he wants to meet?"

She pulled the photo out of her purse and handed it to him.

Rudy pinched his lips together. "Okay, I'll have to make some preparations."

"What do you mean?"

"Since this is in the industrial district, it's probably a warehouse. Let's just say you don't want to be there alone with him."

She put her face in her hands and let out a quivering moan.

Rudy pulled out of the parking garage. "There's something you need to tell me. What's all that stuff about the chickens?"

Her shoulders drooped and she slowly looked at him. He pulled over to the side of the road. "Charlotte. What is it?"

She crossed her arms tight against her abdomen and closed her eyes, tightening her brow. She bowed her head forward and her voice was weak. "We'd only been married for a short while. We were living in a small trailer out in the woods — no neighbors for miles. I guess he wanted me to feel like there was nowhere to turn for help — or anyone to hear. Something I did made him angry one day. I don't even remember what it was. He was always getting angry, and then he'd blame me for it. But that day was worse than any other. He said I was a chicken because I was so cowardly."

She put her face in her hands again. "He said he was going to butcher a chicken for dinner." She started to shiver. "He was cruel. First he plucked it alive, then he tortured it — for a *really long* time. He made me watch and listen to those awful squawks. Whenever I tried to leave, he'd say, 'If you walk out, you're next!' I was so sick to my stomach, I couldn't eat for two days. Then after that, whenever he was really angry, he'd call me a chicken. I *just knew* it could happen at any time." She started to sob again.

"Charlotte, we're all here for you. He isn't going to touch you or your family. I promise you."

"I wish ... I could ... believe you," she stuttered between sobs.

He took a slow breath to control himself. "Oh, you can believe it!" He pulled out into traffic again.

"Please don't tell anyone," she begged after a couple miles down the road.

He pulled over again. "Charlotte. You have to tell your family. None of this is your fault. They love you, and they'll help you."

She gritted her teeth with an awful grimace, and then she doubled over with a deep groan. "I just can't."

He put his hand on her shoulder. "If you want, I can tell Hal."

With tears streaming down her cheeks, she nodded.

Rudy told Hal everything and waited for him to help Charlotte calm down before he left.

When Rudy got home and entered the living room, he stopped in his tracks. "Whoa! I didn't even recognize you."

Georgia smiled. "Doesn't she look nice? Sharon and Callie brought some clothes for her. Sharon cut her hair and Callie dyed it."

"Debbie, you look like a new woman." Rudy was pleased to see the first faint smile he'd seen on her face.

"I want to thank you all. I ... I don't know what I would've done if you hadn't helped me." Tears welled up in her eyes.

Georgia gave her a hug. "You're going to be okay, honey. Come on. We can talk during dinner."

As they ate, she told them about how she had been charmed by Kurt's good looks and interest in her. He had pursued her, and she was flattered that he wanted her to live with him so quickly. "My dad was never home, so I really just wanted someone to love me. My poor mom, she's probably worried sick about me. And I treated her so badly." She looked down at her plate. "I don't know what I'm going to do."

Georgia put her hand on Debbie's shoulder. "Were you living at home when you met Kurt?"

She shook her head. "No. I was a runaway. Tom, uh, Kurt doesn't even know about them. At first, I just wanted to forget about them; I was still angry at them. Then when I saw how he really was, well, I was afraid to tell him I even *had* parents. I didn't want him to do anything to them."

"He was that bad, huh?"

Debbie's face drooped as she nodded.

Rudy clenched his jaw.

"Can I ask you why your hair was so choppy?" Georgia asked gently.

She bowed her head. "Sometimes, when he accused me of something, he'd chop off a handful of hair. At first, I'd try to fix it. But he did it so many times, I gave up trying." She pointed behind her left ear. "He cut off some more right here just before Rudy came to rescue me."

Georgia got up and brought her the phone. "You call your parents right now."

"I don't think they'd want to hear from me. I was pretty rebellious."

"Believe me, they'll be thrilled to hear from you."

"You think so?" She paused. "But it's long distance. I can't afford to pay you."

"Honey, with Rudy's work, we've got unlimited long distance."

Debbie started to cry again. "I don't know what to say. Saying thank you isn't nearly enough." The conversation with her parents took about ten minutes. "Mom and Dad are going to wire some money for a train ticket." She laughed hysterically. "I'm going home!"

"Oh, honey, I'm so happy for you! And you can stay here until it comes." Georgia patted her hand.

Debbie put her forearm on the table, laid her forehead down on it, and sobbed with relief.

Georgia got up and pulled Rudy aside. "Callie said to call her." She whispered. "She was acting kind of weird when she was here, so I'd say it's important."

"Okay. I'll be in my office."

"Hi Callie, what's up? Did you forget something?"

"No. I was going to wait until you got home to tell you. But then I realized it might creep someone out if they overheard this."

"What is it?" He started to pace.

"Well, I decided to start from when the governor was born. I figured I could make better sense of it that way. The records show that he grew up on a farm and had a pretty average childhood. But then I found some pretty weird stuff on him. The more I researched, the more it made me uneasy."

"Go ahead."

"Well, when he was eleven, he was bitten by a dog, and the parents sued the owners. I saw the photo in the paper, and his left hand had a pretty nasty wound. It should have left a big scar, so I decided to look at some current photos of him — Rudy, I didn't see any evidence of a scar."

"Any record of plastic surgery?"

"That's what I thought at first. There's no record of it. But then I looked at all those photos a little closer and I realized something else. You know how people change as they grow up?"

"Yeah."

"Well, I'd heard that the ears don't change shape, they just get bigger. I looked it up, it's true."

"And?" Rudy nodded and raised an eyebrow.

"Rudy, his earlobes are unattached in the photo of him when he was a kid. But in the photos of him after he started campaigning, his earlobes are attached."

"Good work, Callie."

"Oh, that's not all."

Rudy sat on the desk, picked up a pencil and twirled it between his index finger and thumb.

"Well, you know when someone goes to office — the reporters are all over their past trying to find some dirt."

"Yeah. Go on."

"I figured they'd sensationalize a lot of stuff, so I wasn't prepared to find anything substantial or to believe much. I felt kind of sorry for him when I read that his parents died when a burglar entered their home and shot them. Then it got creepy."

"What do you mean?"

"Then I found an obscure article on microfiche about him going missing for a couple of days when he was twenty. Then he reappeared with some form of amnesia. I thought that might be worth looking at a little more, but I couldn't find any other mentions of the incident in any other articles. I thought that was strange so I decided to check on other articles that particular reporter might have written. Rudy, he didn't write *any* more articles after that one. In fact, he died in a hit-and-run two days after it was published."

Rudy let out a low whisper.

"I got goose bumps when I read that. So I looked more closely at all reports before and after he was missing. Before that, he was pretty much off the radar. Then after he 'recovered' from his amnesia, he got interested in politics. There's a lot of coverage from then on."

"Did any of the news reports explain his change in behavior?"

"Just the usual. 'I realized how precious life is.' 'I knew I had to make things better for everyone.' But I don't believe it. It was a total turnaround in personality."

"I think you've just uncovered something big."

"That's what I thought. That's why I called you. What do I do now?"

Rudy sat up straight. "Did you copy all those photos and articles?"

"On the flash drive, just like you told me to."

"Good. I'll pick it up tomorrow."

"You don't have to. I put it into the vase in the living room when I was there."

"Ha, ha!" He slapped the top of his desk. "Excellent! I knew I made the right choice picking you to do this." He quickly frowned. "Don't tell *anyone* what you found. Understand?"

"Are you kidding? When I read what happened to that reporter, I knew it could happen to me. Rudy?"

"Yeah?"

"Is Roy involved in this?"

"No. Right now, I'm concerned about you. Just go on with your usual activities and pretend that the research was for school."

"Okay. But this …."

"I'll take it from here. Okay? I don't want you involved any more than you are."

"You'll let me know how it turns out?"

"I think everyone in the state will know when that happens."

"Wow! Okay. I'll play it cool for now."

"I'm counting on you to do just that. By the way, thanks for doing this. You have a good nose."

"Is Georgia feeling better now?"

"Sure. Why? Are you anxious to learn self-defense?"

"That's for sure. Especially now. I'm feeling pretty uneasy." She paused. "And I'm concerned about her, too." She paused again. "That didn't sound very sincere did it?"

"Hey, I get it. I'll tell her to call you."

After he hung up, he peeked into the kitchen to make sure Georgia or Debbie wouldn't see him. He retrieved the flash drive, put it into his pocket, and went back to his office. He plugged it into the computer and examined all the information Callie left for him. "So, Governor, who are you?" He sat back in his chair to think. "I wonder."

He called Callie again. "Say, I've got another person for you to check out. Just like the last one, be thorough, including pictures." He gave her the name, date and city of birth, and all the rest of the information he had already gleaned.

He put everything in his safe and went back to the kitchen smiling.

Chapter 23

Saturday was finally here — moving day.

Jack helped Sharon put the cooler in the back of the van and drove his truck to meet John. Sharon headed for Charlotte's to pick her up before driving over to get Bonnie and a load of stuff.

John finished helping them load the van with clothes. "Are you sure you don't want directions?"

Bonnie put her hands on her hips. "John, I know how to get there. We've been there four times." She paused briefly. "Or was it five? Anyway, I know the way."

John turned to Sharon. "You've got my cell number."

Sharon nodded. "Hey, Charlotte, do you mind sitting in the back seat?"

"That's okay, I'll be fine."

"Bonnie, you sit here so you can tell me where to turn." Sharon pointed to the seat next to her.

"Okay." Bonnie giggled. "I can't believe it's finally happening."

As Sharon pulled away from the curb, Bonnie reached over to turn on the radio. *Every Breath You Take* by The Police started playing.

Charlotte gasped and pushed her locket under her shirt. "Bonnie, change it!"

Bonnie ignored her and turned it up. Charlotte took off her seat belt, lurched forward between the bucket seats, and pushed the tuner button. The news came on.

Bonnie glared at her. "What are you doing?" She reached over to change it back.

Charlotte grabbed her wrist. "No! Don't do that!" she demanded.

Bonnie rolled her eyes. "You're just weird."

Sharon stopped at a red light. The light turned green, and she started up again.

"Oh, yeah, turn left at the next street," Bonnie directed after a few blocks.

Sharon started to turn, and Bonnie waved her arms. "No, no! You're going the wrong way."

"I'm turning left just like you said."

No! Your other left!"

Sharon frowned. "You mean right?"

Bonnie paused for a moment. "Uh — yeah, right."

Sharon snickered. "Okay. I'm already turned, so I'll have to go around the block. When you want me to turn, just point the way."

"Okay. That works."

Sharon turned around, and crossed the street they turned from.

Bonnie pointed. "When we get to that pretty tree, turn left."

Sharon pulled over to the curb and twisted her hair. "Which pretty tree?"

"That one. The one by the light pole."

"Bonnie, all the light poles have trees by them. How about I just drive slowly and when we come to the corner, you point which way to turn. Okay?"

"Okay. Don't you just love all these trees? That's one of the reasons I like this neighborhood."

Sharon pulled out slowly. "Yes, they are nice."

"Turn right here."

Noticing that turning right would put them in someone's hedges, she asked, "Which direction?"

She pointed left.

"Thanks." She controlled the urge to snicker. When Sharon saw the moving van parked a block ahead, she sighed with relief. Then she saw Jack's pickup in the driveway. She started to pull over behind the van.

"Oh, be careful!" Bonnie blurted out. "He's going to back up — see, his back headlights are on!"

Charlotte put her hand over her mouth and chuckled quietly.

Sharon took another deep breath. "Bonnie, why don't you bring in a box, then you can direct everyone where they can put things? Charlotte and I will get everything else."

Bonnie grinned. "That's a good idea. Thanks."

Sharon opened the back of the van so Bonnie could grab the box on top.

When Bonnie left with it, Sharon quietly turned to Charlotte. "What was that all about?"

Charlotte frowned. "Huh?"

"The radio?"

Charlotte's face dropped. "Uh, I don't like that song."

"That reaction was more than just not liking it."

She started to bite a nail. "I can't listen to it."

"What do you mean?"

"Too many memories."

Sharon put her hand on Charlotte's shoulder. "Charlotte, tell me what it is."

Charlotte closed her eyes as she leaned back against the van. "It was Kurt. He played that song — or he sang it." Charlotte's lip quivered as she emphasized the next three words. "*Over and over.* I suppose it's a song about an aching heart. But the way he sang it — he made it sound like every move I made, every breath I took, he was watching me. Like he was looking for some misstep so he could punish me. Every day, he sang it until it echoed in my head, every move, every word, every breath." She started to shiver. "I started to believe that all his accusations were because of something I'd done or said. I was a wreck by the time Josh ran away." Charlotte chewed on her nails more intently. "I don't know what would have happened to me if it had gone on any longer." She closed her eyes again to take a deep breath. "He even bought a tape of it and he played it over and over. And the looks he gave me as he sang it — I died a thousand deaths." She cringed. "I *have* to turn it off when it comes on. I can't handle it."

"Oh, Charlotte. I'm so sorry you had to go through that." Sharon moaned as she hugged her.

Charlotte started to sob, and she laid her head on Sharon's shoulder.

Just then, Hal drove up. He got out and hurried over. "Charlotte, are you okay?"

She looked at Sharon with horrified eyes.

"Trust me," Sharon whispered. Then she turned to Hal. "Charlotte just told me something."

Charlotte shook her head violently. "No, don't tell him."

"Don't tell me what?"

Sharon squeezed her hand. "Charlotte, he has to know. He loves you and wants to help. Let him."

As Sharon explained Charlotte's story, Hal's eyes widened with horror. He took her in his arms and held her tight until her trembling lessened. "Why didn't you say something?"

"I thought you'd be ashamed of me."

He held her tighter. "I could never be ashamed of you. I thought you knew that." He whispered in her ear as he gently cradled her head.

She cried softly on his shoulder.

Sharon walked to the back of the van to give them some privacy. She picked up some clothes to bring into the house. When she walked in with an armload, John was barking orders to let everyone know where to deposit their loads.

"John," Sharon said, "after the van is emptied, I'm going to have to get someone to help to bring in the cooler. I've made lunch for everyone and it's too heavy for me."

John stopped in his tracks. "Really? You didn't have to do that?" Then he relaxed a bit. "Thanks, you're a peach."

She smiled. "Where's the bedroom?"

"Oh, right. Up the stairs and first door on the left."

When Sharon started for the stairs, Arlene stepped in front of her, stopping her short.

"I should've known you'd be buttering up everybody. You're going to be sorry." Arlene glared at her.

Sharon took in a deep breath and let it out slowly. "Honestly, Arlene."

"I don't want to hear your excuses." She stormed off to another room.

Sharon watched her leave and started again for the stairs, slowly.

After a busy two hours, everyone stopped for lunch. Sharon had spread the food on the kitchen counters, displaying sandwiches, a vegetable tray, a fruit tray, brownies and cold drinks. Everyone walked through buffet style.

After the men went through, Bonnie picked up a plate and stopped at the vegetable tray with a puzzled look. "Sharon? Where did you find white broccoli?"

Sharon cocked her head. "Huh?"

Arlene huffed.

"You've got green and white broccoli. I didn't know it came in white."

Sharon put her hand over her mouth to stifle a laugh. "Uh, Bonnie, that's cauliflower."

Bonnie looked again. "Oh." Then her eyes widened. "Oh! Right." Then she giggled and loaded her plate.

"I'm going to the little girls' room. I'll be right back." Sharon snickered all the way to the bathroom.

Arlene rolled her eyes. "Bonnie, you take the cake."

"Cake? Where?"

"Oh, brother," she groaned.

From the dining room, John shook his head as he watched.

Jack sat down next to him. "Don't take it so seriously. Just laugh, everyone else does — even Bonnie. You'll have good memories instead of irritation."

"I guess so."

Just then, Mel walked up. "Say, John. I've got an idea for your man cave. You could get some room darkening shades for the windows. I know where we can pick up some motorized ones, with a remote even. That would really make it look like a theater."

"Hey, I like that. Good idea." John gave him a high five.

Sharon sat down next to Bonnie in the corner of the living room. "Say, Bonnie, I've been thinking. After you get settled in, why don't you take a break and go to a bed and breakfast for the weekend. It'll be relaxing. It might even spark some romance."

Bonnie thought for a moment. "That sounds great. John does seem a little stressed lately." Then she smiled. "We could be teenagers again."

Then she giggled. "You won't believe the crazy things we did when we were in school."

"Really? Tell me about some of them."

Bonnie giggled again. "We were just friends at first. He lived just a couple of blocks from me. One time, when we were freshmen, we had a substitute in English class. John told everyone to answer to someone else's name." She snickered. "It was so funny because once in a while someone would forget who they were supposed to be. When the sub would call out the name she had written down for that student, someone else would answer. I laughed so hard; I guess I gave it away. John laughed, too."

Sharon smiled at the vision in her head.

"Then at the junior prom, we each went with someone else. Darrel and I were dancing the robot." She giggled. "Can you believe that? I accidentally stepped on another girl's toe with my heel." Bonnie cringed. "I think it hurt pretty bad, 'cause she yelled at me. I tried to apologize, but her date got in my face. He got so angry that he wouldn't listen. Just then, John came up and talked with them. I was so relieved 'cause he rescued me."

"I thought Darrel was your date."

"He was."

"What happened to him?"

"He said he was going to go get us some punch." She paused. "He must have been really thirsty, 'cause he didn't come back."

Sharon gasped. "Ever?"

"Nope. I was stranded, so John gave me a ride home."

"Wow, that was rude."

"Oh, no. John was a gentleman."

Sharon blinked twice. "Uh, I meant your date was rude."

"Oh. Oh, yeah, for sure. But it was after that, that John and I started …. Well, you know, we started to date. I was the damsel in distress, and he was my knight in shining armor." She raised her shoulders and giggled again.

Sharon laughed. "Well, I'm glad your date ditched you. You got John."

"Yeah." She pondered that for a moment. "Yeah, you're right. It *was* a good thing."

"Did his date get jealous?"

Bonnie paused to think. "I don't know."

"Well, didn't she say something on the ride home?"

"No, she wasn't there." Then she sat up straight and her eyes got big, "Oh no! We left without her." She looked confused for a moment. "Do you think that's why she picked on me after that?"

Sharon bit her lip and nodded. "I'd say it's a pretty good chance." She took a drink of her soda. "Don't you think it would be nice to rekindle that feeling with John?"

Bonnie blushed. Then she raised her shoulders and grinned shyly. "Uh-huh. Ooh, would you look up some bed and breakfasts on the coast?" She leaned over to whisper. "That's where we had our honeymoon."

Sharon laughed. "Oh, you little devil. Of course I will."

Bonnie's face fell. "Devil? Did I say something bad?"

"No, no. I meant it in a good way."

"Oh. Okay." She took a bite of her sandwich. "This is going to be so cool."

Jack walked over to Mel. "Where's Arlene going?"

Mel rolled his eyes. "She decided she 'couldn't take any more.'"

"What do you mean?"

Mel's face dropped. "I convinced her to come. But now she'd decided none of us is good enough. She went home."

"Sorry to hear that. Maybe you can talk some sense into her when you get home."

"Actually, she moved out. I won't be seeing her. And I'm tired of trying to convince her of anything."

"Jack's mouth dropped open. "Aw, Mel. I'm really sorry to hear that. You need anything?"

"No. I'll be okay. I've got my work to keep me busy."

"Anytime you need to talk, I'll be there. Okay?"

"Yeah. And thanks. I'm really glad you and Sharon found us. Even though this divorce is the result, I can see it's for the best. Actually, I probably would've filed sooner or later."

They went back to the dining room to finish eating.

Charlotte's phone rang.

After Charlotte said hello, her eyes widened and she walked to the next room. "Why are you calling me? You're the one that decided on Thursday. … No, I can't hurry it up. That's just how it is. … Yes, that's the amount I asked for."

Hal watched for a moment and then came over. He took the phone from her and walked to an empty room.

"Look, Kurt. Harassing Charlotte is *not* going to get that money to you any faster. … And your insults aren't going to move things either. She said she'd call you when we get it. Good-bye." Gritting his teeth, he hung up and paced until he noticed Charlotte in the far corner with her head in her hand. He walked over and held her. "It'll be okay," he whispered.

As Kurt hung up, he snarled and kicked his rear tire. He gritted his teeth as he looked up to watch the police swarming into the bank. *I'll bet she did this. She's gonna pay!*

Inside the bank, Mel Sharpe was directing the investigation. "Roy, since you got the anonymous tip, you can do the fingerprinting."

"I'll get right on it." Roy was careful to follow protocol; he didn't want any chance of Kurt getting off because someone missed a step.

Sharpe spoke with the man in charge of the safe deposit boxes. "I need a description of the man who rented this box."

"It was Mr. Baxter. He's about five feet, eleven inches. He's got black hair, slicked back like a young Elvis Presley, even with sideburns. And hooded, dark brown eyes, olive complexion, and deep dimples. He was wearing dark blue jeans and tennis shoes and a bulky jacket. In fact, he was just here today."

The captain's eyebrows went up. "Really, what time was that?

"I'll have to check the records." He pulled the card out of the box. "Just a couple of hours ago."

"Did he ever say anything?"

"Nope, just asked for the box number and signed in."

"Did you notice anything unusual?"

He shook his head as he thought for a moment. "Oh, wait a minute. … Yeah. But not with him, though. There was this old guy behind him. He kept staring at the card when I pulled it out. Weird thing is, he was gone when I got back from the vault."

"Can you give me a description of him?"

"Sure. He was a couple inches shorter than you. He had horn-rimmed glasses — and the lenses were pretty thick. But it was his black eyes that stood out, especially through those thick lenses. And he had short gray hair — in a butch cut. And even with the pea coat, I could tell he had a beer belly. And he had on faded blue jeans and sneakers."

"You ever see him before?"

The clerk shook his head. "No, never."

Chapter 24

Georgia drove Debbie to the Western Union office to pick up the MoneyGram from her parents.

When she parked in the lot, Debbie started to cry. "You've been so nice to me. I don't know how to repay you." She took a tissue out of her pocket and blew her nose. Then she paused and frowned, "I think Tom — uh — Kurt might have done something awful if Rudy hadn't gotten me out of there." She looked over to Georgia. "You two probably saved my life." Her voice cracked. "How do I thank you?"

Georgia reached over to hold her hand. "Honey, just knowing you're safe is thanks enough."

Debbie sobbed joyfully. "Thank you. Thank you so much." She regained some composure. "If you'll give me your email, I'll keep in touch."

Georgia grinned. "I'd be delighted."

After exchanging information, they went into the office.

When Debbie told the clerk why she was there, he eyed her. "Identification please."

"Uh, oh, no." She stammered and turned to Georgia. "What do I do now? I don't have anything."

Georgia thought for a moment. "Debbie, you can stay with us until we resolve this. Let me think." After moment, she held up her index finger. "We have a few choices here. We can buy your ticket, and then you can pay us back when you get home. Or we can have your parents send a check in the mail, and then we can buy your ticket." Then she frowned. "But with the way Kurt treated you, your parents might not trust us." She looked up with cheerful confidence. "We'll just pay your way."

Debbie's jaw dropped. "Are you serious?"

"Of course, dear. And I'm sure Rudy will agree." She turned to the clerk. "I guess you can return that MoneyGram." She took Debbie's arm and led her back to the car. "Come on, let's go home first."

When Rudy came home, Debbie was helping Georgia put dinner on the table.

Georgia called out from the kitchen. "Oh, hi, honey. We're keeping Debbie for a while. She doesn't have any identification, so she can't collect the MoneyGram. We're buying her ticket for her. Do you mind if she stays with us for a while?"

"No problem." He took off his coat. "Oh, by the way, it's probably a good thing you're here instead of at the trailer."

Georgia turned around from the stove, put her hands on her hips and looked at him with her head cocked. "And why do you say that?"

He grinned. "Well, right about now, the Feds are swarming all over one of his safe deposit boxes and the police are confiscating a second."

Debbie's eyes popped. "Safe deposit boxes? He had two of them? Why the Feds and the police? What could he have in there?"

"Let's sit down to dinner, and I'll tell you."

He told them how Kurt had been pulling money out of the two safe deposit boxes as needed.

Debbie stopped eating. "I can't believe it. He made me think we had nothing." Then she gasped. "Is it counterfeit?"

Rudy put on his business face. "I can't tell you any details yet, but let's just say you're close."

Horrified, Debbie sat back in her chair. She grimaced. "Does that mean I could've been arrested?"

"Don't know, but probably not. But that's not why I got you out of there. I didn't want him to come back and take it out on you."

She let out a sickly moan.

Sharon had just put out the glasses when everyone started to arrive.

Callie decided to join them today, since Roy was out of the picture. She let everyone in and helped them with their jackets. When Bonnie handed Callie her jacket, Callie gasped. "Is that a new purse?"

Bonnie looked at it and then said. "Not really, I pulled out an old one."

Callie's eyes widened. "You made that one, too?"

Bonnie looked at her warily. "Don't tell me you like it?"

"Well, yeah!"

"She's been making them for about five years now." Karen interrupted. "Although this is an exception, she hardly ever uses one for more than a few months. She usually just makes more. You should see the stash she has at home. At least she has storage space for them now."

"Tell me, how did you start?" Callie asked enthusiastically.

Charlotte brought her bottle into the dining room along with her food contributions.

Karen smiled as she walked past Bonnie and Callie, who were absorbed in animated conversation. "It's so nice to see someone interested in her hobby," she whispered to Sharon.

Sharon looked up as she arranged the napkins. "You mean making purses is just a hobby?"

"Well, you know Bonnie's interested in everything about fashion. She always wants something new. But she's pretty particular about her purses. She could never find one that suited her. So she started to design her own. At first, they were glitzy and showy, but I'm glad to see her taste has improved."

"She makes *all* her purses?"

Karen and Charlotte nodded in unison.

"The ones she makes now are pretty nice," Charlotte added. "I had to do a lot of convincing for her to give me one, because no one can convince her they're that good. She just hides them away."

Sharon stood up straight. "Wow, I'm impressed."

Callie pulled Bonnie aside. "I have a confession."

Bonnie looked horrified. "What did you do?"

"When the mugger hit me, he stole the purse you gave me. I feel just awful. I'm sorry."

Bonnie hugged her. "Oh, for Pete's sake, you don't have to apologize. It wasn't your fault. Tell you what, if it's okay with you, I'll give you a couple more."

Callie's eyes got big. "I don't know what to say. That's so generous of you."

"Oh, it's nothing. I'm glad to do it."

After the table was set, everyone filled their plates and glasses and sat in the living room to talk.

The next morning, Callie rang the doorbell twice. "Hi, I'm really excited to start," she said when Georgia opened the door.

"You're right on time. But I should've expected that. Come on in." She led her to the den.

Callie looked around, noticing a few things that hadn't been there before. A punching bag with the outline of a man painted on it had been placed in the corner. An opened package sat on the coffee table, and a large mirror stood next to the closet door. "I was pretty glad you called last night. I was almost ready to call you."

"Well, the timing was right, since Debbie just left. Thanks again for the clothes and help you gave her." She sat down on the couch and patted the cushion next to her.

Callie took the invitation and sat down.

"I just want you to know that I understand what you're going through — the vulnerability, fear, and feeling like a victim."

Callie blushed and looked down. "Yeah. I haven't been able to really talk with anyone yet, not even Mom," she said quietly.

Georgia took her hand. "Like I said, I've been there. Learning how to defend yourself will help you to put all that behind you. You won't forget, but you'll be able to move on and heal. I took several kinds of classes, took those ideas and adapted them to my abilities. Then, when Derik died, I felt vulnerable again. It might seem to take a long time to heal, but it will happen." She smiled. "Ready to start?"

Callie nodded.

I took the liberty of getting you some supplies." She reached for the package and pulled out two items. "Now you take this Taser and Mace, and don't be afraid to use them if you feel threatened. It's all about attitude. If you look like you'll kick someone's behind, you're less likely to be confronted at all. Trust me, just carrying that Taser and Mace will make you feel empowered."

Callie stared at them.

"Don't worry, I'll show you how to use them safely — safe for you, that is."

Georgia started the lesson with the new equipment: how to hold them, aim, and avoid personal injury. "By the way, you're going to have to get a different purse."

Callie gasped. "Why!?"

"You have to have separate, easily accessed compartments for these. Can you imagine how vulnerable you'd be searching through all that stuff for one of them?"

Callie moaned. "But I love my purse."

Georgia put her hands on her hips. "What's more important, fashion or your safety?"

She sighed. "All right." Her lips slowly turned upward. "Maybe I can ask Bonnie to design one."

"There you go. Flexibility is going to serve you well. I'd also suggest it have a long shoulder strap to go around your neck, too. Less likely to get your purse snatched." Georgia put the equipment on the table and turned around. "Now try to grab me from behind."

"What do you mean?"

"Just what I said. Try to grab me from behind."

She made a feeble effort, but Georgia jabbed her with an elbow to the sternum. Georgia spun around, wrapped her arm around Callie's upper arm, put her leg behind Callie's, and dropped her to the floor.

Surprised, Callie looked up at her rubbing her chest. "What was that?"

"Now, *you're* going to learn how to do that." She held out her hand so Callie could get up and she showed her in slow motion so Callie could see exactly how to do it. Soon Callie was able to replicate the moves.

"Wow! This is pretty cool," Callie said proudly.

"There. Now all you have to do is do it a little faster each time. But I'm going to let you practice on someone else. I'm getting a little old to land on the floor like that." She giggled.

Callie laughed. "Okay, what's next?"

"Generally, it will be a man that is most likely to attack. Now, there are three vulnerable spots, I'm sure you know one of them."

Callie turned red. "The groin?"

"Yup. The other two are the Adam's apple and the top of the arch on the foot. But how you hit is just as important as where you hit." She demonstrated slowly and without force. "You might want to get a punching bag like this one and paint the outline of a man on it like I did. Practice hitting it every day. Oh, and one more thing, start running and build up to five miles a day. You'll appreciate having good wind when you need it."

After they spent the next two hours practicing moves and precautions, Georgia smiled. "You already have some of the moves down pretty good. But you have to practice to increase the power and precision required. And you seem timid. Gotta toughen you up."

Callie looked down at the floor. "I've never fought before."

"That's why you need to practice at home. Your actions and responses have to be so natural that they will be a reaction. You won't even have to think about it. I think that's how the military trains, too. And when you get the punching bag, visualize it as your attacker. You'll be surprised at how quickly you'll give it full power. Visualization will develop the desire to overpower anyone."

"Okay." She squinted at Georgia. "Who did *you* visualize?"

Georgia's pupils dilated and she blanched. "It doesn't matter. I think we're done for today."

She watched Georgia pretend like nothing happened. After a few moments, Callie took a deep breath and let it out. "It's a lot to take in. But don't worry, I will."

"How about a quick sandwich?"

"You don't have to feed me."

Georgia put her hands on her hips. "Questioning the sensei, huh? Come on, you're hungry aren't you? Besides, I know for a fact that you haven't been eating properly since the breakup. You have to be well fed to stay strong. Okay? Besides, they're in the refrigerator just waiting for us."

They sat down at the dinette table.

Georgia looked her in the eye. "I know about it."

"About what?"

"About you helping Rudy."

Callie froze.

"He didn't tell me, but I know."

"How?"

"Like your mother, I can read people. You can tell a lot by observing eyes and body language. By the way, that's going to be your next lesson.

Since you're going to help Rudy, that'll be vital." She watched Callie fidget. "See. Your reaction tells me that you're uncomfortable right now."

Her eyes got big. "But …."

"It's okay. I'm on your side. But not everyone is. That's why we're going to have lessons twice a week. Okay?"

Callie's uncertain smile gave way to a nervous laugh. "I guess I have a lot to learn, huh."

"That's okay. That's what I'm here for."

It was less than an hour before everyone's shift started. The captain arrived early as usual and brought his coffee to the break room. He thought about his coming retirement and smiled apprehensively. He had often thought about staying on, not because he enjoyed his job, but because he enjoyed the money that came with the "arrangement" with his contact. But now, with the governor arrested, it would be too dangerous to stay. He'd already had several discussions with his wife about the possibility of retiring in the Bahamas or some other exotic place. But she wouldn't have it; too many of her friends were here. He sighed. Last night, he decided that he'd just leave on his own. Too risky to tempt fate. He was thinking about contacting one of their paid informants to get hold of someone to create a new identity, when Todd walked into the room.

"Hey, Captain. What's on your mind?"

Surprised, he looked up from his thoughts. "Huh? Nothin'."

"Come on, I know you. What is it?"

He shrugged. "Just thinking about my retirement."

Todd smiled. "Oh, right. Just two more months, and we're giving you that party. What are your plans?"

"Still not firm. Sheila's not so keen on what I'd like. So I don't know."

Several officers passed in the hallway preparing for the change in shifts.

"Well, Todd, it's about time to get to our desks."

"I'm almost done with the forensics on that last tape; should have it to you by the end of the shift."

"Thanks. I know I can always depend on you."

In the locker room, Novak and Harrison were changing into their uniforms to start their shifts, along with several other officers. Novak reached down to tie his shoes and he winced with the movement.

Watching Novak struggle, Harrison grimaced as he put on his shirt. Harrison was tall and lean with a slight slouch to his shoulders from too much time at the computer. His low forehead and short blonde hair made his head appear too small for his body. Multiple worry lines made him look older than his forty years. "Hey, Novak. You sure you're okay to work today? It's only been a few days since you got clipped, and you look like you're still pretty sore."

"Well, I don't like it, but a desk job is better than doing nothing. Besides, the captain has a couple of assignments for me that he can't trust to anyone else."

"I've got to give you kudos for that. I wouldn't want to be working if I didn't have to."

Just then, eight FBI agents rushed in with their pistols poised. They commanded everyone to lean against the locker doors, spread their feet wide, and place their hands on the lockers. Novak and Harrison were cuffed and read their rights. Novak cringed with every movement. As they were taken away, the other officers looked at each other, mouths agape.

At the same time, four FBI agents rushed into the break room down the hall with pistols aimed at the captain and Todd. "Freeze! FBI! Down on the floor, face down!"

Todd complied quickly but the captain stayed standing, enraged. "This is my precinct, and I demand an explanation!"

Two of the agents forced him to the floor and cuffed him while they read him his rights, easily subduing his futile attempts to resist.

That night, Rudy worked in his office after Georgia went to bed. He grabbed the phone halfway through its ring. "What took you so long?"

"Look, I had to check them out first. I had to sound like I knew what I was talking about when I gave it to the Feds."

"What'd you think of what was on those the flash drives I gave you?"

"That was a bombshell! I still can't believe it. By the way, how'd you find out all of this?"

"Callie did the research."

"Callie?!"

"Yup. I thought, uh, I thought she'd be the perfect bloodhound, and I was right. You give it to the Feds yet?"

"This morning. Right after I sorted through all of it. And thanks for giving me Pierre's box. I'm pretty sure you're right about the West case."

"Wait, there's more to it."

"Seriously?"

"Oh, yeah. Callie's researching someone, a pretty prominent person — can't tell you who yet, but you'll hear about it. It won't be too long afterwards that it hits the newsstands."

Roy whistled.

"I heard about the take-down at the station."

"Yup."

Rudy could hear the smile in his voice.

"Oh, and the Feds are investigating all those court cases with missing evidence. So far it looks like they were connected to all of them somehow. I'm pretty sure they'll be exonerating a lot of wrongly convicted men.

Chapter 25

The only light coming into the warehouse was from the streetlights outside the door two hundred feet away and from the moon shining in a few windows three stories up.

Charlotte watched Kurt enter by walking between two large crates. She stood in the dim light at the center of the large room as he walked toward her.

"Don't come any closer, Kurt."

"Why?"

"Because I don't want you near me."

"Is that the money?"

"Do you promise to leave us alone from now on?"

"I don't know. This is a pretty good deal for me. I just might stick around."

Although she could see only his silhouette, she knew he had a smirk on his face. "Kurt, you promised!"

"Well, you know how it is. Let's just call this the down payment." He started to walk towards her.

"No."

"Oh, yes! Now let's have it." He walked faster. When he was about fifteen feet away, a clanking sound echoed above them.

When Kurt came to, he blinked and was blinded by the industrial, overhead light shining in his face. "What did you do, Charlotte? Where are you?" Still blinking, he tried to get up, but he was constricted and could barely move. Looking around, he realized he was inside a rope net suspended off the floor. He gripped the ropes as he struggled to get up, but the room started to spin.

"The rope's secure. You won't get out," a man's voice said.

Still adjusting to the light, he blinked several times. "Who're you?"

The man with black hair smiled with intense black eyes as he stepped into the light and sat down on a crate ten feet from Kurt.

Kurt tried to reach behind him.

His captor smiled and held up a gun. "Looking for this?"

Kurt shook the net in a rage. "Where's Charlotte?!"

"Oh, she's long gone. And you're not getting out of there unless I say so."

Kurt's mouth turned down into a sneer. "We'll see about that! Hey! You're that old man that was at my trailer!"

"At least you're awake enough to know that."

"If it wasn't for that giant pile of ropes falling on me, you'd be a bloody pulp!" Kurt yelled as he tried to climb to the top of his prison but the dizziness kept him off-balance. He looked up and saw that the top was gathered too tightly for him to escape.

"I injected you with a drug while you were unconscious. It should wear off in a few minutes. Oh, by the way, the State took most of your money for back child support. The FBI was pretty interested in it, too. Turns out there was a lot of cocaine residue on those bills."

Kurt glared at him. "Are you a cop?"

"Nope. Just a good P.I. But you can call me Butch."

Kurt gripped the ropes. "Who hired you — Butch?"

"It doesn't matter. By the way, you never did have heart trouble, did you?"

Kurt took a deliberate breath. "It *was* Charlotte, wasn't it?" He shook the net as if he was rattling a cage. "You already know that. Why're you asking?"

"Oh, I just wanted to hear you say it. You thought you were pretty smart with that scheme, scamming your son and ex-wife. Since you think you're going to escape and do me in, you might as well fill me in."

Kurt stuck his arm through the net, pointed at him, and sneered. "Look, old man, when I get outta here, you won't have to worry about getting any older." He struggled some more. "I'm the smart one. And, yeah, I am getting outta here, and I'll finish the job on you and that little chicken!"

"Ri-i-ight. And that's why *you're* in that *net*."

Kurt lurched at him, making the net swing wildly.

"Oh, by the way. I've got some papers here that you're going to sign."

"The only thing I'm going to do with those papers is light 'em on fire and cram 'em down your throat!"

"Oh, I'm not worried about that." Rudy stroked his chin. "I am, however, worried about you."

"You're asking for it, you cheap P.I."

"Aw, you shouldn't oughta talk like that when your life is on the line."

"You think you're gonna do anything that I'm afraid of? Hah!"

"Oh, no, I'm not going to do anything. She is." He pointed toward the door behind Kurt.

"Charlotte? Hah! That's a good one." He sneered as he turned to look.

A woman came out from behind several stacked crates and into the shadows. The echo of her heels clicking on the concrete matched Kurt's heartbeat.

Kurt strained to see who was coming. "You think some woman is going to help you?" he growled.

A deeply-tanned, athletic Colombian woman with thick black hair gradually appeared. Her buttery voice was betrayed by a serious smirk. "Ah, pequeño ladrón estúpido."

Kurt's eyes instantly switched from rage to panic. He stopped breathing, pinched his eyes tight, and grimaced. He clutched the ropes even tighter and pressed his forehead against his white knuckles.

"Where have you been? I missed you," she purred with a thick, Spanish accent.

As she came closer, Kurt put on a brave face and smiled weakly, but his trembling voice betrayed him. "Maria — I missed you too, mí bonita amazona."

She stopped within inches of him and stood face to face. She stroked his cheek with the back of her hand and smiled ambiguously. With the flick of her other hand, she placed the point of an eight-inch dagger under his chin. "You've been a naughty boy."

Kurt swallowed hard, nearly nicking his throat.

"Don't worry; I won't hurt you. I'm taking you back to the plantation. Papa can't wait to see you."

Kurt turned white.

"Manny, Geraldo, come here and show him to the car," she commanded.

Two muscular men with tattoos came running towards her.

Kurt flinched when she used her knife to cut into the ropes, barely missing his thigh. "Papa has a surprise for you."

He grimaced as the two men wrestled his arms behind his back and put a plastic Zip-Tie on his wrists.

"Butch, you've gotta help me," Kurt pleaded as he looked at Rudy.

Rudy feigned sorrow. "Now what do you think an old man like me can do?"

"They're gonna kill me!"

Maria flashed a sinister smile. "Oh no, I'm not going to *kill* you."

Kurt slumped.

Rudy turned to Maria. "Oh, there's one more thing."

"Anything for getting my ratero back again." She turned to wink at Kurt.

Kurt shuddered.

"Kurt needs to sign these papers."

"Of course." She snapped her fingers. "Manny, bring him here."

Rudy laid the paper on a short crate, held his pen out to Kurt, and smiled. "Well Kurt, I did pretty well — for an old man." He gave him a menacing glare. "Sign the papers, and you get to live a little longer."

Manny cut the Zip-Tie as Geraldo held onto a fistful of Kurt's hair at the back of his head.

Kurt's lips curled down as he took the pen with a shaky hand.

"Make sure it's legible," Rudy ordered.

As soon as Kurt finished signing it, Manny put another Zip-Tie on him, yanking it tight.

Rudy picked up the papers and checked the signature. He nodded, folded them, and put them in his pocket. "Thanks, Kurt. That's probably the only decent thing you've ever done." He shook his head as he watched the men drag him towards the door. "Pathetic cretin." He turned his attention to Maria. "Thank you for coming so quickly and cooperating with me. Oh, and I'm sorry about insulting your husband."

"No offense taken. As usual, Papa was right. I didn't want to believe him." She straightened her shoulders. "Thank you for finding him." She held her head high. "Papa will get the truth from him."

"Sorry about your money. The police have confiscated it."

She looked towards the door and hardened her jaw. "I'll just have to take it out of his pretty hide." She shook his hand. "As I promised, you and your family will have no problems from us."

"And as I promised, if anyone asks, I never saw you."

Maria smiled knowingly and she turned to leave. The echo of her clicking heels faded as she left the warehouse.

Rudy heard Kurt make a single cry for help. Then there was silence. Since he had promised to wait fifteen minutes before leaving, he sat down on a crate and made some phone calls.

"Hey, Roy. You can tell the Feds I can come and meet with them now. I just finished with Kurt."

"Good. I was running out of delays. How about tomorrow?"

"Got a few loose ends to take care of. Make it Tuesday afternoon."

He called Georgia, and then checked his email. He quickly opened the one from Callie and read it twice to make sure. "Yes! I'll bet my hunch was right! And just in time." He called her immediately. "Tell me what you found."

"I think you already knew."

"It was a suspicion. What is it?"

"I checked out that guy, Barry West, like you asked. I was almost done when I found a wedding photo from the '90s. He was listed as one of the ushers. I almost stopped breathing when I examined the photo. It wasn't very clear, but he looked *just* like the governor would as a young guy — and about the same age. At first, I thought, 'What a weird coincidence.' Then there was an article in the paper about him being arrested for murder, but I couldn't find any police records on it. I thought that was strange. But then I saw another picture of him, just a few months later, in the obituaries." She paused. "Rudy — it was on the same date that the governor went missing. Is it too creepy to think he switched places? I mean, why even *do* that?"

"I can't tell you what I think right now. But you did good. Couldn't have done better. Put it all on a flash drive, and I'll meet you at our coffee shop in half an hour to get it."

Callie was sitting at a corner table when Rudy walked in. He looked around. There were only two other customers sitting at a window table across the room. He got a plain black coffee at the counter before he tapped her on the shoulder and made her jump. "Sorry. I should've let you know I was here before doing that." He sat down and leaned forward. "I've got a tip for you — never put your back to the room."

"Right. I didn't think about that." She flushed.

"It's okay. You'll learn."

"Here." She handed him the flash drive.

He had trouble reading her eyes when she looked at him. He detected a hint of anxiety, tension, and hesitation. "Are you okay with doing this?"

She blinked a few times. "Uh, yes and no."

"You want to explain that?"

"Well, I can't stop thinking about that reporter, you know, the one that was run down. Are you really sure that won't happen to me?" Her eyes were intense. "Because if I'm in some kind of danger like that, I'd really rather do this research somewhere safer rather than in a public library where anyone can enter, kill me, then shove me behind the stacks in the basement where I won't be found for days."

"I can't guarantee that you're completely safe. But then that's generally true with anyone at any given time. I understand your apprehension about being in a dark, scary, library basement, though. Tell you what, if you're sure you want to stick with this, I can set you up on a secure server in my office at home. That way, either Georgia or I will be within hollering range at all times. *But* you don't *have* to do this, you know. I can always get someone else, and I wouldn't think any less of you."

Her eyes got big. "Rudy, everything I just said was the 'no' part. The 'yes' part is that it's totally exciting. I can't put my finger on it. I feel like we're getting the scoop on the news, finding out peoples' dirty little secrets." She leaned forward and whispered again. "It's kind of addicting. I don't know how to explain it."

He wore a knowing smile. "What are you telling me? That you want to keep going or that you want to stop?"

"I want to keep going! You opened a whole new world for me." She frowned and paused. "Where'd you get those names you had me look up? Surely you already knew what was going on. Why'd you need me?"

"I knew something was off, but like I said, I didn't have the time to dig. I had to take care of Kurt."

"He's taken care of?"

"Yup."

"Woohoo!" She looked around to see how many people heard her. Only the barista had looked up. She cringed a little. "Tell me how you did it," she whispered.

After Rudy explained what happened in the warehouse, she laughed. "Serves him right!" She stared at him for a moment. "This feeling of serving justice, is that what keeps you going?"

He looked at her with renewed respect. "You're hooked, aren't you?"

"What do you mean?"

"I can see it. I had that same determination to nail the bad guy and help the good guys. That's what keeps me going." He smiled. "And I see it growing in you, too."

She wrapped her hands around her cup and stared at the rising steam for a moment. "Yeah, I guess that's it. I almost feel like a vigilante."

"I couldn't be more proud of you." He leaned forward. "Ready for another assignment?"

"You bet!"

He pulled two spreadsheets out of his pocket. "This one is a list of dates and dollar amounts. Look up the political contributions to the governor's campaign, clear back to when he ran the first time, and see if any of these amounts are close to the dates listed. When you finish that, check out this other list of court cases, comparing them by date and case number. I want you to look them up and see if there are any trends, similarities, coincidences — *anything* unusual. You'll have to read everything in each file. I'll show you how to look them up. Put your findings on this flash drive as you go. When you're done, just hand it over."

She looked at the list. "Wow. This is going to take a while."

"I know. That's why I'm giving it to you. I just don't have the time. Oh, one other thing. I want you to go to this address and ask for Freddy. Tell him you're interested in this tattoo, that you'd seen it and want to know if he can duplicate it." He pulled up the photo on his phone. "He's seen this photo, so I drew it by hand. That way he won't realize it's from me."

"You want me to get a tattoo? Of that?"

"No, no. I just want you to get him to tell you what he knows about it. When he's ready to actually do it, you'll chicken out."

"What do you want to know about it?"

"Find out who gets them, how many he's done, what do they mean, anything. Of course, you'll ask in such a way that you really don't know anything about it, but you want to be careful that it isn't a gang thing."

"Are you going to tell me what you already know? I don't want to stumble onto something or say something in a way that I'll blow my cover."

"You're right." He took a breath. "I've seen it on three people so far. I believe they're all connected to some crime syndicate." He stared at her for a moment as her eyes widened. "Are you sure you still want to do this?"

"It would've been nice for you to tell me that from the beginning instead of me having to ask about it."

"You're right. I should've been up front with you. I'm sorry. I'm not used to working with a partner. I'll work on it."

"Yeah, 'cause what if he'd said something that freaked me out so much that I blew my cover?"

"You're right." He looked over his shoulder in dismay. "Maybe we should forget this."

She crossed her arms. "Rudy. Will you look at me when I'm talking?"

He slowly turned to look at her. "Yes."

"As long as I know what to expect, or at least what is involved, I can make a more informed decision about whether I want to get involved. You need to fill me in on all the details for any assignment. Even your suspicions. Okay?"

"Absolutely. I respect that. And I respect your honesty, gumption, and your ability to stand up for yourself. You're going to make a fine P.I."

"Are you buttering me up?"

Surprised, his mouth dropped open. "Uh, no. I meant it."

She chuckled at his reaction and pulled out a tablet to take notes. "Okay, I'm ready. Spill it."

He grinned. He told her about Pierre's box, the flash drive, the connection between the crooked cops and the crime syndicate, and that he was going to work with the FBI.

When he was done, she leaned back. "Wow. So Pierre was part of that all along?"

Rudy nodded.

"How long have you known?"

"I figured it out when Ralph was in trouble for gambling last year."

"Those guys are connected, too?"

"Well, they were, until your dad and uncle helped put them away." He hesitated. "And there's something else you should know."

She wilted. "Yeah?"

"Roy's been …."

She set her jaw and thrust her hand out to stop him. "Stop! I really don't want to hear about him. Please, just stop."

He was firm. "You have to know this."

She crossed her arms and glared at him.

He lowered his voice. "Roy's been putting his life on the line. He's working with the FBI and was crucial in getting the goods on the dirty cops that were just arrested."

Her crossed arms loosened slightly.

"We're working together to figure out who the syndicate boss is. That's why I've been so busy and needed your help."

She looked off to the side, revealing all her anxiety and worry. "Is he safe?"

"We don't know." He paused. "I know you still care for him. I had to let you know that he's not a bad guy." He explained how Roy got suckered into helping the syndicate. "It wasn't about the money, at least, not for himself."

A tear slowly ran down her cheek, and she put her hand to her face to wipe it away.

He took a breath. "If we don't get the syndicate, he'll probably have to go into the Witness Protection program." He paused again. "I told him about you helping me."

She glared at him.

"He was even more determined to help when he heard." He paused. "He told me to take care of you, not to let you get hurt." He waited for a response, but when there wasn't one, he added, "Do you still want to help?"

Startled, she looked up at him. "Huh?"

"Now that you know what's involved, do you still want to help?"

"Oh, right," she mumbled. "Can I think about it?"

"Sure. But if you don't, I'll have to find another way to get to Freddy. We do have a time crunch."

"Okay." She frowned. "How will you get Freddy to talk if I decide not to?"

"I can figure that out later. But don't base your decision on that. Whatever you decide, I'll understand. Don't feel pressured."

"That's easy for you to say. I'll let you know tomorrow."

Chapter 26

The next evening, Charlotte was anxious as they got in the car. "I don't know, Hal. Rudy just said that we're all having dinner at their place tonight."

"Are you sure he didn't say anything that might indicate what it was about?"

She shook her head as she chewed her fingernail. "Josh, Cal, he said you guys have to go, too. Not negotiable."

Josh rolled his eyes, and Cal just sat in the back seat with his head hung down.

As Hal drove off, Josh looked over at his brother. "Hey, Cal, I'm sorry. I didn't know he'd be that bad."

Cal didn't look up, "You were right. It was just too good to be true." Then he stared out the window so nobody would see the tears.

"Hey, Jack and Sharon are here," Hal said when they drove up to Rudy and Georgia's house.

Charlotte looked anxious. "What's going on?"

Rudy met them at the sidewalk and escorted them to the back yard.

Jack, who was removing burgers and hot dogs from the barbecue, waved when they rounded the corner.

Sharon was at the picnic table unloading a bag of food. She looked up and shrugged.

Just then, Georgia came out of the house with a bowl of potato salad.

"I got all of you here for an update," Rudy announced. "Please sit down."

"Don't look at me, I don't know anything," Georgia said when Sharon looked questioningly at her.

They finished arranging everything on the picnic table and sat down. All eyes focused on Rudy.

"I have something that you'll all want to hear. I wanted everyone here at the same time — easier than telling you one at a time. Go ahead and fill your plates while I play this recording." He turned on the recorder and they heard Kurt's voice, almost like an echo. "What did you do, Charlotte? Where are you?"

Everyone leaned forward with wide eyes.

"Is this what happened after I left?" Charlotte asked anxiously.

"Yup, just listen."

Jack pointed up for more volume.

They all leaned in to make sure not to miss anything as they listened to the events in the warehouse.

When the tape was done, Josh was wide-eyed. "Does that mean he's gone for good?"

Rudy grinned. "Well, nothing's a hundred percent sure, but I'd say it's pretty close."

Josh stood up and cheered.

Cal folded his arms and leaned back.

Charlotte sat stunned for a moment and then she put her hands over her mouth. Hal held her as she sobbed happy tears.

Rudy pressed some buttons on his phone. "This recording is from the Memorial Coliseum. Cal, I hate to do this, but you need to hear it."

When it was over, Cal's lips were pressed together as he struggled to keep from crying. "Did he really just call me a brat?"

Charlotte put her arm around him. "Oh, Cal. I know you wanted him to be your father. I'm sorry you had to see this side of him."

Cal's lower lip trembled. "No. It's better that I know. I guess Josh was right."

Josh rushed over. "I'm sorry, Cal. I wish I'd been wrong. I'm just glad this is over, and we're okay."

Cal looked to Rudy, tears streaming down his face. "I guess I should thank you."

"I was glad to do it."

Jack frowned. "That woman in the recording, who was she? Didn't I hear her say she was his wife?"

"Yup, that's Maria Perez, Kurt's wife." Rudy finished piling his plate.

"No way! How'd you find her?"

Josh sat down again, listening intently.

"I put Kurt's picture out on every social media website out there asking if anyone recognized him. It wasn't long before this Maria Perez sent an inquiry. She asked all the right questions, so I knew we had a match."

"What's the story?"

"Well, with what Roy and I found out and then what Maria told me, I was able to piece it together. You know that we tracked him down to Nevada, and he seemed to disappear about four years ago. I discovered that just before that, he lived with a guy named Vinnie Peters. Well, Roy dug up that Vinnie was involved in a lot of illegal stuff, including drug deals, and he was pretty high up in a gang with contacts in Colombia.

"Some of my contacts down in Nevada found out that Kurt made a bold move by betraying Vinnie. Shortly after that, Vinnie got shot in a drive-by shooting. Kurt brown-nosed his way up the ladder and eventually got chummy with Maria Perez, the kingpin's daughter."

Jack raised his eyebrows and pointed to Rudy's phone. "You mean *her* father is a *drug* lord?"

"Yup. Well, charming old Kurt convinced her they were in love, and she married him. After living in Colombia for a while, he realized he was in over his head, and he escaped."

Georgia gasped. "How'd he manage that?!"

"He had worked his way up to making deliveries. About two years ago, he was on a small yacht with two other men to make a delivery to a remote beach in Texas. The boat sank, and the two men went down with the ship. Kurt salvaged some packages, and he sold the contents on the streets. That's how he got the money that went in those safe deposit boxes. We think he arranged the whole thing — sinking the boat, killing the men, and stealing the drugs."

Sharon winced. "Wasn't he afraid of them hunting him down?"

"You bet! But he had it all planned out. Remember the drive-by shooting? Remember we talked about the innocent bystander that died, Tom Rance. Kurt took that name, knowing the guy would never show up. And he's been using that name — and others — ever since."

Hal frowned. "But where'd he get the other aliases?"

"I'm pretty sure they were just random deaths. It's pretty easy to find names by searching public records. There doesn't appear to be any connection to him knowing any of them. Apparently, he just randomly chose names from the obituaries and searched the Internet for personal information so he could open accounts in their names."

Hal scratched his head. "If he was invisible, why'd he take the chance on coming here? That's just crazy."

Charlotte sighed. "Nothing was ever enough for Kurt. He must've heard about my inheritance."

Rudy huffed. "You got that right. He just didn't know how much until he got here. When I found Maria, we made this arrangement. I'd help them get Kurt, and she'd make sure we got his signature on this." Rudy pulled a legal document out of his pocket and handed it to Hal. "This is what you wanted."

When Hal took it, his voice cracked out, "Thanks." He cleared his throat. "You don't know what this means to me." A big grin emerged across his face and joy seemed to radiate from him.

Charlotte pulled his hand closer to see the document. "Oh!" She spun to look at Rudy. "Really?!"

"What is it?" the boys asked simultaneously.

Rudy smiled. "This document verifies that Kurt relinquishes his rights as your father. Since I'm a notary public, I notarized it. Hal, you can legally adopt those boys now."

Hal put his arm around Charlotte. "I've wanted to do this for a long time." He looked at Rudy. "At first, we didn't know where Kurt was. Then, when he showed up, I almost lost hope." He gave Charlotte a tight squeeze and she nodded enthusiastically.

Cal looked at Hal with disbelief. "You mean you still want me after I practically threw you away?"

Hal got up and went over to him. "I'd be honored to be your dad — if you'll have me."

Cal stood up, hugged him, and with his eyes pinched shut, pressed his cheek against Hal's chest.

"Oh, Charlotte, you should be hearing from the State in the near future. You'll be getting a check for back child support," Rudy added, after letting them have their moment.

"Don't tell me Kurt's going to do something honorable? 'Cause I wouldn't believe it."

"Oh no, never!" Then he chuckled. "Apparently, someone told the authorities that Kurt had money in a safe deposit box under an alias, so they confiscated it. After everything is sorted out, you're first on the list. It'll probably be a while until that happens, though. There'll be a lot of red tape on this one."

Charlotte giggled. Then she broke out in hysterical laughter.

Josh cheered. "That serves him right!"

Rudy frowned. "Josh, Cal, Charlotte, I'm sorry."

They looked surprised. "For what?"

"I had to let Kurt think his plan was working. That's why I had to let him threaten you and think he was getting the money. Don't worry, I knew he wouldn't do anything to you because then he wouldn't get any money. I'm sorry I didn't let you in on that. I had to let you act naturally, or he'd know something was up."

Josh sat up straight. "Wait a minute. What are you talking about? What threats? You mean at the Coliseum?"

Hal explained Kurt's other extortion threats and confrontations with Charlotte.

Josh's eyes widened and his face turned red. "I knew it! I just knew it."

Rudy looked at Josh hard. "You have nothing to talk about, young man."

Josh's mouth hung open.

Charlotte slowly looked at the both of them and raised an eyebrow. "What's going on?"

Rudy held an open hand out to Josh. "Well, do you want to tell her, or should I?"

Charlotte narrowed her eyes. "Tell me what?"

"Well, I, uh, I was … It wasn't just me. Smitty and Al helped," Josh stammered.

"Helped you do what?" She said firmly.

He swallowed hard. "Well, Smitty's got this hobby. It's a pretty cool one …."

"Oh good grief," Rudy butted in. "I'll tell her. Josh was following Kurt while Cal was out with him. They actually followed Kurt to his home, and I caught them before Kurt did."

Charlotte stood straight up. "What!?"

Josh leaned away from the table. "Well, I thought nobody was doing anything. I knew he was dangerous and …."

"Exactly! What made you think that you could help? You put us all in danger!"

"I didn't know! I was trying to help Cal!" Josh pleaded.

"You're grounded!"

Josh hung his head. "Sorry, Mom," he mumbled.

"Well, you deserve it," Hal added.

Josh grimaced. "Well, that wasn't quite all of it."

Rudy glowered at him. "Okay, spill it!"

"That day that Cal sprained his ankle — well, we were parked in the woods taping everything."

"What!?" Charlotte exploded. Then she started to cry. "I could've lost you."

"I'm sorry, Mom! When I heard Cal cry out, I didn't know what to do! I was ready to go save him, but Al and Smitty made me stay in the car."

Hal took a big breath. "Thank goodness somebody had some common sense."

"I thought Kurt …." He winced. "I thought he killed my little brother." He started to cry. "That's what I was going to tell you when I came home — you know, when I said I had something awful to tell you?"

Charlotte reached across the table to hold his hand. "Oh, honey, you must have been out of your mind."

"Then when Cal came in the room, I was so happy he was okay." He turned to Cal, "That's why I hugged you."

"Don't you mean *mugged* me?"

"Yeah, sorry about that. I was just so happy you weren't *dead.*"

Cal frowned. "So you decided to finish the job?"

"I said I was sorry!"

"Josh, I hope you learned a lesson here." Rudy shook his finger at him.

Josh wilted. "Yeah. I don't ever want to do *that* again."

"Just because you can't see what's happening behind the scenes, it doesn't mean nothing is happening. But more importantly, I told you specifically to stay away from Kurt." Rudy paused. "You said you were taping what they were saying — how?"

Josh explained about the Duck pin. "Oh, Cal, when you get a chance, I'll need the pin back, it really belongs to Smitty."

Cal grimaced. "I'm sorry. I can't."

Josh frowned. "Why not?"

"Well, it's at the bottom of a ravine."

"How'd that happen?"

Cal nervously looked at Hal and his mom. "Well, when I tripped, I almost went over the cliff. But Kurt grabbed my ankle. That's how it got sprained. If he hadn't grabbed me, I think I'd be at the bottom along with my cap."

Charlotte gasped.

"Is that when you yelled?" Josh asked.

"How'd you know?"

"I was listening, remember? When I heard that branch break, I thought — I thought Kurt hit you with it. Then when we heard your yell fade so quickly — well, you know — I thought you were done."

Charlotte closed her eyes and shook her head. "Oh, Josh. You must have been frantic."

Josh's mouth turned down, and he nodded quickly.

Rudy just shook his head. "You don't know how fortunate you are."

"I know that now. I'm sorry. I'm really, *really* sorry."

Charlotte got up, went around the table and pulled him into a hug.

He put his head on her shoulder and cried.

Sharon saw Charlotte's pinched lips as she held Josh. "Charlotte, are you okay?"

"I guess. It's just been so overwhelming. Until Kurt showed up, I really believed I wouldn't ever see him again."

Hal stood up, went over to Charlotte and whispered in her ear.

She nodded, and then everyone sat down.

"Charlotte's had more distress than you know." Hal squeezed her hand. "Sharon, I made her go to that psychiatrist you recommended. Thank you. Without his help, she wouldn't have made it through this." He flinched. "And everyone else's help, too! I didn't mean to diminish that. But Dr. Reed's been awesome."

"Thank you, Sharon," Charlotte said softly. "When I found out Kurt was going to be at our house for the games, we knew I wouldn't be able to handle that. That's when I started seeing him. But I have a long way to go."

Josh leaned back. "Mom, why didn't you tell me and Cal?"

She paused for a moment. "We didn't want to give Kurt any hints that I was getting help." She cringed. "I know him. He would've upped his threats. And I didn't want you boys to be in danger."

Cal's lips quivered. "You mean he could've gotten worse than that?"

Charlotte nodded quickly.

"No …," Cal squeaked.

Rudy picked up his phone and pressed a few buttons.

"What now?" Jack asked.

"Well, since everything's taken care of, I thought I'd cover my tracks by erasing the evidence."

Charlotte fingered her locket.

Sharon leaned forward. "Charlotte, I've been meaning to ask — if it's not too personal. Can I ask what's in your locket?"

She looked down at it and smiled. "It's okay. It's a picture of Mom and Grant when they got married. Grant gave it to me when I moved away from home. He said that wherever life took me, he and mom would always be there with me." She opened it to show her. "Whenever things don't go very well, I clutch it to help me have hope for the better — because they are so good for each other. And when things go well — well, I just think about them and their example." Her face fell. "When I was with Kurt, he threatened to destroy it. I couldn't take that chance, so I had to hide it until he was gone." She squeezed Hal's hand. "After I married Hal, I put our wedding picture in the other side."

He put his arm around her and kissed the top of her head.

"Say, Georgia, what happened to Debbie after we did her makeover?" Sharon said.

"Oh, she's back home with her parents now. We bought the bus ticket for her. Poor thing, she thought her parents didn't want her. She didn't realize how frantic they were *and* how happy they were to hear she was okay and coming home."

"I'm really glad for her."

"Say, has anyone noticed a difference in John?" Jack asked after swallowing a bite of potato salad.

Hal laughed. "I'll say! He's not drinking so much anymore. Man, am I glad about that. I was pretty worried about him."

"You can thank Jack for that." Sharon beamed.

Hal shot a look at him. "What'd you do?"

"Well, we started having a few talks before and after the games at your house. It seems he was having issues with Bonnie and was drowning his sorrows."

Charlotte frowned. "With Bonnie? What'd she do?"

"She didn't do anything. He was just feeling sorry for himself. He was focusing on the wrong things and forgot about all her good qualities."

Sharon put her arm around Jack. "I'm so proud of you, Sweetie. It looks like John's back on track now."

"Thank goodness. What was he focusing on?" Charlotte pressed the issue.

"I'll bet it has something to do with her acting blonde," Georgia piped up. Then her eyes got big. "Oh I'm sorry, Charlotte. No offense intended."

Charlotte giggled. "None taken. You mean because she's clueless?"

Jack nodded.

Charlotte looked puzzled. "But when they were dating, he thought it was cute. What changed his mind?"

"He said he started to feel embarrassed and short-changed. But I helped him to reason it out. He still loves her; he just needed to show it more. And he has been — now."

Charlotte cringed. "Poor Bonnie. She must have been devastated."

"Don't feel bad. She didn't have a clue." Sharon grinned.

Charlotte raised an eyebrow. "Is that a joke?"

"No." She giggled. "Well, maybe. But I don't think she was aware of what was going on. I encouraged her to be more romantic, and now she thinks that's why John is paying more attention to her. They're both happier now." She raised an index finger. "Oh, by the way, they're going to spend next weekend at the coast — at a bed and breakfast."

"I don't suppose you're responsible for that?" Charlotte cocked an eyebrow.

Sharon grinned and nodded.

Hal laughed. "You guys are awesome."

"Thanks. But that's not all. Hang onto your seats — Bonnie actually started a business."

Hal practically choked on a potato chip. "Now *that has* to be a joke."

"No, really. Callie convinced her to sell her compacts and purses on the Internet. Callie takes the pictures so Bonnie can post them. And John takes care of the finances."

Rudy chuckled. "Who would've guessed?"

"And get this; they're selling for quite a bit. John has a newfound respect for her. Instead of just tolerating her purses, he's realized that Bonnie is pretty smart after all. He sees her as a person with value now." Then she quickly added, "You know what I mean. She was always valuable, but now he sees her creativity."

Hal put down his fork and clapped. "Good for her. And for John." Then he became serious. "It looks like you helped all of us. I'm really thankful you came into our lives. We can't thank you enough."

Jack smiled — then frowned. "Well, not everything went so great when we met."

"What do you mean?" Georgia looked puzzled.

"Well, you know that Arlene got it in her head that Sharon was responsible for all the bad stuff that happened. She even rolled it back to when they were little kids. When Arlene found out she was getting part of the inheritance, she filed for divorce."

"Why?!" Charlotte gasped.

"She didn't want Mel to get any of it."

Charlotte gripped Hal's hand.

Hal shook his head and mumbled to himself.

Rudy and Georgia looked at each other.

"She wanted the divorce to be final when the money arrived. Poor Mel, he was shocked when he got the papers. He tried to work it out with her, but she was determined. It took a while for him to realize that the divorce was going to happen. It wasn't long before John said something to Mel about the inheritance, and that's when he knew what her agenda was. He knew reconciliation was out of the question, so he decided to drag it out. He made changes in the paperwork, several times, just to slow down the process, just until the money came in. He just recently started to confide in me."

Hal frowned. "I thought we were friends. Why didn't he tell me?"

"He didn't tell you or John because he didn't want the sisters to talk, especially Bonnie."

Hal winced. "Aw, poor Mel. That must've been tough."

"You have no idea. Mel told me about their blow-out." Jack made air quotes and continued, "She argued that it was *her* money, that she *earned* it by having to take care of Charlotte and Bonnie when they were kids. Since it didn't work out the way she planned, she's really mad — at everyone." He slowly looked at Charlotte, Hal and Sharon. "She thinks you're all against her. And no one can convince her otherwise. She ...." Jack inhaled quickly and then added, "Uh, I'd better not say what he said she called you." He grimaced. "Sorry, I shouldn't have said that."

Charlotte moaned. "I knew she was miserable, but I had no idea what it was about."

"Mel said that even when they were first married, she wasn't very happy. He thought he could make her happy, but of course that never happened. You just can't *make* someone happy. That has to come from within." Jack shook his head. "Then when Sharon showed up, she was the scapegoat and Mel was the target." He let out a sad chuckle. "Mel said when she moved out, she took the desk and file cabinet they got from Alice's mansion. She said it's her inheritance — even though she has no use for them. Mel said she's just being vindictive. But he doesn't care. He said she can have them as long as she doesn't come back."

"I wondered why he's been happier." Hal shook his head. "You know, last week, he even asked me to go fishing with him. I didn't let on that I was busy because of Kurt. I didn't want to add to his misery."

"I think he probably knew. It was pretty obvious," Rudy blurted out.

Hal shrugged. "Yeah. Maybe I was fooling myself. I'll call him when we get home to set up a fishing weekend. Would you boys like to come along?"

"You bet!" they both said.

Charlotte smiled. "I know Hal already said it, but I want to thank all of you for being here, too."

"Well, that's what family's for," Georgia and Sharon said in unison.

Everyone laughed.

Callie's heart pounded as she opened the door to go in. She almost wished she hadn't told Rudy she'd do this. But when she found out that Roy was risking his life for this, she knew she couldn't do any less. She took what was supposed to be a calming breath, but it didn't seem to work. The buzzer sounded and startled her. She looked around.

"Coming!" called a voice from the back room. A man with spiked, blue hair, multiple facial studs, and tattoos on every visible part of his skin came out from the back room. Even though Rudy had described what to expect, she realized that she wasn't as prepared as she thought she was. She could feel the veins in her neck pulse with every heartbeat. And why was her heart beating so loud? Surely he could hear it. "Hey, do you do tattoos that the customer designs?"

"Sure. What've you got?"

She handed the picture to him. "I saw this tattoo the other day, and I thought it was pretty cool. I tried to draw it. The lines aren't very even, but you get the picture." She grinned. "I hope."

She was careful to recall Georgia's lessons on reading body language, and sure enough, she noticed more than she normally would have. He seemed to hold back a gasp as his nose flared, his pupils dilated, and his lips pressed together slightly. She could tell he made a fist with his free hand behind the counter when she saw the muscles in his forearm tighten. Without Georgia's training, she wouldn't have thought to look for it.

"I can't give you this tat."

"Why not? Is it too difficult?"

"Oh, no. What I meant is …. Uh, it's …. Let's just say it's got a reputation."

"What do you mean? What kind of reputation?"

He set his jaw. "It's something bad guys wear." He looked at her sternly. "Enough said?

She feigned shock and whispered, "You mean like a gang thing?"

"I'm sorry, I can't help you."

"I can see it in your eyes, you know," she said softly.

"See what?"

"The guilt."

"Look, you don't understand."

She mustered up all the courage she could. "I understand plenty. I got this drawing from someone we both know. I already know about the tattoos. And just so you know, I've got a fun little device here that interrupts the transmission of any audio or video bugs you might have in your shop. Known or unknown."

He stared at her as the corners of his mouth gradually turned down. Finally, he shook his head and gritted his teeth.

"You want to give me some more details?" she asked.

"What you're suggesting is dangerous — for me and for him." His eyes darted all over the place.

"I should've known," she said.

"Known what?"

She looked at him incredulously. "You're just going to let them all get away with what they're doing."

He seemed to shrink back. "It's not that simple."

"I do understand; you're scared stiff. But if you don't do something now, it's just going to get worse. And can you really live with all that guilt?"

He thought for a moment. "It's been eating me up inside."

"It almost sounds like you're forced to be quiet." She lowered her voice, "If you had a safe way to get out of this — arrangement, would you take it?"

He looked at her with disbelief. "But you can't guarantee anything."

"I'm talking about our mutual friend. You know who he is, right?"

He stared off over her shoulder. "Yeah." Then he looked her in the eye. "You'd better be right." He took a deep breath and let it out slowly between pursed lips. "Those tattoos .... They're like a brand. They mean something ... something pretty grim." He took a deep breath. "This one guy, he always brings in the new guy to get his tattoo. I heard him talkin' during some of the sessions. They didn't spell it out, but after a while, I figured it out." He shook his head again and leaned across the counter a bit more. "Look, these guys are bad news. Just tellin' you, this could get me killed." He tapped his chest with a decorated forefinger.

She saw sweat beads forming on his forehead and temples. "I get it. But you've got to let it out. Do you want to tell R— our friend — instead?" She was horrified that she almost said Rudy's name aloud, but she maintained her composure.

"This isn't a gang. They're worse."

"What do you mean worse?"

"I'm pretty sure they're part of a crime syndicate." He leaned forward to whisper. "And they only get this tattoo when they've whacked somebody."

Even though Rudy had already filled her in, actually hearing this from Freddie made her heart pound even harder; but she didn't flinch.

"I've only met a few of them, but there's someone higher up. His name is Frankie. I don't know anything more, only the first name."

"I'll need the names and information of what you have from your records."

"There aren't any records. It's all under the table. But I can give you descriptions with the names. I think they're probably nicknames." He wrote down everything he could remember.

She looked at the list and folded it before putting it in her purse. "Thanks, and I'll find out what our friend can do for you." She walked quickly to her car and called Rudy on speakerphone, started the engine, and took off.

"He's willing to talk, but you have to help keep him safe. He's really scared. … Yeah, I got a list just in case he changed his mind. … When do you want me to deliver it? … Okay, I can be there in twenty minutes."

Rudy sat at the corner table of the coffee shop with his back to the window to make sure he had a view of the whole place. The only other customer was a man who ordered a coffee to go and was adding cream and sugar at the side bar. Callie walked in, bought a coffee, sat down opposite him and slipped the piece of paper across the table.

He looked at her flushed face as he took the paper. "Are you okay?"

She nodded vigorously with a nondescript look.

"Are you sure? You don't look so good."

Her eyes darted to the ceiling and she blew out a nervous breath. "Yeah, I'm okay. I'm just pumping a little adrenalin right now. No, make that a *lot* of adrenalin. But I didn't show it in front of him."

He smiled faintly. "I've been there. It'll get easier."

He unfolded the paper to see names and descriptions of seven men. He knew his work was cut out for him.

She took a sip of coffee and nodded toward the list. "He said those were probably nicknames."

"Yeah, I figured. And I already know three of them."

Her eyebrows went up. "Whoa." She leaned forward and whispered, "How do you know all this?"

"After all these years, I've learned things. Let's leave it at that." He regretted asking for her help. *She's only twenty — so young and naïve.* Sharon, or Georgia for that matter, would never forgive him if anything happened to her. And after what happened last year, Jack would have his hide. His stomach turned and he blanched at the thought.

"Rudy, what's wrong? What else aren't you telling me?"

Dreading to tell her what the possibilities were, he shook his head. "Nothing."

"I'm not buying it. Georgia taught me body language. I know there's something you aren't telling me." She glared at him. "Tell me."

She's tougher than I gave her credit for. Maybe she isn't so fragile after all. Reluctantly, he decided to tell her the plan to take down the syndicate.

That evening, Bonnie came out of the grocery store with two full bags of groceries. When she got to her car, she saw the keys sitting on her console. She frowned, put her bags down on the trunk and called John. "John, I hate to do this to you. I locked my keys in the car. Would you come rescue me?" she asked apologetically.

She leaned against the car until he arrived. She smiled when she saw him pull up. "Oh, honey, you're the best. At least it isn't raining."

He smiled as he shook his head. "Anything for you, Doll." He reached into the open passenger window and unlocked the door. He grabbed the keys and gave her a kiss as he handed them to her.

"Ooh, I should do this more often."

He gave her a hug. "Do you need help with the groceries?"

She grinned. "Okay, thanks. Just put them in the trunk. Here, I'll even pop it open for you."

He chuckled. "Thanks, Jack," he mumbled under his breath.

"Jack? What did he do?"

"I'll tell you some day." He blew her a kiss, got in his car, and followed her home.

Chapter 27

"Rudy, the deal's all set for two o'clock. Even though they have all the evidence you gave me, they want you to come in and work with them to get the syndicate that's behind the dirty cops."

"What kind of deal did you get me?"

"I made sure that there would be no charges on any of the things you did. You know, breaking and entering and what-not. I didn't tell them you took Pierre's money, though."

"Thanks for that. It'll be a relief to have this over with. What's the address?" Rudy put the address into his phone. "I guess I'll leave now."

"Well, my deal hinges on this, too."

"Got it. See you at two."

Rudy came up behind Georgia in the kitchen and put his arms around her. "Hey, Sweet Cheeks, I've got some business to take care of. I don't know how long I'll be." He gave her a squeeze.

"Take care now." She looked up at him with a knowing smile. "I knew you wouldn't really retire."

"Hopefully, when this is done, I can relax. I wish I could tell you about it."

"I know. It comes with the territory."

"I love you." He gave her a lingering kiss.

"This is serious isn't it?"

Forgetting his poker face, he grimaced. "Can't say."

Her eyes got big. "Be careful. You don't want to do that when it counts."

He nodded. "Yeah," he said, barely audible. He gave her another kiss and left.

On the way, he needed to hear something to cheer him up and the radio was his best bet, so he turned it on. The first station was broadcasting exactly what he wanted to hear, and he turned up the volume.

"Further investigation reveals that Governor Munson is an imposter. The man who has been our governor for the last twenty years is really Barry West. Although he was out of office for a few years in that span, there are reports pointing to criminal activity while he was in office.

Apparently, Barry West took over this identity before he ever ran for governor. And there is new evidence that points to the possibility that the switch was arranged — and that the real Aaron Munson may have been murdered in 1996 so that Barry West could take his place — all this before he pursued political office. From the start, Munson was never the man in the Governor's office.

Even more alarming is that prior to the alleged switch, West had been investigated for the murder of a fine arts importer, but was never arrested because he was pronounced dead as the result of a house fire. This happened at the exact same time that Munson had been presumed missing and just before he was found again. It is almost certain that the real Aaron Munson is dead and that his body was the one assumed to be that of Barry West. Clues are even pointing to West being involved in Munson's death. An investigation is in full swing.

When West was being investigated in the '90s, convincing evidence mysteriously went missing just after the arrest warrant was issued. Now, after all these years, that missing evidence has turned up. With no Statute of Limitations on murder, it appears that Barry West, Munson's imposter, will be going to trial on that case....

And this news update just came in. New evidence implicating Barry West in receiving payoffs to grant early releases for several inmates while he was in office as governor. Those payoffs were apparently disguised as large donations from three local foundations to his political campaigns. Investigation into money trails has given convincing evidence that there have been multiple transactions since Munson, or West, was first elected back in the '90s."

Rudy laughed. *I knew Callie would be thorough. She's the one who found the proof that those "campaign contributions" were really payoffs, just as I suspected.* In a better mood now, he turned off the radio to double-check the address before he parked. Clutching his briefcase, he walked in through the side door of the old warehouse as instructed. It took a moment for his eyes to adjust to the dark expanse after leaving the bright sunlight. A black man in stained coveralls and several days of stubble shut the exterior door, frisked him, checked his ID and the contents of his briefcase, and led him through several rooms. Rudy saw several other men in the room and Roy standing to the right. He nodded, wondering what had caused the anxious look on Roy's face. Then he dismissed it to the situation.

When a bearded man with a ruddy complexion and bushy eyebrows stood up, Rudy figured he was wearing a disguise. "Rudy Burke?"

"Yeah, that's me."

"Agent Rice." He shook his hand.

"Okay, what do we do now?"

"First, we want to thank you for that collection of missing evidence. We're working to overturn all the cases where wrongly convicted people were put in prison. And we're collecting additional evidence to arrest the guilty parties in all those cases."

Without thinking, Rudy laughed aloud and raised his hand for a high five.

Agent Rice responded enthusiastically.

"This moved pretty fast. What happened?"

"Maxwell. You called him Todd?"

"Yeah. What about him?"

"He sang like a canary. Ratted out the captain, showed us money trails, and confirmed the captain's connections. Then when the captain realized there was no escape, he asked for protective custody and relocation in exchange for his help and testimony against the governor and what he knows about his contacts with the syndicate."

"What about Barry West?"

"He isn't cooperating. Won't say a thing."

"I'd say it's probably because he's family."

"Well, with all the evidence against him, his permanent residence will be federal prison. And he's still got to go to trial for that murder charge from twenty years ago. I'd say he'll be locked away for a long time." He patted Rudy's shoulder. "Thanks for getting the information on him. We were suspicious for a long time. We just didn't have any proof until you handed it to us."

"Do you want me to tell you the rest of what I know?"

"We'll get to that. We'd like you to work with a stool-pigeon that has inside information. We'll be recording as you collaborate. With his information and yours, we've already been able to arrest four dirty cops at the precinct."

"The captain, Novak, Harrison and Todd, right?"

Rice nodded.

"I don't know how much this stool-pigeon told you, but what Officer Jackson and I told you should be plenty to get them put away for a long time."

"True, but he had details that glued everything together."

Rudy really wanted to know what this other information might be. "Just for my own curiosity, and if you can tell me, I'd like to know what charges and evidence you've got on them."

"So far, it's tampering with evidence, interfering with a police investigation, aiding and abetting a felony, and obstruction of justice."

Rudy smiled.

"As Officer Jackson told you, since you were so crucial in our investigation, we'd like your assistance in going after the crime syndicate that's behind it all."

"Okay." Rudy assumed he'd be working with a Fed that had been investigating the syndicate.

The bearded man led Rudy out of the room.

"Isn't Roy going, too?"

"No. We have something else planned for him."

Rudy wondered why, since Roy was so crucial in getting everything started. He worried that Roy's deal wasn't as beneficial as they figured. The thought that Roy might be charged and go to prison after all made his stomach turn.

Agent Rice led Rudy into a dark room, stood in front of a one-way mirror, and pointed to the thin man sitting at a table on the other side. "This is the man you'll work with. You may already know him."

When Rudy looked at him, his mouth dropped open. The thin man's brown dye job was nearly grown out, revealing graying black hair; but the pencil mustache was unmistakable.

"Pierre?! He's supposed to be dead!"

~ To Be Continued ~

Family Tree

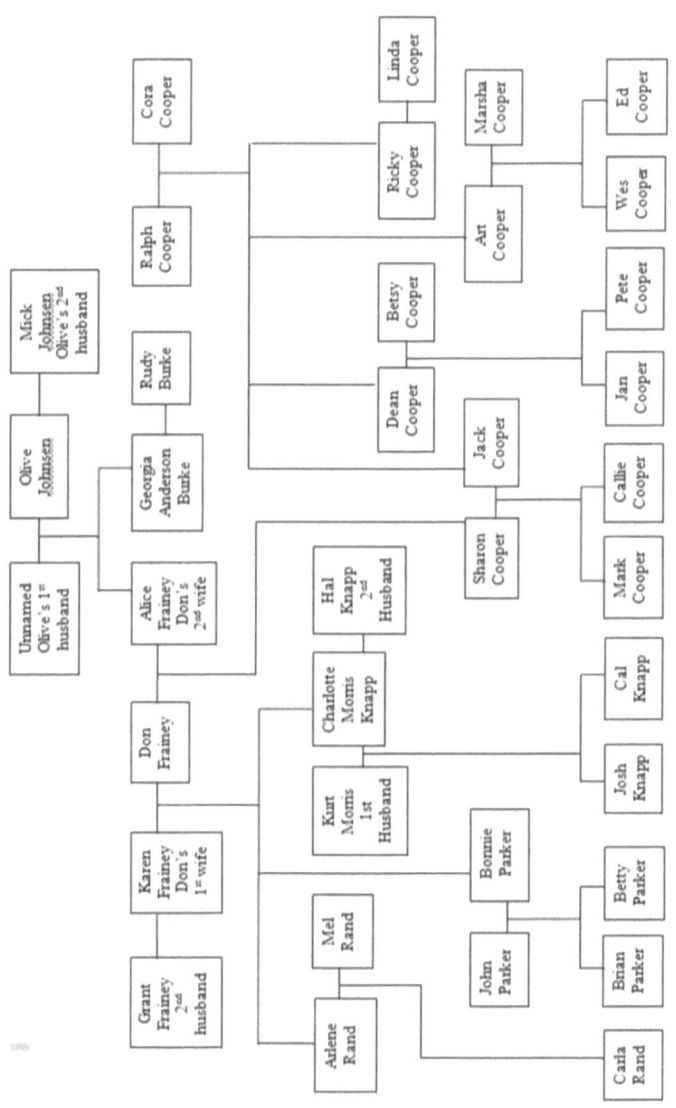

List of Characters

Aaron Munson – Governor

Agent Rice – Federal officer

Agent Riley – Federal officer

Al – Josh's friend

Alice Frainey – Sharon's mother, Don's second wife

Arlene Rand – Karen's first daughter, Sharon's step-sister

Barry West – Distant relative of Pierre Martine

Bonnie Parker – Karen's second daughter, Sharon's step-sister

'Brick' – 3rd thug in Pierre's house

Bruce Wiggins – Gym manager

Cal Morris – Charlotte's youngest son

'Callie' Diane Cooper – Sharon's daughter

Captain Joe Crandall – Police station captain

Charlotte Knapp – Karen's third daughter, Sharon's step-sister

Cora Cooper – Jack Cooper's mother

Darrel – Bonnie's date in high school

Debbie Kruz – Kurt's girlfriend

Dr. Pritchart – ER doctor

Don Frainey – Sharon's father

'Fingers' – 2nd thug in Pierre's house

Freddy – Tattoo artist

Gary Rawlins – Mark's friend

Gene Baxter – Kurt Morris' second alias

Georgia Burke – Sharon's aunt, Alice's sister

Grant Frainey – Karen's second husband

Hal Knapp – Charlotte's second husband

Harrison – Police officer

Jack Cooper –Sharon Cooper's husband

Jerry – Evidence locker guard

John Parker – Bonnie's husband

Josh Morris – Charlotte's oldest son

Karen Frainey – Don's first wife

Kurt Morris – Charlotte's first husband

Mark Cooper – Sharon's son

Mel Rand – Arlene's husband

Mick Johnsen – Olive's second husband, Georgia's step-father

Olive Johnsen – Alice and Georgia's mother

Oscar 'Todd' Maxwell – IT officer at police station

Pierre Martine –Alice Frainey's lover and co-conspirator

Roy Jackson – Callie's fiancé

Rudy Burke – Georgia's husband

Sharon Cooper – Callie's mother

'Shiv' – 1st thug in Pierre's house

Smitty – Josh's friend

Steve Novak – Police officer

Tom Rance – Kurt Morris' first alias

About the Authors

Sandra Denbo and her daughter, Tamarine Vilar, live in Portland, Oregon, which is the setting for their stories. Sandra has five children, Tamarine being the youngest. Sandra has had a wealth of experiences and has met a wide variety of personalities, each with their own idiosyncrasies. This fertile bed is the source of ideas for creating the characters you will learn to love and hate. Sandra has always had the ability to clearly describe ideas and feelings.

Tamarine Vilar has one son and also lives in Portland. She has a Bachelor's degree in English with a minor in writing from Portland State University. Because Sandra loved to read, she read to Tamarine from infancy. As a result, reading became her favorite way to relax. Professors and fellow students alike have enjoyed her natural ability to evoke emotion, even tears, with her writing, and have encouraged her to continue writing.